Dax stepped forward. "You aren't stealing that painting or anything else tonight, lady. So keep your manicure off the merchandise."

"And why are you here?" Raven took in his leather jacket, oxford shirt and jeans. "Bidding on an ashtray you fancy?"

He grinned. "I believe you fancy something else. I saw the way you fondled that painting. I think you need a man."

Her eyes narrowed dangerously. "Number one, it's perfectly legal to cop a feel. No pun intended. Number two, the only man I need is the one with the bull's-eye over his heart at the shooting range. And number three"—her eyes narrowed even more—"you're wasting your time with me. In more ways than one."

He leaned boldly into her personal space. She didn't move a muscle as he ran his gaze along her bare shoulders and down her body. He had to admit, she was pretty damn hot...

SIGHT
UNSEEN

Samantha Graves

NEW YORK   BOSTON

Warner Forever is an imprint of Warner Books, Inc.

Warner Forever is a trademark of Time Warner Inc. or an affiliated company. Used under license by Hachette Book Group USA, which is not affiliated with Time Warner Inc.

Cover design by Dale Fiorillo
Cover illustration by Rob Wood
Book design by Giorgetta Bell McRee

Warner Forever
Hachette Book Group USA
237 Park Avenue
New York, NY 10169
Visit our Web site at www.HachetteBookGroupUSA.com.

Printed in the United States of America

First Printing: April 2007

10 9 8 7 6 5 4 3 2 1

This book is dedicated to my terrific, supportive family:
Ed, Rachel, and Ryan.

Acknowledgments

It takes a village. No truer words were ever spoken. This book is the culmination of the generosity and commitment of many people.

My editor, Devi Pillai, for understanding my fixation with spreadsheets, charts, and details, and using her wonderful editorial guidance to make this book the best it could be despite all that.

Beth de Guzman, Larissa Rivera-Gonzalez, Frances Jalet-Miller, and the Hachette Book Group staff for believing in me and for their hard work and support.

My fearless and tireless agent, Roberta Brown. There simply are not enough words to thank her for always being there.

Lani Diane Rich, who helped keep me afloat for the five months it took to write this book.

Maggie Shayne, whose talent is eclipsed only by her generosity and kind heart.

I love research. It's a good thing, too, because I did more than my fair share for this book. I'd like to thank the following people who put up with my million questions. In no particular order: J. L. Reyes, former police officer; Eileen Toth, actuarial analyst; Linnea Sinclair, author; Bonnie Vanak, author; Patrick Picciarelli, author; and the experts on the Weapons_Info loop. This book would not be a reality without them.

All mistakes made or literary license taken is mine.

Many thanks to RWA, the members of the Central New York Romance Writers, FF&P chapter, Kiss of Death chapter, the Lollies, the Warner Women, and my dedicated critique partners, Patti Newell and Joyce Lock.

And finally, thanks to all you readers out there for allowing me into your hearts and your homes. There is no greater gift for a writer. This book is for you.

CHAPTER
1

God, I love this part. Raven smiled as she peered through her scuba mask.

With one hand, she steadied herself in the water while gently prying the gold medallion from lava stone with her knife. She kicked slowly in the tiny phone-booth-sized alcove, careful not to stir up any silt or bump her gear against the low rock ceiling. The caving dive light attached to her mask penetrated the inky darkness and gleamed off the golden treasure before her.

"Do you have it yet? You've been down there for thirty minutes," a high-pitched, anxiety-induced voice asked in her earpiece.

She grinned at her colleague's typical impatience, which was why he was in the boat, and she handled the acquisitions.

"Relax, Paulie. This thing's been set in rock for four-teen hundred years. Cut me a little slack," she replied. "You got a hot date or something?"

"No, but we have company up top."

Raven stilled. They weren't exactly in the main shipping lines, five miles off the Yucatán Peninsula coast. "What kind of company?"

"Looks like a luxury yacht, but you know, it's raining up here. Who goes for a joy ride in the rain?"

Nosy tourists, that's who. Or worse. An uneasy feeling prickled in her mind. Seventh sense maybe, but it had kept her alive all these years and she wasn't about to ignore it now. "Watch them. I'm almost done here."

She finished running the knife around the edge of the round medallion, liberating sea-crusted lichens. Slipping the blade in a gap, she gently freed the gold disc from its ancient berth and into her hand. A low groan echoed through the narrow passage. Raven turned her head, scanning the cave with her dive light and the sound dissipated.

She shrugged and turned the artifact over. It was in superb condition, which was amazing considering the elements it had been exposed to. The markings were clearly Mayan and matched the design she was looking for. But there was only one way to make sure it was authentic.

She pulled off her dive glove and held the metal with her bare hand. Her fingers tingled. A flash of light behind her eyes signaled a familiar journey into the past. Her physical world faded for a moment as her mind focused on the man who wore this amulet. Gold glinting in the sun and a man, his demeanor analytical, decisive, powerful. Through his eyes, she saw costumed followers, intricate ceremonies, and fervent chants. He was the king.

"The yacht just stopped a hundred feet from me.

I think you better get up here." Paulie's statement wrenched her out of the past.

She moved the amulet to her gloved hand and worked to get her bearings. Her psychic foray confirmed it was the genuine article. A fake would have registered a whisper of existence.

"Heading up now," she told Paulie.

After carefully securing her prize in a pocket of the dry suit and her knife to her belt, Raven backed out of the tiny grotto and into the main passageway of a cave system with no name. She picked up the reel that connected to a guideline, her only link to the entrance.

Black water permeated the undersea cave a hundred feet below the surface. Her light flashed off small silver fish darting out of her way. As she reeled in the line, following it through the complex network of catacombs, she wondered how someone could have embedded the medallion down here a thousand years ago. Even with her specialized dive equipment, it was extremely dangerous.

There were times when the sheer will of man and his reverence for the trinkets of the past boggled her mind. Why anyone would go to so much trouble for a single object—

A hand slashed out from the darkness, knocking off her face mask and taking her light, air, and comm with it. Precious gas free-flowed around her as she struck blindly at her assailant with the reel. A massive fist shoved her in the chest, smashing her against the cave wall as the reel was ripped from her hand.

Raven brought her legs up and drew her knife from its sheath to defend herself. Eyes closed, muscles coiled, she waited. A hard flow of water came from the left, grazing her head as she ducked. She slashed out, snagging something solid, and heard a muffled cry. Pressure buffeted her as she sliced through the water around her, then everything was calm again.

Long seconds ticked by with no movement. With her lungs begging for relief, she fumbled for her mask and found it at the end of its safety tether. She pulled it on and blew air into it to clear the seawater. Cold gas mix filled her lungs, easing the burning.

Her eyes opened to pitch-black—her dive light was gone. Raven retrieved the spare from a pocket and turned it on, which didn't improve the view much. The struggle had kicked up silt from the floor, and visibility was near zero.

As the silt settled, she swept the cave with her light. No sign of the attacker . . . or her reel. However, there was a distinct red tinge that confirmed a hit. Good. She hoped the sharks got him. On the other hand, she was still in the water as well. Sharks weren't picky about their prey.

"Paulie, can you hear me?"

"Yup," his voice crackled in her ear while rock-and-roll music blared in the background. "How's it going?"

She patted the medallion in her pocket with relief. "Well, I was just mugged. How's things with you?"

"Holy shit, are you okay?"

She checked her gas levels—they were in the red. "I have a major problem."

"I knew it. The legend is true. That thing is cursed."

Raven shone her light on two passageways, trying to remember which one she'd come through. If she had a god, she would have prayed. Instead she kicked toward an opening, hoping she picked the right one.

"Trust me. That wasn't a curse that stole my lifeline."

"Oh crap. *Oh crap.* Are you kidding me? You don't have the line? Jesus, Raven," Paulie sputtered.

She could tell he was about ten seconds away from a nervous breakdown. Rough coral snagged her tank and arms as she squeezed through the narrow tunnel.

"Paulie, shut the hell up and listen to me." She took a breath. "I have next to no air left. I want you to drop a tank, mask and all, over the side of the boat. Open up the regulator full blast."

"What? There's no way—"

She breathed, watching the gauge drop. Two breaths, maybe three left. Not enough to argue with. "Just do it."

"Okay, okay. I'll be right back."

The line went silent except for her tank scraping rock. Stay calm. Easy breaths.

Right. Her heart was pounding out of her chest. *Breathe.* Relief pumped through her as her lungs filled.

"The tank is dropped," Paulie's frantic voice came back. "Can you get to it in time?"

She didn't want to answer and waste precious air, but Paulie would throw himself overboard if she didn't. "No problem. Now get out of here."

"No way. No way am I leaving you. And just so you know, next time you get a dive partner," he said. "I don't give a damn how much you hate that. I don't care. Nothing is worth this."

Jeez, you'd think Paulie was the one in trouble. She pulled herself through around a corner and saw light. Hallelujah.

Breathe. The gauge dropped to empty.

Last call on life.

Her lungs ached already from holding her breath during the exertion of swimming, but she worked through the pain as she cleared the cave and entered open water. With a powerful kick, she headed for the surface.

Breathe— Air cut off halfway through.

Oh hell. Don't panic, body. We'll get through this.

Water flowed around her as her legs pumped. Eyes upward, flashlight scanning, she watched and listened. It had to be close.

"Raven? You got it yet?"

She didn't answer this time. Seconds passed like eternity. Her lungs screamed. Her head pounded. And then she heard it—bubbles.

She moved to the right. Pain radiated through her body. The sound drew closer, and she scanned the sea with her light. Thirty feet above her, a white cloud plummeted toward the ocean floor. She kicked once more for position. She'd only get one shot at this. If she missed the tank, she'd be dead. Just about the best motivation she could think of.

"Raven!" Paulie yelled, as if shouting louder would make her answer.

Black started crowding her vision as she grabbed for the tank, missing it but snagging a strap. The force jerked her downward, and she fumbled for the mask shooting bubbles.

The rest was a blur as she yanked off her own mask and shoved the new one over her face. Just before the darkness took her, she purged the seawater and inhaled.

"Did you get it? Did you get it?"

Paulie's voice in her ear drew her out of the fog

that threatened to swallow her up. She was floating downward toward the sea bottom. Cold oxygen filled her starved lungs.

She checked the depth—120 feet and falling. She shook off the stars and shrugged out of her spent tank. It floated off as she pulled on the new gear and headed to the surface. Heavy legs took her up.

Damn, that was close.

"Raven!" Paulie screamed in her ear. She wished she had a volume control on the earpiece, but this was good. If the attacker was listening, he'd think she was dead and hopefully leave Paulie alone up top. If not, they would probably go after her boat, too.

Eighty feet from the surface, she pulled up short. No divers within visual range, and Paulie was still hyperventilating, so he was safe enough. A low rumble permeated the water as the party boat churned up the sea and headed back to the coast. She'd like to be here to give them the surprise of their lives when they came back looking for her body in that cave. *Not today.*

"I'm here, Paulie."

"Thank God," Paulie replied. "You scared the crap out of me."

She could almost hear his blood pressure dropping. "Did you get an ID on that party barge?"

"No, I was a little busy freaking out over you. Besides, the yacht just left."

"Any other boats in the vicinity?"

"Nope." A pause. "Oh hell. They were the ones who mugged you, weren't they?"

Five miles from the coastline. That diver didn't swim all the way out here by himself. "Most definitely."

"Damn scavengers," he sputtered. "Want me to call them in to the authorities?"

"For what? They didn't get anything."

"Oh, right. Maybe we can follow them."

"Forget it, we'll never catch up." She turned toward the surface and kicked. "Unless you mounted a rocket launcher on the deck while I was gone?"

He laughed nervously as if he thought she might actually be serious. "No, sorry."

"Too bad. That would have really made my day. I'll be up after I decompress."

Paulie was hovering like a mother hen by the time she pulled herself onto the swim platform and into the boat. Twentysomething with glasses, a shaved head beneath his Cardinals cap and thin frame under his Aerosmith T-shirt, he could have been any geek on the planet. Luckily, he was her geek.

"I mean it," he muttered, helping her with the gear. "I'm not doing this again unless you get a dive buddy."

She leaned back against the gunwale, unzipped her dive suit, and let the rain trickle inside. These near-death experiences took a lot out of her.

"Save it, Paulie. You know I don't play well with others."

He mounted the cockpit seat and revved the engine. "I don't care. This is absolutely the last time."

While he rattled on, she extracted the medallion from her pocket. Even in the gray rain, it was superb, depicting the Mayan sacred calendar in gold relief. And more than that, it was the real deal. Another artifact unearthed for the world to worship with giddy reverence and kill for. She wondered how many people had died for this one. She was just grateful she wasn't one of them.

The boat lurched forward, drowning out Paulie's lecture. She tucked the medallion into her suit, and a shiver of victory went through her. She'd won the game despite the attack. It'd been too long since she'd had a good adrenaline rush.

She smiled. She really did love this part.

CHAPTER
2

Her footsteps echoed in the marble corridors of the Antiquities Preservation Institute. An enormous window showcased a fifty-first-floor view of the Manhattan skyline.

A few of the office staff did a double take as she passed by them. She supposed it wasn't every day they saw her dressed in a black turtleneck and slacks wearing an ancient medallion around her neck. She stopped at Thomas Bigley's door and planted her hands on his assistant's desk. Gilmore looked up at her in annoyance and made a face.

"Hello, *Raven*," he said in a nasal voice.

"Gilmore." She leaned closer. "Is he in?"

Gilmore sat up straight in his chair and crossed his wrists with a huff. His slicked-back hair looked glued to his pinhead. "Do you have an appointment?"

He enunciated every letter of the last word because he knew damn well that she wasn't on the schedule. The little shit. Over the past year, she'd entertained a multitude of fantasies on how to teach Gilmore some manners. Today's was to take the medallion and shove it—

As if reading her mind, his eyebrows went up. "No appointment? Well, I can pencil you in for next week."

She gave him her most brilliant smile and swung the medallion on its chain in front of his eyes. "This is my appointment. You want me to tell Bigs you wouldn't let me through?"

Gilmore's nose wrinkled, and he turned to check his computer. He finally looked at her. "He's in. Let me buzz him."

She shoved off the desk. "Never mind, I know my way."

Gilmore's sniff was unmistakable as she pushed open the double doors and entered her boss's office. A wide bank of windows surrounded a ring of crimson chairs and a modest mahogany desk. Thomas Bigley, president of API, glanced over his glasses. A smile blossomed on his face as he pocketed the glasses and stood to greet her. With white-shot hair, sharp blue eyes, and tall stature, he looked fit for a fifty-eight-year-old man.

"Raven, you're back," he said.

She kissed him on each cheek. "When are you going to replace that little shit of an assistant you have?"

"Gilmore has been here longer than any of the others, so leave him alone." He raised his eyebrows. "Unless you'd like the job?"

She nearly choked. "Not on your life. Keep him."

Bigley asked, "So how was your trip?"

She unclipped the latch behind her neck and held the medallion up to Bigley by the chain. "Present for you."

His focus shifted instantly. He pulled his glasses back

on hastily and took the piece like it was spun glass. She followed him to his desk where he turned on a magnifying light and inspected the piece through it.

"Oh my," he said in a hushed voice. "Truly spectacular."

His reverence always made her smile. It didn't matter how many pieces she recovered for their clients; each and every one earned the same reaction. She swore the whole reason he created the institute was so that he could get his hands on the good stuff.

She sat on the corner of his desk and crossed her arms. "Worn by King Pacal Votan the Great—A.D. 615–683."

Bigley squinted up at her. "Are you certain?"

She shrugged. "Most likely. I'll leave it up to you to get the provenance. I only do the easy stuff."

Her boss gave a little smile. He never questioned her gift, never pried into how it worked or why. He simply nodded and went back to studying the artifact. "I'll notify the Guatemalan Ministry of Culture at once. They will be happy to hear you got to it before the looters did."

"I almost didn't. Someone paid me a visit while I was in the cave," she said.

Bigley's head came up. "Good heavens. What happened?"

She waved him off, because she didn't feel like another lecture. "Nothing I couldn't handle. I'm just getting damn sick of being ambushed. I hate these government jobs. Politicians can never keep a secret."

Bigley donned a worried frown. "I suppose it's possible the ministry may have leaked the general location of the medallion once their scholars deciphered the scrolls they found."

She nodded. "That's my theory."

"Or you were followed. This is the third time over the past few months." He eyed her over his spectacles. "You are becoming quite famous, my dear."

She gave him a stern look. He knew damn well she wasn't in this for the fame. "It just makes life more interesting."

"It also makes my position more difficult."

She knew where he was heading with this one. "Don't try to protect me. I'm perfectly capable of doing my job. Besides, I am the best recovery specialist you have. How many of your clients have their stolen artifacts back because of me? How many national treasures have I returned to their rightful places in museums and private collections?"

He raised his hands in defeat. "You are the best, without a doubt. I'm just saying, you always have other options in this organization."

"Like replacing Gilmore? No thanks. If my life comes to that, I'm throwing myself off a bridge," she said firmly.

He leaned back in his chair, watching her for a few moments before nodding. "In that case, I have an urgent job for you."

He picked up the remote and clicked it at the forty-inch plasma screen on the wall. A photo of a painting appeared—a portrait of a woman with relaxed realism, rounded features, classic pose.

"Recognize this?"

Raven studied it. "Santo Vassalo portrait. Romanticism, Italian, late 1800s. Private collection, if I recall."

He nodded. "Very good. It's titled *Sad Maria*. Vassalo's wife. Now look at this one."

Another photograph appeared next to the first. Raven narrowed her eyes. It was of a man with the same expression, but his eyes were more direct and intense. Passionate. Angry.

"Is that Vassalo himself?"

Bigley moved next to her. "It's unsigned, but the technique, probably early in his career, is similar, as is the setting. They are companion pieces, separated shortly after his death and never reunited under one roof. In fact, neither of these have been seen in over fifty years."

She turned to him and noted the light smile. There was more to this story. "So how did you get the photos?"

"*Sad Maria* just came on the market."

She cocked an eyebrow. "And the Vassalo self-portrait?"

He winked at her. "I took the photo. This morning."

She blinked. "Excuse me?"

He walked over to an enormous wall painting and touched the side. It swung wide on precision hinges, revealing a stainless-steel vault. He laid his palm across the security panel, and it opened to a deep room with padded walls. From it, Bigley removed a frame and laid it on a nearby table—the Vassalo self-portrait.

A heartfelt "Holy shit" was all she could muster. Then she glanced at her boss. "And how long have you had this?"

He took a deep breath. "Just surfaced last week. No one knows about it except you and me."

She gaped at him in utter respect. "And you kept it secret this long? I'm impressed."

He laughed. "It wasn't easy. I was hoping you could tell me if it's genuine."

She turned serious. A painting this old would have a lot of history, and possibly changed hands hundreds of times. And with each new owner, the imprints of people, places, and emotions—every one of which she would experience vividly. Especially the bad ones. She would never understand why violent emotions always imprinted best.

Using the skills she'd acquired over her lifetime, she pulled insular protection around her, shutting off the flow of emotions. Then she raised her hands over the painting. Lightly, she pressed her fingers to the canvas and closed her eyes. A flood of images flashed as she descended through the layers to the first brushstrokes.

Old Venice, thick Italian voices, the smell of tobacco and wrenching emptiness. She shielded herself from the sudden onslaught of passion and yearning. A lover lost. Crushing depression. Betrayal . . . pain.

Raven extracted herself abruptly from the past and the residual anguish. Damn paintings. Bigley was watching her with rapt interest as she lifted her fingers, still tingling from the images, and shook them out.

She said, "Could be his. And just so you know, he wasn't a happy camper when he painted this one. Why are the good painters always suicidal?"

Bigley frowned. "I'm sorry about that."

"Not your fault," she said, and she meant it. He respected her gift, and his requests were few. "So—" She looked at him. "What's this baby worth?"

He picked it up and placed it back into the wall vault. "Probably close to 1.5 million."

Raven crossed her arms. "Provenance?"

He turned to face her with a shake of his head. "That's the challenge. Authentication will be the best we can do."

"Don't think anyone's going to take my word for 1.5 mil."

He smiled crookedly. "I agree, but I may have the solution. *Sad Maria* is going to private auction in Miami tomorrow evening. I'd like you to bring it back so we can use it to validate this one."

"Another auction," she said. "How very exciting. You really are trying to keep me out of trouble, aren't you?"

He chuckled. "I'm afraid all your recoveries can't be as exciting as cave diving, my dear. Try not to fall asleep. Walter Abbott will be the buyer. You'll be his associate."

She frowned. "Why can't I just go solo?"

He walked by her and took a seat behind his desk. "As a well-regarded art dealer, Walter was invited. You weren't."

"After all the art I've handled over the years, I still get no respect."

She ignored Bigley's warning look as he continued. "And I want you to keep an eye on Walter. He doesn't move as fast as he used to. Besides, this is his last job for API before he retires. He specifically asked to work with you."

She couldn't say anything to that. Walter was a sweet man who sincerely adored and appreciated great art and shared that passion with anyone willing to listen. Over the past ten years, they had worked many jobs together, posing as prospective buyers to locate artwork that had been stolen. Of course, Walter tended to follow the rules and call in the authorities more than she did. Sometimes, it was a lot less hassle just to steal the art back.

"Tell Walter I'll be honored to work with him again," she said.

"Excellent." Bigley hitched his head toward the self-portrait. "Until we have the auction piece, I'd like this Vassalo to be our little secret. Walter doesn't even know. *No one* can know."

"What Vassalo?" she said innocently.

Bigley didn't even break a smile. "No jokes, Raven. This job could become very dangerous. We're talking the find of the century. Separately, the pieces may be worth only a few million dollars each. But reunited as a set after over one hundred years, they could easily top ten million or more. Never underestimate the greed of man."

He didn't need to worry. The greed of man was something she knew all about. Intimately.

The phone was ringing when Raven entered her apartment. She dropped her suitcases at the door, tossed her keys in a crystal bowl, and grabbed the phone on her way to the kitchen.

"Hi, Jill."

"How do you always know it's me?" her sister asked.

Raven opened the refrigerator door and light washed the tile floor. "Aside from caller ID and the fact that only you, Bigley, and Paulie have this number, it's 7:32 P.M. on a Monday night. You're heading out to dinner with Dad, and you are calling to see if I want to join you. You are highly predictable, kiddo."

Raven scanned the meager contents. Half a quart of milk, spoiled no doubt. A six-pack of bottled water.

Leftover pork chop suey with petrified white rice. She picked up a mushy package that was once lettuce and tossed it in the trash.

"You just got back in town, didn't you?" her sister said with a sigh.

"Yup." Raven opened the freezer. A full tray of ice cubes sat next to a Lean Cuisine dinner stuck to the back corner.

"Don't tell me what you were after this time. I don't want to know."

Raven closed the door and stood in the middle of her kitchen. Where were those damn grocery fairies when you needed them? "Not even a hint?"

"No! Good God, Raven. I'm an assistant curator for the Metropolitan Museum of Art. The last thing I need is insider information. I'll *never* get promoted."

Raven paused. "You need to find another job. You bust your ass seventy hours a week for those people, and no one appreciates it. You could put your gift to better use."

"Oh, and what am I supposed to say to potential employers? Hey, I can see ghosts moving around your precious artifacts? That'd go over real well. No thank you. I'll stick to my graduate degree and hard work like everyone else."

Raven sighed. Playing by the rules never got anyone a promotion. She pulled out a stack of take-out menus, leaned against the counter and flipped through them. "We aren't like everyone else, Jill."

"Tell me about it. So come to dinner with the other freak in the family."

"Sorry. I'm beat, and I still have to unpack and repack for tomorrow."

"I'm buying. Free food," her sister cooed. "I know how you cook."

Raven's fingers paused on the menus. That was the problem with sisters—they had ammo, and they weren't afraid to use it. "I've been contemplating cooking lessons."

Jillian laughed. "Don't even try that one. You don't possess the prerequisite skill of water boiling."

Raven found the flyer for Riccardi's Italian Grill and tossed the rest aside. She walked over to the couch, dropped her shoulder bag beside her, and sank into the leather upholstery. "For your information, I'm having manicotti tonight."

"Oh? Dating an Italian?"

Raven narrowed her eyes. "Maybe. How's the dating world treating you?"

Jillian relented. "Fine. I'll tell Dad you were busy again."

Like you do every time. "I've been busy every Monday night for the past two years. I think he's probably figured it out by now."

Jillian quieted, and Raven felt a stab of compassion for her sister. Raven rubbed her forehead. Jill would never understand. She was a far better person, and good people forgave.

"Why do you keep trying, Jill? You know what the answer is going to be."

"Because someday, you might say yes, and I don't want to miss it."

Her sister had the blind faith of a saint. "It'll never happen. Dad and I have nothing to say to each other."

"Never is a long time," Jill quipped.

Raven squinted. "Have you been watching reruns of *Kissed by an Angel* again?"

"That's *Touched by an Angel*," she corrected; then she added a guilty, "No, I haven't."

Raven wanted to laugh. Her sister was such a good Catholic girl. At least one of them would make it to heaven.

Jillian asked, "So where are you off to?"

Raven smiled, knowing her sister was dying to find out even if she denied it. She had adventurer's blood in her veins, no matter how hard she tried to bury it under blind faith and the security of homogeneity. "Art auction in Miami with Walter."

"Oh. That's good," Jillian said with more than a little relief in her voice.

"You just like it when no one shoots at me."

Raven could almost see Jill's eyes glaze over, caught dead center in the middle of the dysfunctional family headlights.

"Don't say that, Raven. Those are the visions that keep me awake at night. You do legitimate recovery operations for API. Period."

Except when I have to steal stuff back from the bad guys, Raven thought silently. "Of course."

Jillian said, "I have to run. If you change your mind, you know where to find us. Love you."

Raven replied with her usual, "You too."

After she'd hung up, Raven sat for a moment in the silence and looked across her apartment. French doors framed a matrix of buildings as dusk weighed heavy on her balcony. Fading sunlight warmed the chrome and glass of her furniture, giving the monochromatic colors a rosy tinge. Funny how there could be a whole city beyond those doors and yet so quiet in her apartment.

From the bag, she pulled out a souvenir and held it up to the waning light. Its crude, classic Mayan face stared back at her—a wooden smile frozen in time.

She set the Mayan figurine in an empty space on the curio wall cabinet. It fit in perfectly with the odd assortment of mass-produced souvenirs from all her travels. Some people collected fine art—paintings, bronzes, sculptures, or antiquities. Some . . . didn't.

Then she picked up the phone and dialed the number for Riccardi's takeout.

CHAPTER
3

"Welcome to Matador's Auction House," the greeter said and handed Walter a catalog. Raven nodded at the young man beneath the brim of her black feather hat as they entered the preauction exhibition. He gave her an approving smile, and she knew he was watching her ass as she swayed by. As long as everyone concentrated on the dress and not her hands, she'd be good.

Her pulse quickened when they entered the great hall with the other patrons. The game had begun, even if it was a simple one. She loved the setup, the preparation, the anticipation. And the sweet smell of victory. Instant gratification. Like chocolate. Like sex. Only without all the calories and strings.

Walter looked every bit the proper dealer in a fine charcoal suit with carefully combed white hair, soft gray eyes, and a face that crinkled when he smiled.

Decked out in a little black dress, a floral black-and-red scarf that brushed her thighs, and Dior slingbacks, she preferred to think she looked more like his daughter than a companion. And if Walter thought otherwise, he was too much of a gentleman to say anything.

Glass cases full of artworks lined the exhibit hall, and potential buyers milled about, hoping for a good deal come auction time. This crowd was more upscale than most, the items demanding top price.

Walter gently held her elbow, and they proceeded slowly through the rows of paintings, sculptures, and artifacts that made up today's bidding lots. His step was light and his face animated as he regaled her with tidbits of information about the pieces, still teaching her, as he had from the first day they worked together. Everything she'd learned about the art world, she'd learned from him. And if not for his great love of art, she would never see artifacts as anything but painful memories.

As they took their time, stopping at various items, she noted four security guards covering the exits, two standing at permanent posts and another two floating.

"We aren't alone," she whispered to Walter.

"Quite," he said, barely moving his lips. "We shall need to be expeditious."

Raven scanned the crowded room until her gaze settled on the Vassalo in the far corner, with a security guard posted nearby. Aside from the security detail, the room also housed a matrix of ceiling-mounted cameras; but all she needed was a few seconds, and since potential buyers had the right to inspect the painting, this should be quick and easy.

However, "easy" usually wasn't part of her job. Thank God, or she would have quit ages ago.

As they approached, the guard gave her a quick once-over and effectively dismissed her. Raven moved to the opposite side of the painting, looking bored, while Walter stood directly in front of it and made thoughtful clucking noises. After due time and with skilled ease, he engaged the security guard in idle chatter about the upcoming auction.

Raven waited until the guard was looking the other way to give Walter directions to the nearest bar before reaching out and lightly brushing her fingers over the painting's surface.

She inhaled sharply at the resurgence of pain and betrayal, concentrating on the surroundings that accompanied creation. Familiar pipe smoke filled her senses, along with the same sights and sounds of Venice that she'd felt with Bigley's Vassalo.

Authentic.

She broke the bond and stepped away from the painting to center herself. When she opened her eyes, she noticed the dark shadow of a man staring at her from thirty feet away.

Penetrating blue eyes full of condemnation bore through her disguise, stripping her of the past year and setting her back to a near disaster of a heist in a small suburb of Miami and a couple of nosy Ouray patrolmen. His hair was longer and the outfit was different, but his expression was still chiseled from pure granite.

Son of a bitch.

She'd remember that face anywhere.

Son of a bitch.

Dax would recognize that face anywhere.

She stared back at him from beneath the fringe of dark feathers, her hair tucked neatly underneath. While her partner in crime distracted the guard, Dax had watched her finger the painting with blatant hunger. The intense look on her face reminded him of a lover's satisfaction. But this woman was no lover. This one was a thief, a player, and potential trouble for his operation.

She raised her chin marginally in silent defiance, and a stony resolve swept across her expression. Then she stepped beside the old man and whispered something. He nodded to the guard, and they turned toward the main entrance for their escape.

I don't think so, Dax thought as he took a route around the room to cut them off. Potential buyers parted in his wake; one of the benefits of being a big man on a mission. He relished the flash of surprise in her eyes when he appeared in front of them just before they reached the main doors.

"Susan Carrey, isn't it?" Dax said.

She narrowed her eyes. "Sorry, I don't know you. Come on, Walter." She tugged at the startled gentleman.

Dax sidestepped in front of them. "No, I'm pretty sure it's Susan. I rarely forget a name. Or a face."

He stuck a hand out to the older man, who was eyeing him with great suspicion. "David Maddox."

"Walter Abbott," he returned in a distinct English accent. "May we be of service?"

Dax grinned. "Actually, I'd like to borrow Susan for a moment." He winked. "We're old friends. Very close."

"Not friends. Not close," she said coolly.

He leaned down, and with a hundred people present, said, "Don't you remember that hot night last summer?"

Her eyes widened a fraction, and he could almost feel the steam coming out of her nostrils.

"Or maybe you don't mind reminiscing about our good times in front of Mr. Abbott?"

She gave him a withering glare as their gazes locked in a war of wills. Finally, she turned and patted Abbott's hand. "It's fine. I'll catch up with you later."

He appeared uncertain as his white eyebrows knitted. "Are you sure, my dear?"

She shot him a quick smile that surprised Dax with its sincerity. "Positive."

Abbott nodded to Dax. "A pleasure meeting you." With that, he left.

Dax dropped the Good Humor Man act and latched onto her arm as he drew her through the patrons and into a nearby corridor. They were going to have a little talk before things got out of hand. He tried a few doors before finding a storage room unlocked, and ushered her inside.

When he turned around to face her, there was a Beretta Tomcat pointed at his head.

Okay. Looked like things were already out of hand.

He took a breath to ease the automatic fight response looking down the barrel of a gun always had on him. Too many witnesses around, and they'd all seen them leave together. She might be a thief, but she wasn't stupid. If anything, she was brilliant. He'd watched her talk his rookie partner into letting her go last year with minimal effort. Of course, that was Nick. Long legs and a hot phone number did that to him.

"You can get into a lot of trouble pulling a gun on a cop," he said, staying focused, which was a definite challenge, considering he was already trying to figure out where she hid a weapon in an outfit like that.

"Self-protection. I don't see a badge flashing. I don't see a uniform. So as far as I'm concerned, you kidnapped an innocent woman, dragged her into a closet, and backed her up against a wall."

"Innocent. Good one," he said with a laugh. "The way you were innocent when we caught you casing the Lowry house last summer?"

She lifted her chin, her expression challenging. "As I explained to your much nicer partner, I took a wrong turn on a late-evening walk. I was venting restless energy. I vent a lot. You might want to remember that."

She lowered the handgun to her side but didn't stow it. Probably a thigh holster. Now there was a visual distraction he didn't need.

Her lips pursed. "Can we just move on to the high points here? I'd like to make it to the auction tonight."

Beneath the smoky makeup and elegantly arched brows, her eyes were sharp and clear. And light blue, if he remembered right. Under the hat, her hair would be long, fine, and a shade of black that shone in the sunlight. And beneath the dress . . . a whole slew of distractions.

Dax stepped forward. "You aren't stealing that painting or anything else here tonight, lady. So keep your manicure off the merchandise."

A flash of anger passed behind her eyes. "Sorry to disappoint you, but no stealing today. Maybe tomorrow."

"So you're here just for the culture, is that it?"

"And why are you here?" She took in his leather jacket, oxford shirt, and jeans. "Bidding on an ashtray you fancy?"

He grinned. "I believe you fancy something else.

I saw the way you fondled that painting. I think you need a man."

Her eyes narrowed dangerously. "Number one, it's perfectly legal to cop a feel. No pun intended. Number two, the only man I need is the one with the bull's-eye over his heart at the shooting range. And number three—" Her eyes narrowed even more. "You're wasting your time with me. In more ways than one."

He watched her bat her eyelashes mockingly and decided that he wasn't above playing the bad-cop card today.

"You can count off all the reasons you want, but the bottom line is that I have the badge. And if I catch you anywhere near that painting, I'm going to use it. *I* won't let you go next time."

He leaned boldly into her personal space. She didn't move a muscle as he ran his gaze along her bare shoulders and down her body. He had to admit, she was pretty damn hot. But regardless of the view, she was standing between him and his quarry. And no one was going to do that. He'd been waiting for this chance for six months.

He looked her in the eye with renewed focus. "I'm watching you. All I need is a reason."

He turned and walked out.

Raven was still fuming when the auction began. The part of the confrontation that pissed her off the most was the fact that for once, she wasn't even planning to steal anything. The lack of any measurable guilt gave her categorical righteousness. How dare he hassle her? She was here as a lawful buyer. The arrogant bastard.

She sat beside Walter in sullen silence amid the rows of well-tailored bidders and spectators that crowded the hall and chattered between lots. One by one, they paraded through the process of selling art. Hundreds of thousands of dollars exchanged for a single object. If she had that kind of money, she wouldn't be buying art. She'd be . . . she didn't know what, but it would be something more important than hanging a painting over a staircase.

She took note of who bought what, but mostly she waited for the Vassalo. God, she was bored.

Beside her, Walter watched the proceedings with rapt interest.

"The house is doing well tonight," he said softly but with as much giddiness as Walter's breeding would allow. "All lots are selling above catalog estimates."

She nodded, half listening to his ramblings about how art continued to escalate in price even as the economies of their native countries crumbled. His monotone melded in with the other sounds.

A movement to her right caught her attention, confirming her suspicion that Maddox was indeed a man of his word. He stood against the wall, parallel to her row. A cool blue gaze met hers. Thick dark brown hair brushed his forehead. His jaw was set—square and firm. Judging from his big frame and the way the supple leather jacket hugged his shoulders, she figured he went for around 190 pounds of nicely distributed muscle. Not bad for a cop. *For a cop* being the operative phrase.

She couldn't believe he'd caught her last year. She'd been so wrapped up in the job that she'd failed to follow her number-one rule: Watch out for the local police. She would still like to know how he and his partner had found her. Probably Neighborhood Watch. She hated that damn program.

Maddox's gaze locked on hers for a moment with riveting focus before he looked away and scanned the rest of the room. She watched for a few seconds longer and realized his concentration was elsewhere. Interesting. That meant he wasn't here for her. Part of her was happy. Part of her was dying to know who here was a bigger threat than she was.

"How do you know Mr. Maddox?" Walter said, finally realizing she wasn't paying attention to the auction.

She gave him a crooked smile. "*Officer* Maddox. Ouray Smalltown PD. Detained me last year while I was on the Lowry assignment."

Walter's eyes widened. "Indeed. He arrested you?"

"I'm sure he wanted to, but I gave his rookie partner my phone number, and the kid talked Maddox into letting me go. But they made such a fuss, my cover was blown. The Lowrys were tipped off, and by the time I went back, they had moved the Remington bronze underground. I lost it."

Walter hummed with a scowl. "We are supposed to work *with* the local authorities. Officer Maddox was simply doing his job, you realize."

"Amateur," she said, ignoring Walter's subtle admonishment. "He has no business being in this world, no clue how it operates."

"If that's true, I wonder why he is here," Walter said, casting Maddox a quick glance.

Indeed, she wondered herself.

"Our Vassalo is up," Walter said to her in a hushed voice.

They wheeled the painting in on a trolley, and the room quieted measurably in respect to a Master. If only they knew what morbid emotions lurked beneath the surface; it wouldn't fetch a hundred bucks.

After a brief introduction of Lot 90, the auctioneer started the bidding at a respectable $1 million, and paddles went up in quick succession. The phone bidders were active as well, but Walter played the game better than anyone. While he worked, she glanced at Maddox, who was watching each bidder with deep concentration. The intensity on his face intrigued her. Why was he here? Who was he after? And what did she care as long as it wasn't her?

Raven turned back to the bidding when she heard, "I have 3.1 million." Twice Bigley's estimate and still going strong, which was not good news. They had an absolute limit of 5 million.

Walter flushed as the price continued to rise in liberal increments of a tenth of a million. Raven listened with growing dismay as the price topped 4 million, then hit 5.

Walter bid at 5 million and again at 5.5, exceeding their approved amount. He was promptly outbid and lowered his paddle. He gave her a disappointed look, and she closed her eyes. Damn. Of all the things she'd worried about, this wasn't one of them. So much for the easy way.

Maddox was watching her when she opened her eyes; then he zeroed in on the final bid offer.

The auctioneer announced, "$6.4 million." There was hushed silence.

Bid, she wanted to tell Walter. But she knew he wouldn't. He had his instructions, and Walter played by the book. And since she didn't have 6.5 million in her bank account, all she could do was watch helplessly as the auctioneer continued.

"Are you done at 6.4 million?" He nodded and banged the gavel. "Sold, then, at $6.4 million. Congratulations, sir."

Raven strained to hear the winning paddle number announced amid polite applause. Number 116. She caught a glimpse of a tall, slight man with thinning hair.

"Do you know him?" she asked Walter.

He nodded. "George Yarrow. A dealer based in Virginia. Representing one of his bigger clients, no doubt."

The next lot came up. Raven whispered, "Stay here and look interested. I'm leaving."

"What are you going to do?" Walter asked, highly worried.

She glanced around to find that Maddox was nowhere in sight. Good. Let him go harass someone else.

"It always pays to have a Plan B, Walter."

CHAPTER
4

Dax stood outside the auction room and watched the bidders exit after the auction ended. His target had to be here somewhere, but he still hadn't found him. But Dax knew one thing for certain—it wasn't the buyer of the Vassalo. Yarrow was a legitimate dealer. Besides, his body type and the way he moved didn't fit.

In fifteen years on the force, Dax had never been so frustrated or felt so out of place. He didn't belong here with these people, but there was nowhere else to go. He was out of options and out of leads. He thought for sure the Vassalo was his ticket. He'd banked on it. Maybe the boys at the station were right. Maybe the Vassalo paintings had nothing to do with the robbery six months ago.

Disappointment settled deep along with the feeling that he was spinning his wheels. Today was a bust. So far, all he had been able to manage was harassing a gorgeous thief. And it looked like she had come up as empty-handed as he had.

The last of the bidders passed by him, and he realized he hadn't seen her leave. Walter walked out alone, and Dax greeted him with a smile. "Nice to see you again, Mr. Abbott."

He looked at Dax with a start. "Yes, indeed. Excuse me—"

"I'm looking for Susan," Dax said, blocking Walter as he tried to pass by.

The old gentleman betrayed a grimace. "She left early. Wasn't feeling well."

Dax said, "That's too bad. I was hoping to catch up on old times."

Walter frowned. "I don't believe she would like that, Officer."

So she'd told him. What was Walter to her? A client? A sugar daddy? Dax didn't want to consider more than that.

He said, "I just have a few questions for her."

Walter lifted his chin. "She hasn't done anything wrong. You have no right to hound her further."

The older man's protectiveness was endearing but unnecessary. Dax had seen her in action, and she was perfectly capable of taking care of herself.

"Can you tell me where I can find her?"

Walter shook his head. "No, I can't. I don't know. Excuse me. It's been a long day." He brushed by Dax and disappeared into the retreating crowd.

Dax watched him leave. Walter's abrupt demeanor wasn't just for his sake. Both he and Susan had wanted that Vassalo badly; Dax had seen it on their faces during the bidding. He had a feeling she wouldn't take losing it well.

Looked like they'd all lost today.

And yet . . . He stilled, cop instincts chiming in.

According to his discussion with the auction folks, the buyer's name was Yarrow. And if Yarrow had the Vassalo, and she wanted it . . .

Dax made for the elevators.

Raven stopped at the hotel room door, pressed her hands along her hips, and smoothed out her black dress. Her hair was down over her shoulders, her makeup perfect, and her mission clear.

She had verbal approval from Bigley for a cool eight million, and although he'd intended that both she and Walter negotiate the deal, she decided to go solo on this one. Walter was a good man, and he meant well, but he followed the rules, and, in this case, they needed more than rules. Yarrow's clients weren't always the most virtuous bunch, and that meant Yarrow wasn't either. He could be bought. She figured between the cash and the dress, she was golden.

Bigley's disappointment echoed in her mind. He had been crushed when she told him they lost the painting, and even though it wasn't her fault, she felt the pinch of guilt. He so hoped to reunite the pieces. She wasn't going to let him down.

With a quick look down the corridor to make sure it was empty, she knocked on the door.

No response. She listened for activity and knocked again. Nothing. Damn. This job was turning into one pain in the ass after the other. She didn't feel like chasing the man all over the hotel. That's when she noticed the door was ajar. With a push, it swung open. Inside, the lights were on, which usually meant that someone was home.

She reached down her inner thigh for her handgun, and after making a final check of the hallway, stepped inside. Weapon first, she moved into the short entry and cleared the bathroom on the right. Toiletries were strewn across the floor.

"Mr. Yarrow?"

Nothing.

She proceeded slowly into the main room and swept the gun left to right from the window to the king-size bed to the wall. Empty and a mess. The room had been tossed, littered with clothing and Yarrow's belongings.

That's when she heard the groan on the other side of the bed. Stepping around, she stopped. Mr. Yarrow was lying on his back with a big, bloody gash in his forehead.

"Oh hell." She stowed the gun and knelt beside him. His eyelids were closed, and his breathing shallow. She reached for the phone.

"Don't touch it."

She froze at the sharp command and turned. *Maddox.* "Are you going to follow me everywhere?"

He reached down and hauled her to her feet. "Why is it wherever there's trouble, I find you?"

"I'm not responsible for this."

He wasn't even listening to her as he knelt and pressed two fingers to Yarrow's neck. He leaned over to look at the head wound, then stood up.

He grabbed a tissue from the box on the dresser and picked up the hotel phone. He used another one to punch up the front desk. "I'm in room 1505. I need an ambulance." Then he hung up, stuffed the tissues in his jacket, and grabbed her by the arm. "Let's talk."

She thought about arguing, but she really didn't want to be there when Security showed up. They were in the stairwell before Maddox spun around to face her. He looked bigger now in the narrow confines of the stairs. The air was stagnant and steamy.

He held out his hand. "Give me the gun."

She glared. "He wasn't shot. He was hit with a blunt object. I thought you were a cop."

"It could have been a gun butt."

"If it was, it wasn't mine. I didn't touch him. I walked in there and found him like that."

Maddox didn't flinch. "Give me the gun, or I'll get it myself."

The thought of him diving between her legs wasn't at all part of her plans for the evening. Intriguing, perhaps, but not tonight. *Damn him.* She reached down and pulled the Beretta from the thigh holster and laid it in his palm. He gave it a quick check and handed it back to her.

"What were you doing in his room?"

She slipped the weapon back into her holster, noting how still Maddox got when he glanced at her bare thigh under the dress. "I went to negotiate a sale of the Vassalo for my client."

"See anyone around?"

"No, I didn't," she admitted. "The hall was clear when I came on the floor."

He gave her a long, hard look, and she knew exactly what he was thinking. *Guilty.*

"Clubbing men over the head isn't my style," she said, brushing past him and descending the stairs. "My dry-cleaning bills would be astronomical."

He followed close behind even as she tried to figure

out how to shake him while wearing three-inch, sell-me-your-painting heels.

He asked, "Who are you working for?"

"None of your damn business."

"You can tell me who you work for, or I can turn you over to Hotel Security as a witness." Then he smiled like the devil, and she knew he'd do it. She was beginning to see the merits of giving him a little info to keep him happy, *then* sneaking away.

They hit the thirteenth-floor landing, and she turned to face him. "I work for API."

"Am I supposed to know what API stands for?" he asked.

She leaned back against the cool concrete wall. "Only if you know anything about art."

His blue eyes narrowed. "Why don't you educate me since you're being so helpful?"

"The Antiquities Preservation Institute. We recover lost or stolen artifacts for various clients. Churches, museums, private collectors, international governments. All legal and everything. The president is Thomas Bigley. You can call him yourself to confirm."

"What about Walter?"

"He freelances for API. Handles the auctions."

"I want to talk to him," Maddox said.

"Why?"

"I'd like to know where Mr. Abbot has been for the past few hours."

Anger welled up. "He's a seventy-year-old man. Besides the fact that he is a complete gentleman, he has a heart condition. There's no way he could have done that to Yarrow." Then she narrowed her eyes. "I couldn't help but notice that you were pretty hot to clear out of the room yourself."

His jaw worked. "I'm undercover. You aren't helping."

She laughed, and it echoed through the stairwell. "You have got to be kidding."

Much to her satisfaction, he looked slightly wounded. "Is there a problem?"

She scanned his jeans and jacket and regulation haircut. "Nice try, but even the bellhop can tell you're a cop." She looked around. "And where's your partner? I liked Junior much better."

Maddox's face hardened in a flash as he moved so close she could see the silver flecks in his eyes. Heat rolled off him in waves. She could have sworn he smelled like the sea.

"I'd really like to talk to Walter," he said softly.

Her heart thumped in her chest but not from fear. That she could control. Heat spread across her body, and moisture built between her breasts. No, this was far more subversive and dangerous than fear.

She exhaled and inhaled with deliberation. "Fine. But after we wake him, you go on your merry way and leave us the hell alone. Got it?"

"Deal." But he didn't look any less intense.

"Nice poker face," she grumbled, and pushed by him.

They walked down the next four flights to her floor. She knocked on Walter's door across from hers. They waited a few minutes but heard nothing.

"Is he a heavy sleeper?" Dax asked.

"How should I know?" she snapped.

That answered one question. After several more attempts, there was still no answer. Just for the hell of it, Dax pushed down the handle, and the door opened to a dark room.

"Oh no," she whispered under her breath, and reached for her Beretta.

"Move back." He drew his weapon. "Mr. Abbott?"

Silence. He slid inside and flicked the light switch. The room was clear. The bed appeared slept in but was cold now. Clothes were draped carefully over the chair back. A suitcase sat in the closet. There was no sign of a struggle or a search. Nothing seemed out of place.

"Mr. Abbott didn't strike me as a late-night partier," Dax said.

"He's not." Her voice sounded tight, and Dax turned as she stood in front of the mirror above the dresser, looking at a note taped there. He moved next to her and read it.

Dearest Raven,

The price for Walter Abbott's life is the Vassalo painting, Sad Maria, *to be delivered to the Financial District Station Metromover in downtown Miami by 8 A.M. on Friday. Put the painting in a steel suitcase and wait for instructions on your cell phone.*

I knew it was only a matter of time before the two of you sought me out. This time it will end differently. And tell Mr. Maddox no cops, or Abbott dies.

For a moment, neither one of them moved. Then she turned to him with anger in her eyes. "What the hell is this? You *know* this guy?"

Dax knew he'd been made. The good news and the bad was that he was on the right trail. "Looks like he knows you, too. Raven, is it?"

She rounded on him, toe-to-toe, rage clouding her expression. "It's an alias. Don't you dare pin this on me. Who is he? Who is the guy you came here to find?"

The woman was quick. He gave her a hard look. "A thief."

"No self-respecting thief kidnaps someone else to get what he can steal himself. So who is he?"

"If I knew, he'd be in cuffs by now," Dax told her truthfully.

She stared at him with ruthless accusation. "And tell me why on earth he thinks we are working together."

"No idea. Unless he saw us at the preauction," Dax said.

"He kidnapped Walter because you dragged me into a closet?"

Maybe she was right. Had he spooked the killer? Damn. He didn't expect this. "I don't know."

"Is he serious?" she asked.

Deadly serious. "Unfortunately, yes. Is this Walter's handwriting?"

"Yes," she said.

He pulled the note from the mirror. "I doubt we'll get any prints besides his, then."

"What about the rest of the room?" she asked.

"This guy wears gloves," he said absently. *At least he did six months ago.* Generic hotel stationery with a hotel pen. Nothing there. On the upside, there was no detectable sign of blood or a struggle, which meant that they walked out quietly. Maybe someone saw them leave.

"The guy wears gloves," she repeated. "You know all this. How many others has he kidnapped?"

"This is the first one," Dax admitted. Usually he just shot people.

She squinted at him, then said, "He got to Yarrow, too, didn't he? That's why you showed up. So while you were grilling me in the stairwell, this psycho was down here kidnapping Walter."

When Dax didn't reply, she put her hands over her temples and shoved her fingers through her hair. "Lovely, Maddox. Just fucking lovely. You got any last words before I kill you?"

He didn't. What he did have was a big-ass mess. This little foray had spun out of control faster than he could have imagined. An innocent man was now involved. This changed everything.

"Right," she said, rubbing her arms. "You don't give a damn about Walter. You just want your man."

Dax stared at the note, willing something to jump out at him. "He knows you, knows your name. Any idea who he might be?"

"None," she said as she gazed around the room in disgust.

"I realize this is an all-night question, but do you have any enemies?"

"Besides you?" she said, and paced the room. "Of course I have enemies. But this isn't one of mine."

"How do you know that?"

She stopped. "Let me see that note."

He handed it to her, and she turned around while she read it. Then she gave it back, her face pale and strained.

"What?"

"Nothing." She looked him in the eye and said, "Don't even think about calling in your pals, Maddox. Because I swear to God, if anything happens to Walter—"

"Nothing will," Dax said with conviction as he shoved the note in his pocket. "Let me find out if anyone on staff saw them leave. We'll go from there."

She watched him for a moment. "You do that. I'll be waiting in my room."

Raven alternated between fury and fear as she threw her clothes in her bag. Poor Walter. How could she have let this happen? She scooped up her toiletries and shoved them in the case.

The only thing she could pick up from the note was his fear. He hated guns, and there was no doubt in her mind that the kidnapper must have used one. It was enough to make her want to puke, especially after seeing what the kidnapper had done to Yarrow. Walter was in real danger, and Maddox knew it. In fact, based on his casual reaction to Walter's abduction, she could only assume Maddox wasn't surprised.

Whoever this bastard was, he wanted that painting. And Maddox wanted the bastard. Well, they were both bastards, and they deserved each other. Her priority was Walter, and the truth was, she didn't need Maddox for that. She could fix this.

She stuffed her bag with one hand and dialed Bigley's number with the other. He picked up on the second ring with a curt "Yes?"

"Sorry to bother you so late, but we have a slight problem."

"What happened? Yarrow wouldn't sell?"

She took a deep breath. "Not quite. I lost Walter."

There was a long pause. "Pardon me?"

"I went to see Yarrow myself. Someone knocked him out and tossed his room. When I got back, Walter had been kidnapped."

"Oh dear God. Why would anyone kidnap him?"

She mentally conjured up a photographic image of the letter. "The ransom is *Sad Maria* in two days."

"And you don't have it."

She zipped the suitcase closed. "Correct. But I'm going to get it. I promise I'll bring Walter back safely."

"And you are calling the police. This is nothing to fool around with," Bigley said firmly.

"I already contacted the cops," she told him. "They are working on the case." It was true. Mostly. Maddox could do whatever the hell he wanted as long as he didn't endanger Walter's life.

"So while they are doing their thing, I'm going to concentrate on the Vassalo. The auction house already shipped the painting to Yarrow's storage facility in Richmond. I have an early flight out. I'll need Paulie and all his tools when I get there."

Bigley quickly put two and two together. "We can buy the painting from Yarrow."

"No, we can't. Thanks to our kidnapper, Yarrow is lying in a hospital bed somewhere with head trauma. No idea if or when he will recover. There's only one way to get the painting by the drop date."

"We've discussed this, Raven. API isn't a ticket for you to steal."

She clenched her jaw. "Then I quit."

Bigley gave a sigh. "You know that's not necessary. But it's . . . wrong."

"And holding an old man for ransom is right?" she said with more anger than she'd intended. She took a deep breath. "I have to do this, Thomas. The kidnapper knows who I am, he knows what I do, and he's obviously watching me. If I don't go after the painting, he'll kill Walter."

She let that hang between them. *He knew who she was.* How? She always used multiple aliases when working, even when she'd been caught in Ouray. But worse than that, she had a sinking feeling that Walter was kidnapped *because* she was a skilled thief. And that she couldn't live with.

Bigley asked, "What if we offer him money instead? I'll pay any ransom."

She picked up the suitcase and walked to the door. "Possible, but I doubt money is what he wants. He's going to a lot of trouble for this painting. Besides, I have no way of contacting him. So I'm going to do what I can do, and that's get the Vassalo." She opened the door and scanned the long corridor. "Trust me. I'm good at this, remember?"

"Yes, I know. But let's hope the police find Walter first."

Don't count on it. Raven stepped out and closed the door behind her. "Right. I'll call you later."

She was gone.

Dax stood in the middle of her empty hotel room after Security had let him in. This just wasn't his day.

"Looks like she checked out early," the hotel guard said to him.

"It would appear so," Dax replied with a grin. "I thought something happened to her when she didn't show up for our date. Guess she just changed her mind."

"Yeah, women. Never know what they'll do." He shrugged a shoulder. "Maybe she'll be back."

"Maybe," Dax said with a tight smile. *No fucking way.* "Hey, thanks for getting up here at 1:00 A.M. I appreciate it."

"No problem. Anything for love." He nodded and was gone.

Dax looked at the bed that hadn't been slept in since yesterday. Love was the furthest thing from his mind. Murder, however, was right up top.

The drawers and closet were empty. No one abducted her; she would have put up one hell of a fight, and he was pretty sure shots would have been fired. No, she left of her own free will after they'd split up. He should have taken her with him when he canvassed the hotel staff. He thought she would at least wait until he gave her whatever he'd learned before trying to split.

He sat down on the edge of the bed and stared at his mirror reflection in shades of gray that matched his mood. When he'd heard about the Vassalo up for auction, he'd taken a chance that the killer would be here.

He'd been right. Then he'd lost him. Again.

And this time, he'd involved two more people, one whose life hung in the balance. No one he talked to remembered seeing Walter leave. For all Dax knew, he could already be dead. A cop killer would have no problem offing an old man.

It was obvious that the killer had recognized him. Had Dax spooked the killer? Was he responsible for Walter's abduction? Christ. He couldn't take another life on his hands, and he wouldn't.

He pulled out his cell and dialed. It rang twice before being picked up with a terse "Kilroy. This better be god-damned World War III."

Dax couldn't help but grin. "Did I interrupt something, Harry?"

"Yeah, my beauty sleep. Jesus, Dax, can't you ever call me at a decent hour?"

"Don't want Marianne thinking you're having an affair?"

"Hell no, but I gotta live with her. And I'm telling you right now, I'm not responsible when she kicks your ass next time you stop by for barbecue."

Dax laughed. "Deal. Listen, I need some help."

"I had a feeling this wasn't a social call. Give me a minute."

Dax heard a door close, and Harry Kilroy came back. "Where are you?"

"On the trail of a cop killer."

There was a long pause. "Tell me you got that son of a bitchin' bastard cornered like a dog."

Dax stood up and walked to the window. The Miami skyline blinked back at him. Neon lights that only flashed black and white for him. "Not yet, but I might be close. I need some info."

Kilroy said, "Anything."

"For starters, a complete background check on a Susan Carrey. Address unknown, but she works for

an outfit called API. Antiquities Preservation Institute.
See if she has any known aliases."

"Is this for a date or something?"

Only if he completely lost his mind. "No."

"Too bad. What else?"

Dax gave him the name of the hotel and the info on
Walter and Yarrow.

"Yarrow was assaulted earlier this evening. I think it
was our man. See if you can pull the report filed by the
locals."

Kilroy said, "Got it. You know it's too bad you left
the force. We could really use your help. You're officially closer to this guy than anyone else at this point."

As it should be. A familiar headache was forming
behind Dax's eyes, fueled by frustration and words that
haunted his every waking minute. *You blew it, Maddox. You didn't cover Nick's back. You didn't follow
protocol.*

Dax rubbed his neck. He had a choice to make. Tell
Harry about the kidnapping and bring in the Feds, or take
it and run. Not much of a choice, really. The killer knew
he had a cop on his tail. If Dax brought anyone else in
now, he was pretty sure the trail would end quick and
bloody. "I'd appreciate it if you kept this between you
and me, Harry."

He paused on the other end. "You aren't going to do
anything stupid, are you? Because you know how much
I hate cleaning up after you."

"Define *stupid*," Dax said.

"Like not calling me when you have him dead to
nuts."

Dax felt the empty inside pocket of his jacket. "You think I'm going to blow him away like he did Nick?"

"Yeah, that's exactly what I think you're going to do. Look, I want this guy as much as you do, but I need to know that I'm not helping you on the road to twenty to life."

"He killed my partner, and no one cares that he's walking around like it never happened," Dax said, cold hatred heavy in his chest.

"We care. Everyone cares. We just haven't caught him yet. We will never stop trying. But if you take him out, we'll have to come after you. And I'd hate that even more."

"Nick was just a kid," Dax said. "He deserved more than what he got."

Harry sighed in commiseration. "It wasn't your fault, Dax. You gotta let it go."

Dax stared out into the night. It could have happened yesterday, the memory was so clear. For fifteen years, he'd followed the rules of justice laid out in procedures and protocols. And for the past six months, he'd been waiting for justice to be served. He was sick of waiting, and letting go wasn't an option.

"I'll do the right thing," he finally said because it was what Harry wanted to hear.

"Good." He yawned. "I'll get this info for you first thing tomorrow."

"Thanks, Harry. Tell Marianne sorry for me."

"Always do." The line went dead.

Dax pulled out the ransom note and reread the line that confused him the most.

Only a matter of time before the two of you sought me out.

What the hell did that mean? Why would he think they were working together? Until a few hours ago, Dax had no idea where Susan had been for the past year. How was she tied into this? And how did the kidnapper know that alias when Dax ran the background check on her last year and didn't pick it up?

Dax had a real bad feeling that their kidnapper knew a whole lot more about them than they did about him.

The best bet was to follow through with the ransom and try to nab the kidnapper at the drop. Which meant Dax needed the thief, and he knew just where to find her. He folded the note and stuffed it in his pocket on his way out the door.

According to what he'd learned from the auction people, the painting had already been shipped to a warehouse in Virginia. He supposed he could just sit tight, let her do all the work, and wait at the Metromover, but hanging around here doing nothing for two days wasn't too appealing.

Watching her in action, however, just might be.

CHAPTER
5

These warehouse districts all look the same. Generic, gray, and damn ugly. A crime against architects everywhere," Paulie said. Green images flashed across the screen in front of him as he scanned the complex with the long-range night-vision camera mounted atop the fifteen-foot surveillance truck.

"At least they're standardized," Raven said, leaning in for a better look. The storage complex sat on the eastern edge of Richmond in the middle of an industrial park. Things were nice and quiet at 2:00 A.M. "Give me top shot."

Paulie pulled up a satellite image and zoomed into focus. The facility was bordered by roads on three sides and a wooded area along the back edge.

"What are we looking at for a perimeter?"

"Typical setup for the age of the complex. Galvanized commercial-grade chain-link fence surrounding a sixty-four-unit matrix of concrete buildings. One main gate for entry here and one side gate." He pointed to each one.

"I'm sure they are both wired for intrusion. You'll want to cut through the fence instead."

"Tree-line side," she decided.

"Yeah, that's definitely the best bet for access. Floodlights on the fence and interior. Probably motion detectors as well."

"Guards?"

He shook his head. "No guardhouse. These places don't usually provide that kind of service. And I haven't even seen any security units drive by in the past four hours."

"Dogs?"

He grinned at her. "All the bad guys you've faced, I can't believe you're afraid of dogs."

She frowned. "Try having one bite you in the ass, and you'll see my point."

"Don't see any signs of dogs either, but I can't guarantee that one."

She patted the canister of pepper spray on her utility belt just in case. "What about the structures?"

"Poured-concrete walls. About twenty feet high, probably ten inches thick. Steel roofs. No windows. One primary door and one vertical-lift loading door. Both would be wired with magnetic switches. Standard keyed or keypad entry. The lessees of each building are responsible for their internal security systems after that."

"Which could be anything," Raven noted.

"Correct."

She would prefer to know how much Yarrow was willing to spend to protect his goods, but that wasn't an option. She'd have to assume a worst-case scenario. "Can we cut the power and phones?"

Paulie checked one of his monitors. "Most of these systems have wireless signals and backups. Problem is, there's no way of knowing which building has it and which one doesn't. Could lead the cops right to you."

And if the alarm went off, she probably wouldn't even know. Silent alarms were a bitch. "Which one is Yarrow's?"

Paulie tapped the screen near the wooded edge. "Second structure in from the back."

"The main gate is on the other end," Raven noted.

"And opposite the side gate as well. That location might get you a little more time. But we won't know what he's got inside until you get there. My guess would be motion sensors, cameras, independent arming panels. The tricky part here is locating the painting."

Not tricky. Time-consuming. "How much time do I have if I just run it?"

"I checked the local logs. Response goes through the sheriff's office, so it would be as quick as eight minutes if they've got nothing better to do."

Breach the perimeter fence, reach Yarrow's unit, pick the door lock, gain entry, defeat the internal alarms, locate the right cage, snip and duck inside, retrieve the Vassalo, and retreat to the truck. On a good day, that would be fifteen minutes.

"I need more time. Any other options?"

He grinned. "We haven't played Keystone Kops in a while."

She grinned back. She really liked Paulie.

And then there was a loud banging on the back door of the truck. "Open up!"

"Jesus!" Paulie jumped three inches before trying to

switch his cameras to get a bead on who had snuck up on them.

Raven scooted through the narrow walk-through doorway to the front cab area and looked through the dark windows. No people. No flashing lights. No other vehicles in sight along the street.

By the time she returned to the back, Paulie had a fix on their man. Even by the green night vision, she knew who it was.

Maddox.

That man was impossible to shake.

More banging. "Police. Open up."

All the color drained out of Paulie's face as he tangled himself up in his headset. "Oh my God. Oh my God."

Raven put her hand on his arm. "Easy."

"It's the cops," he said frantically. "I've never been to jail, Raven, but I hear it sucks."

"One cop," she corrected him. One pain-in-the-ass cop who was not going to screw this up. "Move into the driver's seat and get ready to take off if I bang on the side."

She pushed by him and out the rear door as Maddox was coming around the corner.

"About damn time," he said, looking highly pissed even in the darkness.

"What do you want now?" she snapped.

He stopped in front of her. Without her three-inch vamp heels, he stood a good six inches taller. The night temperature was warm, around seventy degrees, but he wore a long-sleeved black shirt and dark pants. She had a bad feeling she knew why.

He said, "I want in on the heist and the drop."

"Heist?" She cocked her head. "Heist. Hmm. Sorry, I have no idea what you are talking about."

His teeth gleamed in the night. "I'll bet if I checked the inside of this delivery truck, you and API would have some explaining to do."

Bastard. "You're a long way from home, Maddox. You have no jurisdiction here."

He lifted a cell phone. "All I have to do is make one call."

She gritted her teeth. She didn't need this. It had cost her a day to fly here, rendezvous with Paulie, and wait for nightfall. The painting needed to be back in Miami in twenty-eight hours. It was tonight or never.

She hissed, "Why are you doing this? Why are you risking Walter's life?"

"I won't risk his life," Maddox said firmly.

Did he really believe that? She doubted it. So far everything he'd done had been for his own case.

"We'll get him back," he added. "But I want that kidnapper."

His conviction made her go still. There was something he wasn't telling her. "Why? Why is he so important? What has he done?"

Maddox hesitated. "He killed a cop."

Raven's breath caught. Killed? *Killed?* A cop? Then anger waged in. "And you didn't think to tell me this back at the hotel?"

"Need-to-know basis."

She was so furious, she could hardly breathe. A cop killer had nothing to lose. Walter— "Well, here's something you need to know. If anything happens to that sweet old man, I will come after you. I don't care who you are."

That hung in the warm summer air for a moment as they stared at each other.

"That sounds a lot like a threat," he finally said.

"Threats are for wimps. That's a goddamn promise. Now if it's okay with you, I have work to do." She turned to go, and he snagged her arm.

"I'm coming with you. We're partners," he said. "Says so on the note."

"Don't *ever* say we're partners." She shook her arm free. "I don't need to be babysitting you. I work alone."

"Not tonight, you don't. I can almost guarantee that you'll try to lose me once you have the painting."

"Really? And how do I know you won't arrest me and make the drop yourself after I go to all the trouble to get the ransom?"

His eyes narrowed. "Your imagination scares me."

"It also keeps me alive."

"You have no idea how much better that makes me feel," he said. "I guess you'll just have to trust me on this."

"Don't count on it." She glared at him. "Make no mistake. If you turn on me, I will be sure the authorities know that you were in on this."

He smiled slowly. "Wouldn't have it any other way, partner."

Be careful what you wish for, Dax thought as he followed her into the night. He was now wearing a black balaclava, a TASC headset for communications with someone in the truck, and carrying the bolt cutters. He was about to turn to the dark side. Nick was probably rolling in his grave, loving this.

The truck pulled away, and she moved across the road like a ghost. Dax dropped into the dry ditch beside her as she swept the area with night-vision binoculars. One hundred feet of wide-open, hard-packed Virginia clay stretched between them and the chain-link fence. Beyond that was row upon row of concrete, boxlike structures.

"The truck is set, Raven," Dax heard. So it *was* Raven.

"I don't get to meet your friend?" he asked.

"Cops make him nervous, and I don't need him distracted tonight."

Dax studied her profile as she concentrated. She was all business now. Gone was the eyelash-batting sweet thing who had conned Nick into letting her go last year. Gone was the rich buyer at the auction. This was the real Raven. The thief.

She lowered the binocs. "Stay close to me. Keep your eyes on the target. And do everything I say."

"You sound like one of my sergeants."

Her eyes were like daggers through her balaclava.

He smiled. "Except none of them ever threatened to kill me."

"I find that extremely hard to believe." She slipped the binocs into her jacket.

"What kind of name is Raven anyway?"

He could see her freeze for a second. "What kind of name is Dax? Sounds like a video game."

His turn to glower. "So what's the plan here?"

"We wait for the signal. After that, follow my lead. With any luck at all, it'll be over in fifteen minutes."

"Fifteen minutes?"

Her eyes met his, direct and sure. "Only because I'm not exactly sure where the painting is."

"Christ," he muttered. Welcome to the dark side.

"Plus I have you along, which will slow me down because you won't be quiet," she added coolly. "Try to keep up."

Seeing her in action wasn't quite as much fun as he'd expected. His comm crackled, and a young man's voice came on. "Get into position."

"Game on," Raven said.

She scrambled out of the ditch and raced toward the fence, with Dax behind her. They crouched at a spot between floodlights where it was dark. She held the links, and he made the first cut on the bottom row. Pieces of steel flicked through the air as he worked his way up. When the hole was up to his chin, Raven yanked on the fencing and it rolled back, stretching a hole big enough for them to slip through.

They sprinted down two rows before Raven stopped at one of the units. As she knelt in front of the door and pulled out a pick set, Dax looked around. No alarms. No blue flashing lights. So far, so good.

"Ready here," she said into her mike.

A split second later, a chorus of alarms rang out.

Dax froze. "Was that us?"

"My assistant." Raven worked the lock. "He set them all off."

Dax frowned at her. "Doesn't that defeat the whole idea of stealth?"

"Not if the local authorities have to check every single unit," she said. "They'll start from the front and work their way back. About halfway through and finding nothing, they'll decide that it's a false alarm and head for the nearest Dunkin' Donuts."

He shook his head. The criminal mind never failed to amaze him. "And we're in the back."

She stood up and swung the door open. "Precisely. Shut the door behind you and lock it."

The interior was lit with diffused light, but it didn't matter because there wasn't much to look at. A series of mesh cages embedded in the concrete floor fit inside, each containing crates, boxes, and a few large statues.

Dax glanced up and saw cameras. "Smile. We're on *Candid Camera*."

Raven was studying a grease board on the wall. "Relax. Half the time they aren't even plugged in." She pointed to a small electronic box on her belt. "Besides, we have a scrambler. It'll screw with the video, and all they'll see is static. Just stick close to me because it has a short range." Then she walked by him. "Although it would do my heart good to see you caught stealing on tape."

He narrowed his eyes and followed her between the cages. "I'll bet. What happens when we get out of range?"

She shrugged. "They can see us. Don't look into any cameras."

He shook his head. Some plan. "You're pretty good at this."

She stopped at one cage containing a single large crate and glanced at him. "So are you. I think you have an affinity."

Just what he wanted to hear.

"The cops are on their way. Three minutes have elapsed, Raven," Dax heard in his earpiece.

"Almost done," she replied, and pointed to the cage in front of them. "It's this one."

It looked just like every other cage. "How do you know?"

She knelt in front of the door and worked on the lock. "It's on the warehouse grease board. Vassalo, delivered this morning."

"Very thoughtful of them. You think they had any idea it's worth six mil?"

The lock clicked open, and Raven stepped inside. "None. Would you?"

"No," he admitted. "I can think of a lot better uses for six million dollars."

"There's something we agree on. But apparently, that's the price for one man."

Dax helped her set the crate on its side and pop the latches. The plywood top came off easily, and inside lay the Vassalo in all its glory. His ticket to a killer.

Raven shook out a padded bag and slipped it around the painting. Then they replaced the top on the crate and put it back into position.

A more frantic-sounding voice came through. "Five minutes are up, Raven. ETA on the police, less than two."

"Must have caught them between coffee breaks," she replied with more than a little sarcasm.

Dax ignored the jab. All he wanted to do was get out of here before more hell let loose.

She tucked the painting under her arm, and they headed for the door. The alarms were still wailing when they ran back to the hole in the fence, across the open field, and into the woods behind the complex. In the

distance, Dax heard the sirens. His body responded automatically with adrenaline he would have used to catch
bad guys.

He shook it off. He'd spent every moment of the last six
months waiting for a break, and now he had it. No turning
back. He watched the patrol cars roll in, lights strobing
in the night. They wouldn't find anything. No prints. No
recordings. In fact, no one would even know the painting
was gone until Yarrow's people opened the crate.

Raven pulled off her balaclava, her long hair spilling
out around her shoulders. Her lips were curled into a
smile, her eyes bright as she watched the action.

"Enjoying yourself?" he asked.

She turned to him, and her enthusiasm faded. "I'm not
the one who got us into this mess."

"Don't be too sure."

Raven stared at him for a moment before she looked
away and adjusted her mike. "We're clear."

"You got it?" the young voice came back.

"Got it."

A whoop went up on the other end. "Yes!"

"Thanks for all your help," Raven said.

Dax added, "Yeah, thanks."

There was a pause on the other end. "Uh. Uh—"

Raven cut in. "We're going to get Walter. Head out."

"Okay. Be careful."

She yanked off her headset. "Stop scaring him,
Maddox."

Dax smiled a little at shaking her cool. "He should be
scared working with you."

She walked up to him, her face resolute. "I would never
let anything happen to him. I take care of my own."

Then she pulled a GPS unit from her pocket and checked it. "My bag is fifty meters north. From there, we'll hike to your car and get on the road. It's a fourteen-hour drive to Miami. I want to be in Florida by dinner, get a good night's sleep, and arrive at the drop location early Friday morning." She pocketed the GPS. "Since you're so all-fired up to play partners, you can take the first shift driving."

Dax watched her head into the woods with the painting. He was getting pretty damn tired of being ordered around, but that was about to change. They were heading into his territory now.

CHAPTER
6

Raven jolted awake when the car door slammed, disoriented at being the passenger in a car she didn't recognize with a driver she'd like to forget. They were parked at a low-rent diner surrounded by tractor trailers and cypress trees.

Maddox handed her a bag. "Grub. Eat at your own risk."

She took it and inhaled the welcome smell of pastries and coffee. "Where are we?"

"Just south of Savannah."

The car clock said noon. She'd slept for four hours after nodding off during Maddox's silence. The man wasn't much of a talker when he was wound up. She thought it might have been the adrenaline rush, but decided from his crabby demeanor that it went deeper than that. Or maybe he was just plain crabby.

At least they were making decent time. Good enough to reach Miami in seven hours, clean up, and get some sleep before picking up Walter tomorrow morning. She felt a pang of worry. Was he okay? Was he being treated well by a killer?

As much as she wanted to lash out at Maddox, the truth was that the kidnapper had targeted Walter for a reason, and she couldn't shake the feeling that *she* was that reason. Why else would the kidnapper pick her? How else would he know her name? Maybe he had tried to get Yarrow to tell him where the painting was, and when he couldn't get it for himself, he decided to let a recovery specialist do it for him. But if he needed her, why drag Maddox into this, too?

She glanced in the backseat where the painting sat in a Samsonite suitcase, relieved for the hundredth time that she was in possession of the one thing that would save her fellow agent and friend.

"Still worried I'll take it from you?"

Raven swung back to face him. "Don't expect me to trust you, Maddox. Not after you lied to me."

He grinned a smile that didn't quite reach his eyes. Even after hours of driving and no sleep, he looked good in a rumpled, sexy kind of way. How did men do that? It was the curse of women everywhere.

"Goes both ways, Raven," he said, emphasizing her name. "So how many aliases do you have?"

Great. Seven more hours of this. With any luck, he'd fall asleep. She bit into a glazed cruller. "More than you'll ever know," she said. "I'll drive the rest of the way."

He nodded and took a sip of OJ. They ate in silence for a few minutes before Raven asked, "So when did you get promoted from patrol to detective?"

His donut paused halfway to his mouth. "Recently."

She eyed him. "And you're working solo? Don't you guys usually play tag team?"

He shrugged. "It's a small department. Besides, he said no cops, remember?"

She narrowed her eyes. Something wasn't right. Maddox wasn't being forthright with the pertinent info.

Raven crumpled up her bag and stepped out of the vehicle a little stiffly. Savannah heat swept over her. The sky was gray, air thick and moist and mixed with the smell of diesel fuel.

She reached down and let her spine stretch as she touched the ground. Her body was still a little wired from the job last night, and she knew from experience that it would take a while to come down. Normally, she'd go for a run or get a workout to purge the aftereffects, but time was short.

She'd have preferred a flight from Richmond to Miami, but not with a stolen painting in tow. A private charter wasn't much safer. The less of a trail she left, the better. So instead she was stuck in a car with a man with the words *Stop! Thief!* written across his forehead. Only for Walter would she do this.

When she stood up, Maddox was leaning on the hood of his Ford Explorer watching her, looking far too alert for this early in the morning. A fleeting glance of interest was replaced by indifference as he turned away. Even in faded jeans and a plain white T-shirt, he stood out from most men. Maybe it was his loose stance. Or the sharp blue eyes that didn't miss a thing. Or maybe it was that he didn't talk much. She especially liked that one.

She reached in the Explorer and grabbed her bag. "I'm going to wash up," she said before stopping midstep. She cast a quick look to the backseat, then at Maddox.

One corner of his mouth rose. "Don't think you can hold out for seven hours."

Dax watched uncertainty play across her face. She wouldn't leave him alone with the painting and the car keys. This should be interesting.

He crossed his arms. "Hell of a dilemma, huh?"

"Don't suppose you'd give me the keys *now*?" she asked.

He grinned. "Sure. On one condition."

Her eyes rolled upward. "This is exactly why I don't do partners."

"Your real name."

She looked annoyed. "Raven."

"No. Not one of your aliases. The name you were born with."

"And why can't Raven be my real name?"

"Because you picked it yourself."

She glared at him.

"And if you give me another fake name, I'm going to know," he added.

"Live in disappointment. The name is Raven Callahan." She thrust out her hand. "Keys."

He dug them out of his pocket and pressed them into her palm. The skin-to-skin contact shot through him, far more intimate than he'd expected. Her expression told him she'd felt it, too.

"That wasn't so hard, was it?" he said as he shoved his hands in his pockets.

"Excruciating," she replied, but her fingers were clenched white around the keys as she walked away.

He watched the sunlight pick up the sheen of her loose hair and the subtle roll of her hips. Long legs flexed under the short shorts she'd changed into. The snug tank top hugged her breasts. There was a body built for distraction. He'd had a hell of a time keeping his eyes and mind on the road while she slept beside him. He could only imagine what she was going to do to the truckers hanging around inside. Probably the same thing she did to most men. Make them forget so she could get her way like she had with Nick. She was a player, above all else. The only time she wasn't acting was when she was stealing.

Well, she wasn't going to play him. He had other plans for her. He pulled out his cell and dialed Harry.

"Kilroy here." Dax could hear dispatch squawking in the background and the familiar sounds of patrol life. He shook off the regret.

"Morning, Harry."

"I didn't realize it was you, what with the normal calling hours and all."

Dax grinned. "Thought you might appreciate that. Got any info for me?"

Papers rustled. "Here we go. A lot of Susan Carreys out there, but none of them work for API."

"Try Raven Callahan."

"Will do. Yarrow has a concussion and is still unconscious. The locals are calling it a robbery at this point. His wallet, watch, and valuables were gone. API checked out as a legitimate art recovery company based in New York City. They claim to provide investigative services to help their clients recover stolen art by working with the authorities."

Dax almost laughed. He would bet his life Raven had never once cooperated with the local authorities.

"And Walter Abbott is listed as a consultant. Couldn't

find a whole lot on him. He lives a pretty quiet life in the Big Apple. No criminal record. Nothing out of the ordinary."

"No prints in Yarrow's room?"

"It was clean."

As expected. "Are you on duty tomorrow morning?"

"No. You want to go fishing?"

"In a way. Do me a favor and hang around the downtown Metromover, say about 8:00 A.M."

There was a pause. "Something going down?"

"Maybe. I'd like some backup that doesn't look like backup."

"I see. You'll explain this great mystery to me at some point, right?"

"Right."

There was a grumble on the other end. "Be careful."

"Thanks, Harry. Later."

Dax climbed into the passenger side, pushed the seat back, and closed his eyes. Sleep would be a welcome respite from reality. In the past forty-eight hours, he'd threatened a woman, walked out on an assault victim, gotten an innocent man kidnapped, lied to one of his best friends, and stolen a priceless painting.

He was going to hell in a big way. The sad part was he wasn't even enjoying himself in the process.

A few minutes later, Raven slid into the driver's seat and started the SUV. Raindrops hit the windshield.

Eyes shut, body exhausted, Dax said, "Make sure you stay around the legal speed limit."

"You're a cop. Just flash your pretty badge as we blow by them at a hundred miles per hour."

"That's not what the badge is for. Besides, you want

to explain the hot six-million-dollar painting in the backseat?"

There was a lengthy pause. "You were a Boy Scout, weren't you?"

He opened one eye with a halfhearted glare. "Those days are long gone. Don't think I won't bust your ass if I get the chance."

She gripped the steering wheel with a vague look, like her mind was far away. It was the same expression she'd had after reading the kidnapper's note.

"What is it?" he asked.

She blinked a few times. "Nothing."

She was probably trying to figure out how to lose him again. Not until he was through with her. He closed his eyes. "Wake me when we hit Florida."

At 10:00 P.M., Raven stood in the entry of a grimy, orange, no-tell motel room off the interstate. There was one double bed that looked like it'd seen a whole lot of action, a chair that she wouldn't let a dog sit in, and enough matted shag carpet to hide a hoard of locusts. The room still held the heat of southern Florida, which only added to the claustrophobia.

Maddox came in after her and shut the door, plunging the already depressing interior into a coma. He surveyed the devastation. "Nice hiding place. Our boy will never suspect we'd be desperate enough to stay here."

She set the suitcase containing the painting on the bed. "You're the one who wanted to wait until ten o'clock to find a hotel. This is what you get."

He tossed his jacket on a chair, and something scurried across the rug. They looked at each other.

"The Explorer's looking better and better," Maddox said.

"Feel free. I'll take my chances in here," she said.

If she sat in that SUV one more minute, her head was going to explode. She squeezed the bridge of her nose where an I-95 under frickin' construction forever headache was throbbing. Their seven-hour drive had turned into ten thanks to traffic delays and rain, and she had the strongest urge to run down every orange cone she saw.

He turned on the ancient air-conditioning unit in the window, and it shuddered to life. "You just can't wait to get rid of me."

"Hey, anyone ever tell you you're pretty sharp for a cop?"

She walked past the bed and peered into the bathroom. Ancient, water-stained, and it smelled like urine. Maddox moved up behind her.

After a moment, he looked down at her. "If you aren't out in ten minutes . . . you're on your own."

She smiled. "You first."

He held out his hand. "Keys."

"On one condition."

His eyes narrowed.

"Tell me what your friend had to say when you called him on your cell phone back at the diner this morning."

He arched an eyebrow. "You think I have friends?"

"It could happen. My bet is that it was another cop. So what did you find on me?"

He turned serious. "Nothing on Susan. Raven Callahan should be much more interesting."

"It will be," she said. "What else?"

"API is legit. Walter works there. Yarrow hasn't recovered yet. No prints in the room."

Frustration seeped into her voice. "And that's it?"

His lips tightened. "That's all I got."

There was something he wasn't telling her. Something he knew she wouldn't like. "You didn't mention the kidnapping to him?"

"No."

"And there will be no cops at the drop, right? Nothing that would put Walter in danger?"

"Right."

She studied him for a minute. Poker face. Great. Always the cop, first and foremost. They never change. At least the good ones.

She dropped the keys in his hand, careful not to touch him again. Once was enough. She had no idea what happened in the last exchange, but her fingers were still tingling. He grabbed his bag and disappeared into the bathroom. As soon as the shower came on, she dialed Paulie.

A drowsy voice answered on the fifth ring. "Yeah."

"Where are you?" she asked.

"Jeez, is that any way to talk to a guy who's been driving all day? I just got to sleep two minutes ago."

"Where are you?"

He gave a groan and made a bunch of noises that sounded like the phone falling off the table before finally coming back. "Marriott near the Miami airport."

She cast a look around her abysmal room. Not the Marriott. "Remember you need to get to the station early tomorrow."

"I know, I know. I'll be there."

"I also want you to do a little research on Officer David Maddox. He works for the Ouray Police Department. It's a small resort town just south of Miami."

Paulie yawned. "Will do first thing in the morning. Any particular reason? I mean, we're out of there as soon as we get Walter, right?"

She stared at the suitcase in front of her. "Maddox can have his kidnapper for all I care. My job is to make sure Walter is back safe and sound. The cops are on their own."

"Works for me. Good night." He hung up.

She held the phone, debating whether or not to check in with Bigley while she had the privacy. But then the ugly cloud of guilt descended and ruined everything. Not tonight. Besides, she was beyond tired, and it wasn't all from the long drive.

She'd spent the day with her hands on Maddox's steering wheel. Unfortunately, her psychic abilities didn't come with an on/off switch, and the more tired she got, the more she picked up. He wasn't a happy man. There was guilt, frustration, and a little anger, mostly directed toward her.

And then there was the other stuff. The hot stuff. The kind of base sexual male flashes that would keep her awake at night. Raven glanced at the lone double bed. Especially this night. She really needed to date more.

The shower shut off, and she hid her cell before Maddox emerged from the bathroom wearing only a pair of jersey shorts.

Nice chest, were the first words that registered in her mind. Broad, tanned, deep, and connected to equally nice biceps, shoulders, torso, legs . . . An all-male body to go with the all-male thoughts. It was going to be a long night.

He paused briefly when he noticed her staring and locked on her with blue eyes that looked right through her. Damn. If he put that kind of focus into everything he did—she might have to make this a cold shower.

She picked up her bag. "Any words of wisdom before I go in?"

He rubbed a towel across his head. "There's something in the corner by the ceiling. Don't make eye contact with it."

"Do I need my gun?"

Maddox looked her up and down, lingering briefly on her mouth. "You can take him."

She held out her hand. "Keys."

He stopped drying his hair and pulled the keys from his shorts pocket with slow deliberation. He held them above her hand, and she waited for the bribe to begin.

"So what do you like?" he said.

Her eyebrows hitched along with her breath. "Excuse me?"

He gave her a little "gotcha" grin. "Cheese or pepperoni?"

Ten minutes later, the urge to run over construction cones had subsided significantly. The water was luke-warm, the soap barely lathered, and the towels were like sandpaper, but Raven didn't care. She was clean, and her thoughts were once again her own.

And then she smelled pizza.

She hastily donned a T-shirt and shorts and flung the door open. Maddox was leaning bare-chested against the headboard flicking through the TV channels. Half a large pepperoni pizza lay on the bed next to him.

It was every woman's fantasy.

Blue eyes skimmed over her for a moment before he said, "Better get some pizza before the resident vermin carry it off."

"I take back almost every homicidal thought I ever had about you," she said, crawling onto the bed.

She took a bite and moaned. It wasn't the best pizza she'd ever had. It didn't even rank in the top five, but right now, it was perfect. She inhaled the first slice, licked her fingers, and reached for another.

Maddox's gaze lingered on her mouth, then dropped to the open V of her T-shirt as she leaned over. Their eyes locked, and his darkened slightly before he looked away. She felt the heat to her toes and smiled.

He was human after all.

"So," she said slowly as she took a nibble of pizza. "Speaking of the art world, which I know you know nothing about, how did you figure your killer would be at the auction?"

He gave a shrug. "I'm working on a theory."

She stared at him, waiting. "Which is?"

He set down the remote and crossed his arms, giving her his full attention. "I think he's after the Vassalos. He was stealing a Vassalo painting when he killed the officer. In fact, it was the only piece he took. Do you thieves usually go after a particular artist, or is it based on value?"

He smirked knowingly when he said it, and all those homicidal thoughts came back. "We thieves work for all kinds of reasons. In fact, you should know that firsthand."

His expression remained unchanged, but she knew better. She finished off her slice. "Novices usually go for quantity, ease, and opportunity. More experienced thieves are selective, choosing pieces that have value but not too much. A high-profile piece is difficult to move unless you have the right connections."

"What about Vassalo?"

"He's considered an Old Master. Very recognizable. Hard to sell."

Maddox frowned in thought. "So what's our boy doing with his ill-gotten gains?"

Raven got up and placed the pizza box outside the door. The parking lot was quiet. She couldn't imagine why. She shut the door and bolted it. "My guess is he's working for someone else. Plenty of rich, obsessive private collectors out there."

"Anyone come to mind?" Maddox asked.

She peeked under the covers for unwelcome guests. "No. And before you ask, I don't have my finger on the pulse of the art theft world. I do my job, and I go home at night like everyone else."

He stood up as she slipped between the sheets. She plumped the anorexic pillow, aware that he was watching her.

"Don't bother, Maddox. Nothing you can say will make me change my evil ways."

"Wouldn't think of it. You're having too much fun."

She had a "damn right" on her lips but decided it wasn't worth the battle. Tomorrow morning she'd be rid of him. She just needed to get through one night.

He lifted the sheet and slid in next to her. The bed dipped under his weight, and they rolled to the middle.

"What are you doing?" She sat up and pushed herself away from him.

He put his hands behind his head and settled in the center of the bed. "I'm not sleeping on the floor in this place, for you or anyone else."

"At least stay on your side," she said, trying to keep some space between them, but gravity was against her.

He just grinned and closed his eyes like this was no big deal. Great. She looked over at the suitcase. After running through a very short list of options, she did the only thing she could, which was to put her back to him.

Within seconds, his body heat seared her from her shoulders to her legs. Her ass was wedged against his hip. Every breath pressed his bare skin to the thin fabric of her T-shirt.

Her body responded with a special heat of its own. She hated to think about how long it had been since she'd been in bed with a man. Midnight runs to the ends of the earth and too many secrets made it impossible to have a lasting relationship.

And then there was the psychometry. There were things that two people should never share, but she didn't have that luxury. Once she opened up, she couldn't pick and choose the visions or emotions that came through her fingers. No secret was safe from her—a cheating heart, childhood abuse, a dark side. The stronger the emotion, the faster she'd pick it up.

She stared at the wall and tried to think about something other than Maddox. Like poor Walter. She'd get him back tomorrow like she'd promised—safe and sound. And then, after this, she'd work alone. No more partners, no more associates, and no more cops.

Damn, she was back to Maddox again. The man had *dangerous* written all over him. She was acutely aware of how good he felt, and the A/C unit was doing a pisspoor job of cooling her down.

With a sigh, she had to admit that Maddox might be good for something after all.

CHAPTER
7

Is he ready yet?"

A bright yellow ceiling loomed above Dax. He tried
to look around, but he couldn't move. Somehow he knew
he was strapped onto a gurney. Trapped.

Nick's young face moved into view—big Italian head
with a brazen streak of black eyebrows and a shit-eating
grin.

Nick. Who was dead. Wearing a blood-encrusted uniform with a big red hole in the center of his chest.

What are you doing here? Dax heard himself say. *You
died. You're not supposed to be back.*

Nick's grin didn't falter. "Time to operate, Senior."

Dax felt his chest squeeze. *What? No, wait. I need to
talk to you . . . Nick, I'm sorry, man,* Dax said, the sudden
guilt suffocating him. *I should have handled it. I should
have . . .*

To Dax's dismay, Nick faded into the background as
if he hadn't heard a word. The walls began to close in;
then Walter stuck his head in. "Shall we begin?"

Next thing Dax knew, he was being moved through a tunnel. Blue and red lights flashed around him, and it banged like an MRI.

Begin what? he asked.

"Don't worry. We're going to fix ya right up," Nick said. "It's just your eyes."

It started getting hot, burning his face and his skull. Panic rose in his throat. He tried to get off the gurney, twisting and fighting with the certainty that something horrific was about to happen.

Colors began to fade.

"What's wrong with my eyes?" he yelled.

Nick answered, "They don't work right. They have to come out."

The banging turned into gunshots, and everything went black.

"No!" Dax sat up in bed. The dark hotel room slowly came into focus. Sweat soaked the sheets, and he fought to catch his breath in the stifling air. The still shadow next to him brought his head around.

A dressed Raven was standing beside the bed with a glass of water in hand, and he realized his world had returned to gray. He could just make out the wariness on her face. Not exactly the way he pictured waking up to the woman whose heat had kept him restless most of the night.

Her voice was quiet. "Bad dream?"

He rubbed his eyes. Still there, such as they were. "I always wake up like this. Not a morning person."

He peeled off the sheet and swung his legs off the side. "Why is it so fucking hot in here?"

"A/C unit died. Be grateful it didn't torch the place when it blew." She handed him the water.

"Thanks." He drained the glass in one swallow, the cold water putting out the fire raging in his head. The nightmare was going to take longer to dissipate. The memories were there forever.

Raven watched him for a moment, looking as if she was going to say something else, and he froze. He didn't want her pity, and he sure didn't want to explain what had just happened. Then she shook her head and opened the drapes to a view of a wooden two-by-four railing and a couple of parked cars bathed in dawn.

She said, "Time to get rolling, sunshine."

Miami was already steamy as they walked through the parking lot of the Financial District Station with the suitcase at exactly 7:30 A.M.

She'd opted for the tourist look this morning with a blue peasant blouse that showed a lot of cleavage, a short linen wrap skirt that showed a lot of leg, and low sandals so she could move fast when she needed to. The Beretta was tucked in a pocket of her handbag.

Dax looked as inconspicuous as a cop could with a black silk T-shirt, khaki shorts, and a light Windbreaker that concealed his Glock.

Yup, just a couple of well-armed sightseers.

Raven glanced around the parking lot and spotted a white delivery truck. She adjusted the tiny communications headset in her ear that looked to anyone else like an MP3 player. "Can you hear me?"

"Loud and clear," Maddox replied into an identical unit tucked in his ear, unaware that she wasn't talking to him.

The lights flashed on the white truck. Paulie was in the house. He could listen to their conversation and talk to her without Maddox knowing. He held his secrets. It was about time she kept a few of her own.

They walked to the station building, which was little more than a two-story concrete loading platform and a pair of escalators. The entire rail platform was elevated above the bustling city streets. The place wasn't too busy for a Friday morning, mostly commuters and vacationers. She didn't notice anyone watching them, but that didn't mean anything. Out here, a good pair of binoculars would betray them.

She stopped at a Metromover map system displayed on the wall. "So how does the system work?"

Maddox handed her a brochure with the schedules and map. "It's a free service. Cars run the loop north and southbound across metro Miami, stopping at twenty stations. It's fully automated, no operators. Cars show up about every two minutes during rush hour, which is right about now."

He pointed to a colorful knot of tracks in the center. "The southern Brickell loop runs from this location, around downtown, and back. The Omni loop runs around downtown, then north. The inner Downtown loop circles the business district in one direction inside both loops." He tapped two hubs—Brickell and Government Center Station. "These are transfer points to the Metrorail railroad service that covers Miami-Dade."

Far more complicated than she had anticipated. She had a feeling she was going to be seeing a lot of Miami today. They headed for the glass-encased escalators that led to the loading platform. A boxy white car sporting green and blue stripes was just departing, heading north on the track.

Raven felt Maddox move behind her, and her body reacted by freezing like it had this morning when he shouted in his sleep. She'd seen the anguish in his face before he could conceal it. Whatever he had dreamed, she didn't want any part of. She didn't do other people's nightmares.

Still, it made her wonder: What could strike that kind of fear in a man like Maddox? Whatever it was, he didn't want to share, which was fine with her. They had another hour together; then she'd be on her merry way.

Behind her, Maddox leaned in and asked, "So how's your partner in crime doing this morning?"

She pursed her lips. "I wouldn't know."

"Why don't you ask him since he's sitting out in the parking lot? Or maybe I should wave to him?"

Raven turned to face Maddox, who was inches away, wearing a smile she really wanted to wipe off. She hadn't gotten a whole lot of sleep last night between the hot room and the hot man, and she really wasn't in any mood to argue with half of her problem.

His eyebrows rose as he waited, and she huffed. "He's just here for surveillance."

"And what would he be surveilling?"

So much for secrets. "A GPS tracking device in the suitcase. Just in case we get separated."

Maddox's jaw muscle twitched as he tapped his earpiece. "Introduce me to him."

Raven sighed. There was no getting around this. "Paulie, say hi to David Maddox."

"Crap," Paulie came on, and added a curt "Morning."

"From here on in, Paulie," Maddox said, "we have

a regular three-way relationship, got it? Whatever Raven hears, I hear."

"I got it," Paulie replied.

Maddox reached out and ran a finger along Raven's jawline and up to the communications device tucked under her hair. "Anything else you'd like to share with me?"

She tamped down the heat-induced tremble her body was working on. As soon as this job was done, she was getting a date. "That's it for me. So where's *your* man?"

Maddox's hand stilled, and his eyes met hers. Exactly what she figured. He had someone inside, too, the bastard.

"No cops, Maddox," she said. "You *promised,* no cops."

"I'll only call him if things go bad," Maddox said as he turned and checked the platform.

She glared at him. There was always such a fine line between "if" and "when." *You better not screw this up, Maddox.*

The next car left the station, and her cell phone rang. They glanced at each other. The screen displayed BLOCKED.

She answered it. "Hello."

"Raven, please listen carefully. I am only allowed to say these instructions once. Get on the next northbound train with the Vassalo. Alone."

Thank God he was alive. "Walter, it's so good to hear your voice. Are you all right?"

No reply, and she frowned. "Walter?" She checked the cell. He had disconnected.

"Problem?" Maddox asked.

A bad feeling settled in her gut. "He hung up. I'm supposed to get on the next train heading north. Alone."

Maddox watched the oncoming car. "You think he would notice if I was there?"

"He called just as the last train left. He either got lucky, or he's here somewhere."

Maddox nodded. "I'll take the one after you. Paulie, how familiar are you with Miami streets?"

"I'm not, but I have online maps."

Maddox looked at Raven in concern.

"He's the best. He'll be fine," she said. The next car pulled up, and the doors opened automatically.

Maddox caught her arm just as she was ready to get in. "Be careful," he whispered in her ear. She looked at him, surprised by his sudden concern.

What's your story, Maddox?

Then she shook her head. She didn't want to know.

"I'm always careful," she said. And boarded.

"She's on car number 3," Dax told Paulie as the car pulled away and he waited impatiently for the next one. His instincts were screaming that he should stay with Raven, but he couldn't chance it. They didn't need to give a killer any reason to kill again. It was always easier the second time around.

"Coming up on Brickell Station," Raven said in his earpiece.

Minutes later, the next car pulled up, and Dax got in along with a dozen other people. He stood where he could keep an eye on everyone. Most had briefcases and disappeared behind their newspapers when the car started moving.

Ten minutes later, Raven said, "Getting off at Knight Center Station."

"Location verified," Paulie chimed in. "Moving in."

Dax gripped the vertical pole and tried to see ahead as his car lagged behind.

Not that he didn't trust her.

Hell, he *didn't* trust her.

A few seconds later, she came back with, "Now he's sending me on the Downtown loop heading north."

The moment the doors opened at Knight Center, Dax was out and racing to catch the next Downtown unit. It pulled away just as he got to the platform. Now he was two cars behind.

"Paulie, are you with her?"

"Stuck in traffic on South Miami Ave."

Dax swore softly and hopped on the next car.

"I'm in number 12, hitting Government Center now," Raven said. "Big place."

"The busiest station on the system," Dax told her, ignoring the curious glances from bystanders as he talked to himself. "Also, the most security. I doubt he'd make the switch there."

"You're right, he's not. I'm exiting. Jumping on the Omni loop heading in the opposite direction."

Son of a bitch, Dax thought. They were on a wild-goose chase. "Paulie, did you copy?"

"Turning around now. What is this asshole doing?"

"Losing us," Dax said. "I can't catch her coming back at me. My loop diverts."

There was a pause before Paulie came back. "He knows that, doesn't he?"

Dax looked out the window of the elevated track. He knew that. "Where are you now?"

"Almost to Government Center Station."

She'd passed right over Paulie's location. "Park on the street and stand by."

"Seriously?"

"We might be doing this for a while."

Raven cut in. "Still on Omni. We just left Knight Center heading east."

"Is anyone following you?" Dax asked.

"Not that I can tell."

Dax got off at Government Center. The station was packed with morning commuters transferring from the railroad to the Metromover. He stood in the middle of the platform wondering where to go next. Raven was now five city blocks from him on the other side of the business district. If she stayed on the Omni loop, she'd circle the city, then head north, and he'd never be able to catch her. She would be facing the killer alone.

His chest tightened, and he shook off the feeling of impending doom. It was not going to happen again.

He raced to catch the Downtown loop.

Raven stood in the car and watched another station come and go. *Bastard, bastard, bastard.* She hated this, being strung along like a puppet. And Walter couldn't even talk to her; all she was getting were sound bites. The kidnapper must have planned this all out ahead of time and forced Walter to record each step. Probably afraid that Walter would try to give her a clue to his whereabouts.

Her cell phone rang again, and Walter said, "Exit College Bayside Station."

It was the next station on the route, and she wondered again how the kidnapper knew the system so well,
because no one was following her. Either he had a man
at every station and an operation bigger than anything
she'd imagined, or he was intimately familiar with the
transit system.

"I'm getting off at College Bayside Station," she told
Maddox and Paulie.

"I'll be there in three minutes," Maddox said.

The doors opened, and she stepped out and scanned
the platform. Students from nearby Miami Dade College
milled about, but she didn't see Walter. The disappointment evaporated when her cell rang.

"You have thirty seconds to catch the Brickell loop
south," Walter said.

"Or what?" she snapped.

Disconnect.

Raven swore out loud, and several people looked over
as she raced by them to the other track.

"I'm getting on Brickell heading back toward Government Center," she yelled as she ran.

"I just passed the last station. Wait for me," Maddox
said.

"Can't. I only have thirty seconds."

"I'll catch up as soon as I can," he said, sounding
equally frustrated.

Raven hit the platform and slid between the doors
just as they closed. She took an open seat to catch her
breath. The car pulled out as Maddox's pulled in parallel
to hers. His expression was grim through the layers of
glass between them.

She leaned back and surveyed her car. There were

only about fifteen people, most standing. They passed two stations before her cell phone rang again.

Walter's voice sounded distant and flat. "Get off at Government Center Station. Leave the suitcase in the car. I'll be waiting for you on the platform."

He hung up. Her heart thumped in her chest, adrenaline pumping.

"The drop is Government Center. I'm in car number 8," she told the boys.

"I'm right behind you," Maddox said. "Paulie, she's all yours."

"I'm a block away, moving as fast as I can."

Her hopes rose. "You want the incoming Brickell platform."

"Got it."

"Wait for me once you have Walter," Maddox said. "We need to follow that suitcase."

"No problem," Paulie said.

I don't think so, thought Raven. She and Paulie were going to grab Walter before Maddox got off his ride and get the hell out of here. Knowing Maddox, he already had the cavalry ready and waiting. She was in no mood to explain all of this to anyone, or drag API and Walter into a cop's murder investigation.

The Metromover car turned the corner in front of the Miami Arena. As they pulled closer to the Government Center, she stood up and looked out the window for Walter.

Seconds ticked by, and the automated PA announced the station stop.

"Paulie, do you have a visual on Walter?" she asked.

"I haven't even gotten to the parking lot yet."

Her heart was racing now as she scanned the faces coming into focus on the platform. Where was he? Then she noticed a tall man with thick white hair waving at her. He was wearing the same suit he'd had on at the auction. Relief poured through her. It was going to be okay.

"I got him," she said, and dropped the case on the floor. The doors opened, and she jumped out and ran through the crowd to where Walter was waiting.

As she approached, he turned around.

She stopped in her tracks.

It wasn't Walter.

The man looked at her and frowned.

Raven turned around in time to see her car pull away. She spun back and stared at the man. He looked too much like Walter for this to be a coincidence.

"Where is Walter?" she asked the man, stepping up to him.

He swayed a little. Stale liquor breath belched. "Huh?"

"You didn't get him?" Maddox said in her ear. "What the hell happened?"

"You said you had him," Paulie said in her ear.

"I don't, but I found someone who knows where he is," she said, barely controlling the rage in her voice. She stepped up to the man. "You waved at me."

He lifted his hands. "I don't know who yer lookin' for, lady." He tried to sidestep her, but she blocked him and grabbed his jacket sleeve. The station faded slightly as she let her psychometry work.

Walter's thoughts. Walter's jacket.

She let go. "What did you do to him?"

He shook his head and stumbled backward. "Yer crazy. Get away from me."

Raven tried to stop him; but when she noticed a security officer in her peripheral vision, she had to let him go. The decoy moved quickly toward the guard, and she couldn't follow. She had to get that painting back, or she'd have nothing to bargain with.

She started walking to the station exit just as another car pulled up, and Maddox stepped out. He ran to her, taking in the station guard on the platform looking in her direction.

"No Walter?" Maddox asked her as he caught up.

She shook her head. "There was a decoy waiting instead, someone who looked just like Walter." Wearing Walter's clothes. She was going to be sick.

"Where's the case?"

"On the car," she said. "I thought I had him."

He gave her a hard look. "You *left* it on the car? You didn't tell us you were leaving it."

"Those were my instructions," she said with a glare, daring him to give her a hard time. "I am not going to risk Walter for you or anyone else."

In the corridor ahead of them, a man wearing a blue polo shirt and jeans stepped out of the crowd. He made eye contact with Maddox and started walking toward them. Without easing his tight grip on her arm, Maddox stopped and exchanged a few words with the guy, who eyed her speculatively. Another cop.

He finally nodded and kept walking. Raven turned to see him head up the platform.

"Your man?" she asked Maddox.

"Yeah. He's going to track your impostor."

"Good. I want to know how that son of a bitch got Walter's clothes."

CHAPTER
8

In the parking lot, Dax got his first glimpse of Paulie just before he ducked in the pass-through doorway to the back of the delivery truck. Dax took the vacated driver's side while Raven jumped into the passenger seat, and yelled, "Got a bearing on the suitcase, Paulie?"

He answered through the doorway. "GPS says it just passed the Third Street Station. Looks like it's still on the Brickell loop."

"Best chance at intercept?" Raven asked.

"Hold on," he came back. "First Street Station across town. Three city blocks, due east."

"I know where it is." Dax pulled out of the parking lot and drove toward NW First Avenue.

"No guarantees," Paulie added. "He could take the case off at any point along the way. There are two stations between Third and First."

Dax said, "Just let me know if it makes a detour."

"He set us up," Raven said, her expression fierce.

He wasn't the only one, Dax thought.

She stared straight ahead, her body tense and her face pale. "Do you think Walter is dead?"

Dax didn't want to voice what he was thinking, so he lied. "No," he said and took a right on NE First Street. "We'll be there in a few minutes. Paulie?"

"Still on track. It would help a lot if you could step on it. It's going to be close."

As soon as they reached the station, Dax and Raven were out and running, reaching the platform just as the transit car pulled in. The doors opened, and Dax waited for the people to depart before going in. The suitcase was sitting on the floor, and he grabbed it and exited.

Raven looked mildly relieved when she saw it. "The lock is intact. That's good."

They left the station together to return to the truck. Now that he had one problem under control, he could handle the other one. Dax waited until they were outside before pulling Raven behind a concrete column. He pinned her with an arm on either side. All his anger came front and center. "What the hell do you think you were doing back there?"

She raised her chin defiantly. "I don't know what you're talking about."

Dax moved closer, and her eyes widened. "I'm talking about leaving the case on the Metro, grabbing Walter, and taking off while I was stuck on the rail."

Her eyes narrowed. "What do you expect, Maddox? You think I want to be around when your buddies climb out of the woodwork? You think I want cops crawling all over me?"

"As opposed to me crawling all over you?"

Her pupils dilated just enough for him to realize he

was making her uncomfortable. He'd take the advantage any way he could get it, so he leaned in until he could feel her breath on his face. "I have my reasons for caution."

"Caution? Lying is not caution. Not when a man's life is at stake. You're a cop. You should know that." She finished with a hint of desperation that caught him off guard.

For a moment, they didn't move. She was right about him sharing the info, but he couldn't allow another mistake with this killer. He was taking the lead this time, and nothing was going to distract him, not even a woman with a mind of her own. But he couldn't find the words to explain to her how much this meant to him. So he stepped back, picked up the case, and made his way to the truck.

"Don't do it again," he said. "We are in this together or not at all."

"*Not at all* was an option? Since when?" she asked.

"And here I thought you were warming up to me," Dax said.

"Maybe with a flamethrower," she muttered, and climbed into the truck where Paulie was waiting, surrounded by more high-tech equipment than Dax's entire Ouray PD had.

Paulie turned out to be a rail-thin, twentysomething kid with a shaved head that gleamed in the glow of monitors. In fact, he reminded Dax of Nick.

Paulie brightened when he saw the case. "Excellent."

Dax handed the suitcase to Paulie and dropped onto a makeshift seat. Raven sat across from him with her head in her hands. She looked like he felt.

The bastard had gotten away. Again.

Paulie worked on the combination lock. "I don't get

it. What was all that about this morning? Why didn't he grab the suitcase? Why go to all this trouble if he didn't want it?"

Dax had been thinking about that, too. Why the games? Why the mystery?

Raven said, not looking up, "You didn't tell me this guy was nuts, Maddox."

Dax leaned back and stared at the ceiling. "Thought you'd figure that out yourself."

So much for his theory about the Vassalos. How could his cop instincts be so far off? Why kidnap a man for a ransom he never planned to collect? It certainly didn't bode well for Walter.

He glanced at Raven. "How do you know the impostor was wearing Walter's clothes?"

She answered wearily, "I have an excellent memory. And the jacket still smelled like his Grey Flannel cologne."

The suitcase made a loud click as Paulie opened it.

She lifted her head and looked at Dax, determination on her face. "No more secrets, Maddox. I want to know everything about this nutcase. Start from the top, and don't leave anything out. Because obviously, he's more than your average criminal, and there's more to this game than I'm privy to. That's going to change as of now."

Despite the fire in her eyes, there were parts of his story he wasn't ready to share yet. If ever.

"Uh, guys?" Paulie said, holding up a single piece of paper that he'd pulled out of the opened case. "We have a slight problem."

Raven jumped forward and looked inside the suitcase. It was empty.

"Bastard," she said. "He took it."

"Must have gotten to it between stations," Paulie said. "Used a master key maybe. Slipped the painting out and the paper in. Pretty slick, actually."

Dax took the note and read it out loud.

An admirable effort. Your father would be so proud. Did you think it would be that easy, children? That I would forgive so quickly? There is one more painting I want. The Vassalo Young Virgin *hanging in la Catedral de los Ángeles in Havana, Cuba. I will call Raven with delivery instructions Sunday morning.*

"Are you kidding me?" Paulie blurted. "Another painting? How do we know Walter is even alive? We could go all over hell's half acre for this asshole for nothing."

Raven took the sheet and read it. Her eyes closed for a moment before she handed it back to Dax.

"Walter's handwriting," she said. "He was alive when this was written, but I don't know when that was."

Nothing in the note indicated a time frame. And Dax noticed something else. "You only talked to Walter on the phone?"

"Yes." She studied him warily. "Why?"

"Because so far, all the contact we've had with the kidnapper has been through Walter. The notes, the calls."

Raven's eyes widened in quick anger. "You think Walter staged all this?"

"Someone staged it."

Dax watched her fury build.

"Don't you dare go there," she said. "Walter Abbott is above reproach. The man has been a professional art dealer for over forty years. He loves his work, and he adores art."

Dax said, "Maybe he adores it too much. Could be he's looking for a little retirement fund."

The cold, hard look she gave him was practically lethal. "I guess there's only one way to find out. I'm going to Havana."

Paulie groaned. "Oh man. Not Havana. Illegal to get into, illegal to get out of. And *extremely* illegal to steal a painting from a church. Not to mention, you want God pissed off at you, too? I think you get struck by lightning for that."

Dax watched as Paulie's words bounced off her without effect. No doubt about it, her mind was already working. Planning. She was going to Cuba. And that meant he was going, too. He wasn't letting her out of his sight. She was his ticket.

"You can stay here, Paulie. I'll take her," Dax said, his eyes fixed on Raven.

She raised a single eyebrow. "Is that right? What makes you think I need you?"

He grinned. "Because *I* have a boat."

"He wasn't kidding. He has a boat," Paulie said as they stood on the dock and looked at it.

At one o'clock, the sun was already high in the sky, bringing the sultry heat and blinding sunshine that the central Florida Keys were known for. A leisurely onshore breeze swayed the palm trees lining the small bay. Azure ocean peeked through the small entrance at the head of the marina.

Behind them, a main building emblazoned with the words BIG BOB'S in boxy, black letters housed a general store and bait shop. Tropical music wafted from an octagon hut and patio that served as a snack shack set back in the palms. Miscellaneous structures dotted the rest of the sandy marina.

About forty slips were home to as many powerboats hooked up to a tangle of utilities. The core population consisted of older, shorts-clad owners and geriatric dogs. It was like a nautical trailer park.

And then there was Maddox's boat, dubbed *Breaking Wind,* bobbing in the water in front of her. Raven stared at it from the pier and tried to figure out why her gut was twisted up. It wasn't just because the exchange had gone bad, although that was enough to do it. There was something here that didn't make sense.

Paulie walked along the finger pier that hugged the right side of the boat and whistled.

"Nice," he said, nodding his approval. "Nineteen-eighties Hatteras Sportfish Convertible in primo condition. Looks about forty-six foot. Twin Detroit diesel engines. Cruising speed twenty-two to twenty-six knots. Hydraulic steering. This baby rocks."

Raven eyed his ghostly white legs sticking out from under baggy shorts and the sunburn he was already getting on the top of his shaved head in the fifteen minutes they'd been here. "You know a lot about boats for a city boy."

He grinned beneath his sunglasses. "Always wanted to move to paradise."

Paradise. Hardly. Everyone here had one speed: sloooooooow. She was already itching to get under way to Havana.

"You'd miss all the action," she told him.

He shook his head and made his way back to her. "Nah, I wouldn't. My only problem would be the lack of high-speed bandwidth. Give me that, and I could live on a boat like this, too."

Raven frowned. "Too?"

"This is Dax's permanent residence."

Her gut twisted again. "That's over an hour commute to work every day."

Paulie's eyebrows went up. "He quit."

For a moment, Raven couldn't move. Quit? From the police department? Then that meant . . .

Paulie turned serious. "He didn't tell you? My background check turned up that he worked patrol for fifteen years until something happened six months ago. He took a workmen's comp settlement, sold his house, bought the boat, and moved aboard. He's doing charters for Big Bob's now."

The rage started in her belly and moved out. "No, he didn't tell me."

"You thought he was a cop all this time?" Paulie said in obvious surprise. Then he put a hand on his belly and started laughing. "That's funny."

She didn't smile back, and he sobered with considerable effort. "Sorry. I just assumed . . ." He rubbed his head and blew out a breath. "Never mind. I'll get the report from the truck—" He stopped midsentence and focused wholly on something behind her.

Raven turned to see a young blond woman, wearing a floral tank, pink shorts, and a big island smile, approach.

"Can I help you?" she asked.

Paulie nodded adamantly. "Uh, yeah." Then his face turned beet red, and his mouth moved a few times before he aimed a thumb at the boat. "We're friends of Dax."

Her blue eyes brightened. "In that case, I'm Shelly Henkel. Bob's daughter. I help him run the place." She shook both their hands, then looked around them. "Is Dax back?"

"Inside," Raven said.

"Oh, good," she said, looking relieved. "Chuck's been covering his charter fishing appointments, and he needs a break." She leaned in. "He's pushing seventy."

"I doubt Maddox will be available for a few more days," Raven said, and eyed her new source of information. "Do you know him well?"

Shelly gave a shake of her long blond hair. "Not really. I book his charters and work as first mate. He keeps to himself a lot, but he's been a big help to me and my dad."

"You can handle one of these boats?" Paulie asked.

She nodded. "I do most of the engine maintenance, too."

Paulie looked like he'd been hit by Cupid's two-by-four. Fortunately, Raven had bigger issues at hand than puppy love. Murder, to be precise.

"It was nice meeting you, Shelly. Excuse me."

Raven boarded the Hatteras and entered through the rear door into the salon, which contained an L-shaped built-in sofa along the left side and two chairs on the right. A media center sat directly ahead, surrounded by a bank of wide windows and dark paneling. Narrow stairs led down to a galley kitchen and berths belowdecks. Dated beige shell-design fabric covered the interior.

Maddox was nowhere to be seen, which was probably a good thing. Betrayal seeped through her in increments. He'd lied to her, deliberately using his "power" to manipulate and humiliate her. After this morning, she'd had her fill of being used and abused.

It was time David Maddox coughed up his secrets.

A group of photos was tacked to a corkboard beside the door. Most black-and-white. Some of them were obviously charter customers showing off their trophies. Men with beer bellies, women in skimpy bikinis, and a bunch of dead fish. Then she found one of Maddox surrounded by people who bore a striking resemblance to him—a young woman and two older people, probably his parents. Raven reached out, touched the photo, and focused.

He had held this photo with love and reverence, definitely family. She delved deeper for the true ugliness that existed in all familial dynamics. Duty. Responsibility. Deeper still, and feelings of failure and guilt rose to the surface. Shame.

She withdrew from the power of the last emotion. He definitely had issues with his family. Or himself. Was it connected to the nightmare? She'd probably never know. She doubted he would discuss his family with her, and unless it affected Walter directly, she didn't give a shit.

Another photo caught her eye. It was of Maddox and the young rookie, Nick Cabrini, who had let her go last year, standing in front of the boat, flashing big smiles and a couple of beers. She pressed her fingers to the photo and closed her eyes. Immediately, she recognized Maddox's thoughts where he had touched the photo. Images flashed—laughs, fishing, friendship, and pride, followed by a blinding rush of regret and grief, then loud pops that shattered her connection.

She shook her head and stepped away. The back of her skull burned. The pain was fresh, and so deep that it haunted her bones. What the hell was that? Had he been shot? Was that why he took workmen's comp? And what about the guilt and grief? What were those from? No wonder he had nightmares. The man was a mess.

She breathed long and slow, purging his emotions from her body and mind. Whatever had happened was driving his actions, which meant she needed answers.

She checked every other picture. There wasn't a single one with him in uniform or with any other officers. No hint whatsoever that he had ever been a cop. You'd think a man who had served all those years in the police department would have something to show for it.

Paulie said something had happened to him. What? He certainly didn't look like he had a physical disability, and she'd pretty much checked out every angle. Then it dawned on her. Maybe it was mental. That would explain a few things.

"Lovely," she muttered. Usually, she could pick out the nutcases.

She scanned a row of books on photography and history, touching each spine. Interesting reading for a cop. At the end was a photo album, and she pulled it out. Inside were loose eight-by-ten monochrome photos stacked haphazardly, and they were amazing. The lighting was used well and with much control. Some were close-ups of parts of the marina. Dark, angry oceans. Solitary figures on the beach. Portraits of old faces, no doubt the residents. All of them were captured with an expert eye.

Did Maddox take these?

Raven turned as Dax walked up from the lower level and tossed a blanket and pillow on the sofa. He said, "I'll sleep up here tonight. You can have the queen berth below, and Paulie can sleep in one of the bunks for—"

Dax stopped, riveted by the way her expression shifted and hardened. He was in deep shit, and he bet he knew why.

Well, it was fun while it lasted.

She shoved one of his photo albums back onto the shelf and said, "You're not a cop anymore."

He could try to deny it, but it really wouldn't do any good. He walked past her and out the door into the sunshine. "Took you long enough to find out."

She trailed behind him. "That's it? That's all you have to say for yourself? After all the times you used that as leverage against me?"

Dax paused when he saw Shelly and Paulie making googly eyes at each other. "What's with them?"

"Don't ask, and don't change the subject. I want answers."

He swung up onto the ladder to the upper bridge deck that housed the boat controls. "I quit. There's your answer."

Raven followed close behind him as he ducked under the canopy and turned the ignition to check the gauges. He needed to fuel up before they left. Everything else looked good.

As he worked, Raven didn't say anything, but he knew better than to think she wasn't going to. The woman was like a pit bull once she decided she wanted something.

He stepped back to adjust his seat, and turned to find

her between him and the instruments. There were equal parts anger and dread in her eyes. He knew she had a right to be pissed at him. He'd abused an authority he no longer had, but it was for a good cause. The twinge of guilt hardly hurt at all.

"Where's Nick?" she asked.

"Dead."

She nodded as if she wasn't surprised. "This isn't an official investigation, is it? It's some personal vendetta. You're after the guy who killed your partner."

He took a breath. "That's right."

She watched him calmly, but he could sense the hum of anger and harnessed energy beneath the thin blouse and skirt. It was taking every ounce of self-control she had to stand there. Waiting for him to explain. He actually expected her to be furious, to lash out. It didn't happen.

Instead, she said, "What about the men in your department? I would think a cop killer would be a top priority."

He shook his head. "They won't catch him. They don't know shit about the art world. And neither do I."

Her gaze leveled. "Which is why you need me. The big question is, why do I need you?"

He lifted an eyebrow. "Boat."

"I can get a boat anywhere," she said coolly.

He looked around. "Today? And a captain willing to take you to Havana to help you steal a painting? I don't think even you can pull that off."

She clenched her jaw. "You lied to me, Maddox."

He laughed at the obvious. "And this surprises you? We've been lying to each other from day one. I can hardly wait to see what you've got for me next."

"Death and dismemberment," she said.

He didn't doubt that. "We aren't making any inroads into the whole trust thing, are we?"

"Are you willing to let Walter die to catch Nick's killer?"

He didn't hesitate. "No."

She searched his face. "That better be the truth, Maddox."

He stepped a little closer to her, backing her up to the controls. She didn't even try to escape. Fearless. "That goes for you, too, lady. Remember that next time you think you're going to run out and leave me empty-handed."

Her gaze held steady. "I want to know what happened six months ago during that robbery. All of it. Think of it as a peace offering."

There was no getting around this, especially since he was stuck with her for the next forty-eight hours. "And what are you willing to give me in return?"

He meant it to sound like a bargain, but it came out rougher and quieter than he'd intended. He caught the flicker of awareness in her eyes as she narrowed them to a smoky gaze. His entire body tensed in response. It was his own fault for getting too close. Normally, he tolerated the Keys' heat pretty well. Apparently, not so much with Raven around.

"I'll buy you dinner," she finally said. Her voice wavered just a little.

He grinned slowly, enjoying her obvious unease. "Then you'll get the story at dinner. Right now, I need to make the boat ready to move out tomorrow morning." He turned and headed down the ladder before the heat got the better of him.

CHAPTER
9

Bigley called my cell and left another message," Paulie said. "We're going to have to talk to him sooner or later."

"Later," Raven said as she sat in a lawn chair and read the report that Paulie had given her. Maddox grew up in Chicago with his parents and sister, who was married with kids in Baltimore. He was thirty-six years old, single, and worked for the Ouray PD on patrol until he left six months ago.

The official news release on the robbery was next, containing just the basics of the fallen officer, Maddox's injuries, and the fact that the killer got away. If she wanted details, she'd have to wait till tonight. She hated to admit that Maddox made her uneasy. Maybe because she couldn't seem to get rid of him. The fact that he made her mind and body scatter every time he got too close had nothing to do with it.

Paulie stretched out on the lounge next to her in the breezy shade between the palms and the harbor. "Fine with me, but the longer Bigs waits, the crazier he's going to get. And I ain't gonna be the first one to talk to him after he's stewed all this time."

"No problem," she said absently. "Did you get any fingerprints off the note?"

"Just Walter's."

"What about the suitcase?"

"Nope. And before you ask, no, I can't get access to the Metromover's security tapes."

She folded up the report and handed it back to him. "Any word on the impersonator?"

Paulie's head bobbed to the reggae music filtering through the trees. "Dax said he'd let me know what he finds out."

Raven squinted at him. "He did?"

"Yeah."

"Voluntarily?"

"Yup," Paulie said.

Great. For Paulie, Maddox was cooperative. For her, nothing.

Raven scanned the vicinity. "Have you noticed anyone watching us?"

"You think the kidnapper might be here?" Paulie asked with a quick look her way.

She shrugged. "If you could locate Maddox, so can our man. What about transients? Any new faces in town lately?"

He shook his head. "Don't think so, but I'll ask Shelly."

Raven drummed her fingertips on the chair arm. "I'm going to keep Maddox busy for a few hours tonight. I want you to sweep the boat for any listening or tracking devices."

Paulie's eyebrows shot up over his sunglasses. "Keep him busy, huh?"

She gave him a warning look, but Paulie just grinned.

Then he shifted in his chair. "I've been thinking about what Dax said about Walter's being our only contact. You know, he has a point. What if Walter went bad?"

"Don't start," she said.

"Hey, it happens in this business. We work with million-dollar items. The temptation is there."

"Knock it off, Paulie," she said as she glared across the marina at Maddox's boat. "I've been working with Walter for ten years. He wasn't in it for the money."

Paulie raised his hands in defeat. "Okay, okay. I agree with you. It just needed to be said."

How could she explain to Paulie and Maddox the fear that she'd felt in the notes? She shivered in the heat from the unpleasant memory recall. Walter was so scared, trapped by a madman. No one could fake that. No one could hide from her.

And then Paulie started singing a reggae tune, and she was dragged back to the present.

She eyed him. He was singing to Bob Marley. Badly. In fact, he looked pretty comfy with a mango daiquiri and a loud tropical shirt covered with multicolored parrots. "Where did you get that shirt?"

He looked down at it and smiled wide. "Shelly picked it out for me at the store. You like it? She's really something." He paused long enough to take a draw on his daiquiri. "Do you know she does everything here? Cooks at the shack, runs the store, works on the boats, does the paperwork. And she's like twenty-two. I met her dad,

Bob. Nice guy. He is big, too, thus the name. He said he doesn't even own a pair of real shoes. Just sandals. Can you believe that?"

They'd been here only a matter of hours, and Paulie was already gone. She waved her hand in front of his face. "Stay with me. Did you do the recon work on Havana yet?"

He smacked his head. "Forgot. No problem, I'll have it for you tonight."

Raven sighed. Definitely gone. "I also want you to track down the current location of every Vassalo painting known to man," she said.

Paulie looked worried with that. "You think he's going to play this game until he gets them all?"

She hoped not. "It's a theory. I also want a record of transactions or robberies involving Vassalos in the past five years."

"Will do. By the way, I checked your cell phone records for those incoming calls from Walter."

Hope surfaced. "And?"

"Seriously blocked. Whoever this guy is, he's good at cleaning up his tracks."

If she got her hands on him, he'd be dead. "So how did he get my cell number?"

Paulie blinked. "I assumed Walter knew it."

She shook her head. "No."

"Crap."

"My thoughts exactly."

She stood up and looked over the marina. Most of the tenants were strolling the decks or hanging out drinking. Occasionally, someone would start up an engine and drown out the music. But mostly, they just . . . sat.

Good God. She was marooned in the most boring place on earth.

"This is killing you, isn't it? In all the time I've known you, you've never taken a vacation," Paulie said from his chair.

She looked over. "I don't do vacations."

Paulie held up his drink. "That's because you don't know how to party."

"I can't party when I don't know what's happening to Walter."

Paulie nodded, sobering quickly. "Yeah, that's true. But it's too late to leave for Havana tonight, so you might as well enjoy a free day in paradise."

Raven put her hands on her hips. This was torture.

"I don't suppose Big Bob has a gym?" she asked Paulie.

He hitched a thumb behind them. "No, but there's a real nice beach and a walking trail on the other side of these palms."

Dax was going through the kitchen cabinets when his phone rang. He answered it with a quick "Yeah."

"You want to tell me what the fuck is going on?"

Dax smiled at Harry's no-bullshit way of saying hi. "You don't want to know."

"Actually, I do. I think it's time you explained why I played footsies for two hours with the homeless crowd."

Dax tossed a carton of eggs in the trash. "Let's just say our boy was having some fun with us. What did you find out on the old guy?"

"Not much. He's a local vagrant by the name of George Smith. No record. No address. Says some guy gave him the clothes and paid him a twenty to stand on the platform for fifteen minutes and wave."

That's what Dax was afraid of. "Did you get the name or description of the guy who hired him?"

"Old George was half in the bag. I'm surprised he was even able to find the platform. So short of hauling his ass into the station long enough to sober him up and let him talk, I got nothing. And I had no reason to haul him into the station because I didn't know why I needed to know."

Dax blew out a breath. He hated lying to Harry. "He was supposed to be our man."

There was a pause. "Jesus, you can't lie for shit. Just tell me you don't want to tell me."

"I don't want to tell you."

"Fine."

Dax bagged up the trash and took it up the stairs into the parlor. "Did Raven Callahan turn anything up?"

"Sure did. You got yourself some girlfriend there."

You have no idea, Dax thought.

"She didn't exist until around ten years ago when she enrolled in Columbia U and quit after a year. She moved to Manhattan and started working for API as a recovery specialist. She was questioned once in connection with a stolen property case but never charged. Since then, she's changed addresses a bunch of times and kept a low profile. Real low. In fact, she's off my radar until you guys picked her up last year sitting outside a well-known art dealer's house using an alias."

No surprises there. He tossed the bag on the pile of fishing gear in the center of the floor. "Okay, thanks."

"Okay, thanks? This woman is a professional thief."

He looked out the window across the harbor where Raven and Paulie were sitting. "It's possible."

"Christ, you already know that. Why do I bother? And I don't suppose you know anything about Yarrow's Vassalo turning up missing in Richmond?"

Dax stilled. "Is that right?"

"It was the damnedest thing. Alarm systems were overloaded all at once in the warehouse complex where it was stored. Next thing they know, the painting—the same painting you were tracking—is gone without a trace."

He exhaled in relief. *And miracles never cease.* "How is Yarrow doing?"

"Still unconscious, but I'm sure he's not going to be too happy when he wakes up and finds out his six-million-dollar baby is missing."

"I bet," Dax said, distracted with the disappointment of being so close. If Yarrow could only give them a description of his attacker. Something, anything to go on.

"Yeah, right."

Dax noted Harry's frustration, but he couldn't do anything about it. The last thing he wanted was to involve a good cop in a bad mess.

Harry asked, "So what are *you* up to these days?"

Dax looked down at the pile of prohibited stuff he needed to off-load before he entered Havana illegally to steal a painting from a church to use as ransom in a kidnapping he never reported. "The usual."

Harry swore, then came back, "We didn't have this conversation. If you need to get bailed out again, you know where to find me."

"Thanks, Harry." He hung up.

Dax's gaze settled on the photo of his family. His father's piercing eyes stared back at him. His dad wouldn't understand any of this. He wouldn't understand that Dax quit the force to find justice. He wouldn't approve of Dax's breaking every law he had to for vengeance.

Then again, his father wouldn't have screwed up and gotten his partner killed either.

Raven traded in her blouse and skirt for a pair of Nike jogging shorts and a bikini top in deference to the ninety-degree heat, and hit the beach. A couple-mile run should help to purge the restlessness of staying in one place for too long with nothing to do.

She eased into a steady jog, the sand white and soft under her running shoes. Nimble ghost crabs scattered in her wake. On her left, turquoise water stretched out to meet clear blue sky. A lone kid on a sailboard skimmed the deeper waves, and fishing boats dotted the horizon. An onshore breeze cooled her skin while she dodged the edge of the surf. Palm trees and scrub rustled to her right. An occasional birdcall broke the serenity.

Another fifty feet, and she ran past a group of teenagers. The boys surfed while the girls stretched out on beach towels, all brown and chatty. Where the biggest concern was whether to use SPF 4 or 15. She smiled at their careless youth.

Hers had never felt careless. It had been too full of secrets and shame and despair. Having to grow up too soon. Having to be the adult when the parents fell apart. Watching love die a slow and painful death. That was her youth.

She shoved the memories aside. Ancient history never to be repeated. She'd mastered the ability to block pain and ugliness long ago when her gift first emerged and threatened to suffocate her. One moment of weakness could resurrect memories—hers and every person's she'd ever touched. It was a vulnerability she couldn't afford.

A narrow crescent beach stretched in front of her, and she ran easy, lulled between the roar of the surf and the peace of the land. It really was beautiful here. She could almost see why Paulie was smitten.

It didn't take long to run out of beach. The nature trail started at a low grassy berm before crossing into a tropical forest. Raven skirted a small gathering of sunbathers and sandcastles at its entrance. An endless array of trees and shrubs lined the narrow path, and she found herself slowed by walkers stopping to take in the flora and foliage.

The forest opened to spindly mangroves and lowlands. A great white heron launched itself into the blue sky above. Yellow blossoms and red berries brightened the green and brown of the hardwoods. An occasional butterfly slid silently through the hush of the leaves. It was so serene, she could hear her heart beat.

The trail ended a mile later at Old SR-95, and with a little disappointment, she turned back.

The ocean was still blue when she broke through the trees. The waves still rose gently to breach the sand. Contentment filled her body, probably from the run, she reasoned. Or paradise. She'd been to beautiful places all around the world, but she'd never stuck around long enough to really see them.

Her feet moved soundlessly over the packed sand, paralleling her footsteps out. She passed the surfers and sunbathers laughing on the beach with music blaring from a boom box. Farther down the beach, she ran past an abandoned wind sail nudging the shore.

Raven was nearly to the marina when she stopped in her tracks. Adrenaline shot through her. Something was wrong. She turned around and looked at her two sets of footprints in the sand with a feeling of dread in her bones.

And then she realized that the only tracks in the sand were hers.

Where were the tracks for the windsurfer?

She shaded her eyes and scoured the incoming waves. No sign of him. Maybe he'd come ashore somewhere else. Maybe he'd gone for a swim. Or maybe not. It wouldn't hurt to find out. It wasn't like she had anything better to do.

Raven pulled off her sneakers and socks, stepped into the warm water to inspect the wind sail. The rig and board appeared undamaged. He'd probably just ditched it and went for a swim, but there was only one way to know for sure. She wrapped her hands around the boom and concentrated. Wind, water, exhilaration, a quick snap, pain in her right shoulder, panic, and defeat. She shook her head as realization set in—the kid was out there somewhere.

Behind her, two of the surfers were carrying their boards, and she flagged them down.

"He-yyy, Mama," one of the blond guys said in his best laid-back drawl.

"Do you know the kid who was windsurfing out there?" she asked them.

"No, but . . . ," the other one said, and shifted his weight to one hip while he checked her out. "You live around here?"

She ignored him. "I need your board."

"Huh?" was all he got out before she grabbed it.

She ran into the water. "Go to Big Bob's Marina and tell them we have a possible drowning."

Without waiting for an answer, Raven hurdled over the incoming surf and dove in with the board under her. As she stroked hard into the sea, she mentally calculated the current, the wind, and where she'd last seen the kid.

Fifty feet from shore, she pulled up and balanced on the board for better visibility. Sunlight flashed off the waves, but she didn't see any head bobbing. Nothing.

"Where are you, kid?" she whispered to the sea.

She dropped down to the board. Ocean currents pulled north around Florida's coast, so that's the direction she headed. Another fifty feet, and she stood up to scout with growing desperation. He had to be here. He had to be alive. She'd been in his head. He was a part of her now. He couldn't die.

"Hey, kid!" she yelled over the sounds of the ocean.

Something white moved thirty yards to her right, but she lost it as the wave crested. It was probably a seagull, but she headed toward it anyway, pushing the board over the rolling waves.

A male voice carried on the wind. "Help!"

Relief poured through her, and Raven stroked hard as a hand rose above the blue water. She reached him just as he went under again. She slid off the board into the water and grabbed his left arm, careful not to touch his right shoulder. He surfaced with a sputter, and she helped him to the board.

Exhausted and in pain, he managed to climb on and collapsed on his belly. He was probably all of fourteen years old. Why the hell was he out here alone? Where were the parents? Didn't people watch their kids anymore?

She saw his blue lips and tamped down her anger. "Are you okay?"

His eyes fluttered open. "Wind shifted, and I lost the boom. Swung around, clipped my shoulder. Hurts like a bit—." He grimaced. "Sorry."

She smiled. "I think you are entitled to one swear word. Try not to move."

Raven maneuvered the board around and got behind it to kick toward shore. They were at least 150 feet out with the sun dipping low over the horizon. She was going to get a decent workout today after all. Then she heard the small motorboat.

It plowed through the water in a beeline toward them, and she recognized Maddox at the helm with a mammoth of a man who could only be Big Bob next to him. The engines cut out a short distance away, and she pushed the board to meet them.

"Easy," she said as they lifted the kid aboard. "Dislocated right shoulder."

Under the sunglasses, Maddox frowned. "How do you know?"

She lied to cover her slip. "He told me."

Big Bob grinned an equally big grin. "Nice work

there, girl. He's one lucky boy. Don't know how you found him so fast. Hop on. We'll bring you in."

Her heart was still pounding from the close call, and her mind swam with too many what-ifs. She needed to be alone. "Thanks, but I have to return the board."

Raven straddled the board and stroked toward shore under Maddox's silent stare.

CHAPTER
10

Two hours later, Dax found her under the marina's public shower wearing a sport bikini that wrapped around one hell of a body. He knew it was there all along, but even his imagination wasn't that good. Well-defined shoulders, full breasts, a narrow waist, nicely flared hips, and long, strong legs. Tight nipples pushed through the thin fabric, and for the first time since he was twelve, he wished for X-ray vision.

Dax leaned against the side of the building behind her and said, "You missed all the excitement. The EMTs were here and everything."

Raven turned to look at him, water rolling down her face and dripping from her long hair. "I know. My job was done." She shut the water off and reached for her towel.

"Don't you want to know how he's doing?" Dax asked.

She dried her body. "He's in good hands. He's young. He'll be fine."

Dax studied her. "He wanted me to thank you. His name is Tommy Yeary. He's here on vacation from Michigan with his family. They're staying at the campground across the road."

She squeezed water out of her hair. "That's nice."

What is your story? he thought. She'd found the kid just in time, saved his life, and now she didn't even want to know his name? Dax recalled her expression when they picked up the boy. She'd been emotionally drained. She cared. So why the chill now?

Raven ran her fingers through her hair to shake it loose, cinched a sarong around her waist, and, just like that, she was ready. No fuss, no muss. He'd never met a woman who was so comfortable in her body.

And then she turned to him. Intelligent gray eyes locked on his with a singularity that took him by surprise. When Raven focused on something, she was unstoppable. Fearless. Guileless. And sexy as hell. He was kidding himself if he thought the next forty-eight hours were going to be anything but trouble.

"What I don't get is how you knew he was hurt," Dax said to her.

Her mouth turned up, and her eyes widened dramatically. "Maybe I'm psychic."

He stilled. He sure hoped not.

"Ready?" she said.

He cocked an eyebrow in silent question.

She picked up a picnic basket that sat by her feet. "Dinnertime."

Then she gave him a deliberate smile and walked past him to the beach.

The sun was setting over the trees, and the shore had

emptied out. A pelican squad flew overhead on their last run of the day, leaving only a warm breeze, the endless shooshing of the waves, and the promise of a starry night to keep them company.

Raven spread a blanket for them, gave him a cold Samuel Adams beer, slapped a pulled-pork sandwich from Big Bob's Yak Shack into his hand, and said, "Dinner. Now talk."

He looked at her. "You ever hear of foreplay?"

She twisted the cap off her beer and took a drink. "In my opinion, foreplay is overrated."

Dax grinned. Now there was a challenge any man would have the obligation to rise to. "That's because you don't have the patience for foreplay. I'll bet you wouldn't last fifteen minutes without cracking."

Raven gazed at him over her bottle. "I haven't met a man who can wait fifteen minutes."

She might have a point there. He stretched his legs out and tipped back the beer. "You've been seeing the wrong men."

Raven gave a low, throaty laugh and pushed back onto her heels. "The only problem with the men I date is that they talk too much." She cocked her head. "And then there's *you*."

He liked that he was different from the other men she dated. Not that he planned on dating her. In fact, he shouldn't even be entertaining the thoughts that kept popping into his head or other parts of his body. Dating Raven? About as dangerous as it got.

"So," she said. "What happened six months ago, Maddox?"

And to top it all off, she was relentless.

Dax took a breath and stared out over the eternal ocean, old guilt seeping into his bones. It was inevitable. A lump was forming in his throat already, and he hadn't even started talking yet.

"We responded to a security system alarm at the Lowry house." He looked at her. "Same place we found you casing."

She only smiled and bit into her sandwich.

He shook his head. An exercise in futility. "Nick was primary on the call, and I was backup. We found the back door open and entered the home to investigate. A little terrier greeted us, so we figured it was a false alarm. The burglar caught us by surprise." He paused to take a long draw on his beer. "He came from behind and almost killed me with a marble statue. I went down. Then he shot Nick. He died while I was doing CPR."

He looked at Raven, who was watching him intently.

"Did you get a look at the killer?" she asked.

"What is it with you?" he said bitterly. "Do you have *any* compassion in your soul?"

Her eyes narrowed. "You don't know anything about my soul. And the truth is, if I told you, it wouldn't make a difference. You've already condemned me, and nothing I do or say will change that."

"You don't want to change," he said.

"I don't have a reason to."

They stared at each other, and even in the twilight, he could see the fire in her eyes, and he remembered all the reasons why he couldn't trust her.

Dax finished his beer. "He was wearing a full mask. I only saw him from behind for a second. He was about five-ten, 150 pounds, small build. After the shooting, he vanished with the Vassalo. We had no witnesses, no prints, and no leads. The investigation is going nowhere. Happy now?"

Ambient light from the marina lit the hard planes of his face. He was in another place right now. The past. Raven knew from experience, the past mostly sucked. They finished their sandwiches in silence while she pondered her next question. No doubt, Maddox was not going to be happy with it.

"Did you interview the Lowrys?" she asked as she gathered up the empty wrappers and bottles.

"They didn't have much to say except that they were art collectors. They didn't seem very upset about losing the Vassalo. In fact, the only reason we knew it'd been stolen was because he cut it from the frame."

She gave a short laugh. "That's because they didn't want you to look too closely at their operation. Most of their inventory is stolen."

He frowned. "They steal art?"

Raven shook her head. "The Lowrys are more like a pawnshop for fine art. They just find the buyers and broker the sales."

"So why were you planning to steal stolen art?"

She pursed her lips. Was it worth the battle? Probably not. What did she care what he thought of her anyway? On the other hand, maybe it was time for Maddox to get a clue into her world. Either way, dinner was over. She grabbed the basket and stood up.

"I traced a Remington bronze stolen from an upstate New York museum there. My job was to return it to its rightful owners." She stood up and looked down at him. "The night you stopped me, you and Nick cost us a national treasure."

Dax got to his feet. "You expect me to believe you're the Robin Hood of the art world?"

The one time she tells him the truth . . . "Don't care if you do or don't."

"If you knew the statue was there, why wouldn't you tell the local authorities and let them handle it? I thought that's what API was all about."

She laughed. "Right. I'm sure you boys would believe me if I walked in there with just my word. Even if you did, by the time you got legal entry, it'd be gone. The Lowrys have been operating all over this country for the past ten years, and no one has been able to stop them. No one cares."

Dax stared at her. "Maybe if we'd *known* they were dealing stolen art, we'd have been able to shut them down."

"You can't even tell the good guys from the bad guys," she said with more than a little irritation. She turned and marched back toward the marina. "The Lowrys weren't victims. *They* are the criminals. I'm just righting a wrong that no one else will. You care to guess what the recovery rate of stolen art is?"

He walked next to her until they reached the dock. "No, but I can tell you what the annual murder rate is."

She stopped and turned to face him. "Just because you don't think it's a priority doesn't mean it doesn't matter. That artwork is probably in South America by now or being traded for drugs. Every day, our cultural treasures are stolen and lost forever. You know, Maddox, the world isn't black-and-white. There's a lot of gray out there."

"You don't have to tell me. In fact, thanks to our mutual friend, all I see is gray," he said with such bitterness that she blinked.

"What do you mean?" she asked.

His lips thinned as though he'd said too much. "Didn't it show up on my background check? I'm color-blind."

And then it all clicked in. "That's why you quit?"

His jaw set. "I left for my own reasons."

This was personal. The killer had cost him more than just his career and more than his partner. Every day he saw a gray world. He couldn't escape his past if he wanted to.

"I am sorry. About your partner and your eyesight," she said.

He stared at her suspiciously, then shook his head. "We leave bright and early tomorrow morning," he replied, and boarded the Hatteras. She watched him close the door behind him.

"Wow, he's not too happy. What'd you do to him?" Paulie said behind her.

She took a breath. This day couldn't end soon enough. "I guess you heard all that."

"Everyone heard all that. You guys argued all the way up the beach," he said and handed her a folder. "Havana entry info, your passport and copies for the Cuban officials, and the Vassalo report. And I checked the boat for bugs and trackers. It's clean."

She took it. "Thanks." And pondered whether or not it was safe to go into the boat.

Paulie said, "It must suck to live in paradise and not be able to see it."

Raven looked out over the horizon, where the sun had

set in a glorious palate of oranges and reds. "Can you lose your color vision by being struck in the head?"

He shrugged. "I suppose if there's enough nerve damage. Detached retina and all that."

"Would it be enough to fully disable a cop?"

"Maybe. I don't know. He might not be able to work the streets, but he'd probably be okay at a desk job."

That's what she thought, too. So why did he quit? Why are there no scraps of that part of his life in his home?

She turned to Paulie. "Are you staying aboard tonight?"

He shoved his hands in his pockets and rocked on his heels with a sheepish grin. "Actually, Shelly gave me a cabin. I already moved all my stuff in."

Raven gave a sigh of resignation. Alone with Maddox. "We'll be leaving at dawn. I'll contact you when I can."

"You won't have cell phone coverage unless you register with the Cubans, which you don't want to do," he warned her. "Coverage in the Gulf is spotty at best. Also, you should leave your weapon here. The Cuban authorities will search the boat coming in and going out. They are good to tourists, but they are methodical and deliberate, so *be patient.* And for God's sake, try to act like a tourist and not a thief."

Okay, so maybe she wouldn't mind losing him for a while.

"Is all this in the report?" she asked.

"Yeah. And you should destroy that before you hit Havana," he added, pointing to the folder. "Burn it. No, wait—you're on a boat. Don't burn it. Just toss it overboard.

But shred it first." He paused and frowned. "A shredder would be best. You think Dax has one?"

She started to the boat. "Good night, Paulie."

Dax lay on the gurney, unable to move. The ceiling above alternated yellow and gray. He tried to hold on to the yellow, but it kept fading. It was too hot, and Dax could feel sweat on his face. He heard voices murmuring around him.

"Who's there?" he asked.

Nick's face appeared above him. "Hey, Senior. Can you see me?"

"Yeah—"

"He can see me," Nick announced to someone beside him.

"About damn time," came the gruff reply. Dax froze. It was his father's voice.

"Dad?"

He heard movement; then his father said, "I keep giving you my stuff, David. Someday you're going to have to give it back."

Foreboding filled Dax's bones. He knew his father was standing beside him, just out of range. "What stuff?"

Suddenly, he could move his head, but he didn't want to even though he knew it was inevitable. His punishment for failure.

Dax looked over at his father.

His eyes were gone.

"No!" Dax lunged forward, off the gurney with the word ripped from his throat. He slammed into a body and fell to the floor. "No. Don't do it. Not for me."

"Maddox, stop!"

He opened his eyes to find Raven on the floor, pinned partially beneath him. His heart was racing, his body was slick with sweat, and his hands were wrapped around her wrists. Dawn had begun peeking through the blinds. He was on the boat. Safe.

"Christ," he said aloud, and let go of her wrists. What was happening to him? Was he losing his mind?

She gazed at him with deep concern. "Are you all right?"

She felt good, a link to sanity, and since she wasn't pushing to get away, he rested on his elbows and absorbed her into his senses. Maybe she'd be enough to purge the remnants. "Fine."

"If you say so," she said softly.

There was just enough light for him to watch her lips move, only inches from his. He wished he could see her in living color. He'd have to settle for the other senses, which were kicking in nicely. Her steady breath cooled his face. Her scent filled his head. The warmth seeping through the thin layer of fabric between them . . . he shifted, and her eyes widened marginally. Okay, maybe a little too nicely. But at least the dream was long gone.

"Did I hurt you?" he asked, easing off her and pulling her to her feet.

"No. But you're a lot faster than you look."

She handed him a glass of water from the end table.

He eyed her in amazement. Again. How did she always know? Was he yelling in his sleep? Thrashing around? He didn't want to explain his nightmares to her or to anyone. Hell, he didn't want to explain them to himself.

He took it. "Thanks."

Then, without another word, she went down the stairs

and belowdecks. Dax took a sip and ran a hand through his damp hair. Why the nightmares? He'd never had them before. In fact, he hadn't dreamed much in the past six months. So he finally dreams again, and it's all bad.

He checked the time—5:00 A.M. Time to get this show on the road. That's when he noticed the folder on the table. He turned on a light and opened it.

It was full of documents on Havana entry and exit. He also found a listing of Vassalo paintings and current locations, including *Young Virgin* in Havana. He glanced down through the list of thirty-some paintings attributed to the artist and noticed that quite a few had been reported stolen recently. Their thief had been busy.

On the bottom of the folder was Raven's passport, under an alias of course. He looked at the picture inside. Even in shades of gray, she was the most beautiful woman he'd ever seen.

He closed his eyes and remembered her jet-black hair and the palest blue eyes that shone with a light of their own. Golden skin. Lush lips. Then he opened his eyes to gray, and the sting returned.

It wasn't her fault, and he knew it, but he couldn't seem to separate her from what happened that night. He kept wondering what she would have done if she had been there instead. Would she have surrendered to the police without a fight? Based on what he'd seen, he doubted it. Which put her in the same place.

He glanced at the glass.

Or not.

Still, how far would she go to get what she wanted? He had a feeling he was about to find out.

CHAPTER
11

Probability. The measure of certainty about a certain outcome. The calculated likelihood of a particular event occurring. The management of risk.

Clayton Fauss flipped a quarter and let it bounce on the desk. With the curiosity of a man who had just risked something, he watched it roll in a large circle, spiraling ever smaller, sounding like a roulette wheel churning to its inevitable stop.

The coin finally revealed its outcome with a quick rattle.

Tails. Again. The count was now ten tails to six heads.

Common wisdom stated that the odds would balance out if given enough tosses. The truth was that even if the coin was true, the tosses consistent, the surface the same, and the variables controlled, in the short run, the odds were already against heads catching up.

The coin could not remember the past.

Unlike people.

A green night-vision video played on his laptop of two thieves stealing a valuable painting from a Richmond, Virginia, warehouse.

He paused the image of Raven picking the lock. Resourceful and skilled woman. Her exploits never ceased to amaze him. His analysis of her had taken the longest of any of the components.

Behind her, David Maddox kept watch. Another interesting component. One who would hound his partner's killer until the day he died. A certain event Fauss needed to neutralize.

His cell phone rang, and Fauss answered it. "Hello."

"Did you get the video clip?"

"Reviewing it now. The quality is acceptable."

"They took the bait."

Fauss nodded. "As predicted in the model."

There was a brief pause. "Right. Is everything set for tomorrow?"

"Of course," Fauss said.

"And what about your guest?"

"Resting comfortably. There is nothing to worry about."

"Nothing for you. I'm the one taking all the risks here."

Fauss smiled. "Your risks are minimal."

"Because it says so on the model? Well, that makes me feel a whole lot better."

"Because the model is never wrong," Fauss corrected. "You will see."

"Whatever." He hung up.

Fauss closed his cell phone and sighed at the impertinence of youth.

He brought up the model diagram on his laptop. As it loaded, pride filled him. He'd done well. It was laid out to perfection, every element designated with a unique color, every variable noted and contained. A mixture of independent events, conditional probabilities, impossible and certain events. He couldn't control every variable, but he could reduce their damage to the integrity of the model.

But the main players, he could predict, and therefore, control. He knew from past experiments and careful analysis of the elements themselves what their choices would be. For the past ten years, he'd studied them, watched them, and set the events up accordingly.

The anticipated outcomes would follow, and his current probability of success stood at an admirable 99 percent.

Wind buffeted Raven's face as the boat cut through the water. From the bridge deck settee that flanked the boat's control station, she looked out over dark blue ocean and endless sky. Shallow rollers rippled the straits between Florida and Cuba. Traffic was confined to large freighters, pleasure craft, and tugs. Occasionally, a white triangle sail would pass by. Otherwise, a quiet sea lay before them, which was good because the last thing they needed was the U.S. Coast Guard stopping by to ask questions.

In the six hours they'd been en route, Maddox hadn't said a word about what happened this morning. She'd awoken when she heard "Dad"—partially from the spoken word and partially from the raw desperation in his voice. She could understand having nightmares about Nick's death. But why the father? What did he have to do with it? The impressions she'd pulled from the family photo hadn't been ugly, just sad and filled with regret. Was there a past she hadn't seen?

Raven shook her head. None of her business. This was what happened when she stayed in one place too long.

The only people who could understand what it was like to know too much were her mother and Jillian. There were emotions and memories that deserved to be buried forever. Whatever Maddox was reliving was a hell she had no intention of entering, regardless of how much she'd wanted to help him this morning. Besides, she hadn't been able to save her own mother. What could she do for a man she barely knew?

Maddox stared straight ahead over the wheel, square-jawed and unreadable behind his sunglasses. Since she was also wearing her sunglasses, she took the opportunity to check him out.

Tanned beneath a snug black T-shirt and khaki shorts, he could be any captain on the water. But there was something uniquely sexy about him, besides the 190 pounds of solid muscle, which she could now personally vouch for. In fact, he was pretty much branded into her skin. For a moment this morning, she thought he was going to kiss her. And she had been hot enough to let him.

Maybe the real turn-on was a former lawman surrendering to the dark side. Her fault, that, although she didn't feel much guilt over it. He had his reasons, and he would have come over with or without her. Besides, he was a big boy. All grown up and hot and all. She wasn't responsible for corrupting him. At least not in the theft arena.

He flexed his shoulders, and for a brief moment, she contemplated foreplay.

"Ever been to Havana before?" she asked him over the rumble of the engines.

"Once, last year. An international fishing tournament with Nick."

"Did you two catch anything?"

"Only if you count the women Nick picked up."

"What about you?" she asked.

Maddox turned to her then, and she knew she had his full attention. She smiled. He grinned back but said nothing. For some reason, that bugged her. And it bugged her even more that it bothered her. Then she remembered something.

"I thought you only bought the boat a few months ago?"

"I did. From Nick's estate."

"This was Nick's boat?"

Maddox nodded. "It was part of his grand plan to get rich doing fishing charters. Conned me into getting my captain's license so I could drive while he sat back and drank beer all day. Never did see him catch any fish." That admission brought a smile to his lips.

"Well that explains the boat's name," she said with a laugh. "I'm surprised the family didn't want it."

"Nick didn't have much of a family."

She noted the heaviness in his voice. He was living on his dead partner's boat with all those memories. That would be enough to give *her* bad dreams.

Long minutes passed before Maddox said, "Tell me you left the Beretta at the marina."

She already felt naked without the gun against her thigh. On the other hand, she felt much better that there were pieces of a SIG-Sauer .45 stashed in various places inside the boat. Perhaps it was better not to tell Maddox about that just yet. "I did. You?"

He nodded. "It's all brains from here on in."

"And a hunting knife, diving knife, and butterfly knife."

His forehead furrowed, and she added, "For cooking."

Maddox muttered something low. "Anything else?"

"I might have a lipstick knife in my bag."

"Of course," he said with a certain amount of resignation. "Any toys from Paulie?"

She rested her arms on the ledge of the boat. "The MP3-style communications earbuds. A pick set disguised as hairpins, miniflashlights, cell phone stun gun, and other miscellaneous gadgets. Nothing we can't talk our way out of if the Cuban officials give us a hard time."

Maddox shook his head, and she heard him utter, "Famous last words."

He looked at one of his instruments, then scanned the horizon. "Coming up on Cuban territorial waters."

Raven could just make out a few tall buildings of Havana's skyline. Minutes later, a mountain range appeared to the east. At the twelve-mile point, Maddox picked up the radio and started hailing Guarda Frontera in Spanish for entry clearance.

While he waited for a reply, Raven asked, "So we're going in legal?"

He nodded. "We'll get our tourist visas and a berth at Marina Tarara. It's about fifteen miles from Havana, but it's a lot smaller and quieter than the Hemingway Marina."

"So we can get out in a hurry if we need to," she added.

His lips thinned. "Precisely. Leaving port without exit processing is seriously frowned upon."

Fifteen minutes later, Marina Tarara responded. Maddox gave their boat and crew information, and received instructions on passing through the channel.

"We're in," Raven said. "That was easy."

"We still need to meet Immigration, Agriculture, Customs, and Coast Guard. Everyone's going to know we're here."

"Lovely," she said.

"My thoughts exactly. What color is that buoy at ten o'clock?"

She turned to look at it. "Red."

He nodded and adjusted course. "Thanks."

"Anytime," she said.

Entry formalities consisted of two hours of paperwork and a parade of officials who were pleasant and methodical. All the while, Raven offered them sodas and asked about the best tourist sites, even though she'd already memorized every scrap of paper in Paulie's file before they tossed it overboard. Between the act and the lace-trimmed, fitted white sundress, she made certain the last thing the guys were thinking was "thief."

It was late afternoon when Maddox maneuvered the Hatteras into a slip and they tied off. He chatted briefly with the dockmaster and gave him a bag of goodies—shampoo, aspirin, and beer. The man was very gracious, and Raven felt a pang of humility. Such small gifts for so much appreciation. They hailed a taxi for a ride into the heart of Old Havana.

Green countryside rolled down to white sand beaches

they'd seen on the way into port. On winding roads, they passed oxcarts and automobiles, chicken farms and extravagant residences. Everywhere they were greeted with waves and smiles.

As they drove along the harbor edge, the city of Havana rose before them. Palm trees swayed between early Colonial and Baroque architecture, modern austere towers, and military monuments dedicated to the Revolution.

Tourists strolled along wide sidewalks. Locals congregated on front steps and outside tables. Cigar ladies worked the crowded streets, while taxis and bicycles darted about. The atmosphere was steamy and relaxed.

In a white shirt and faded baseball cap, the taxi driver chatted with Maddox, while Raven concentrated on the layout of the city. She'd managed to commit most of Paulie's maps to memory and worked to get her bearings.

The deeper into the city center they went, the older, more decaying, and pressed together the buildings became. Some stretches were better than others, where care had been given. But peeling paint and grimy fronts couldn't detract from the architectural beauty.

Then she smiled. "Look at all these old Chevys. It's like stepping back in time."

Maddox shifted, and she inhaled the smell of the sea lingering on him as he pressed closer to look out her window.

She had a sudden itch to run her hands over his bronzed skin, just to see what it felt like. Or slip her fingers through his thick brown hair, just to see what his reaction would be. Who would win? The man or the cop?

He caught her staring at him, and the heat in the taxi

jumped. Blue eyes studied her face, then traveled down her throat to her breasts.

"Nice dress," he said roughly.

"I wore it for the Cuban officials," she said, feeling subtly vulnerable. The smile he gave her curled her toes. He didn't believe her for a minute.

The taxi driver asked if they were married.

Maddox replied, "Not yet," and Raven was surprised when he drew her closer with one hand. His fingers gripped her waist, pressing her against him. Her hands splayed across his chest, because she knew what he was going to do.

"Play along," he whispered in English over her mouth just before he kissed her. She heard the driver chuckle; then she was lost in his lips against hers.

Foreplay had its moments, and this was definitely one of them. She heard him suck in air as he wrapped his other hand around the back of her head to capture her better. His tongue slipped along her lips, and she opened to the invitation. She kissed him back as heat trembled in her belly. *Be careful what you wish for.* It was the only thought that came to mind before her nails sank into the thick muscles of his chest, her thigh rubbing his.

He broke it off and looked at her in mild surprise. Then he turned to joke with the driver. Raven realized she was still gripping his shirt in her fist. She released the shirt and pushed him back to his own space. He just smiled tightly and looked out the window.

Having lost her concentration thanks to Maddox's little diversion, she strained to see street signs as they cruised by. The streets had narrowed between tightly packed two-story tenements painted in pastels.

Seconds later, the driver dropped them in a narrow alley near la Catedral de los Ángeles, and with a wave and a smile he was gone. The smell of cigars and petrol wrapped around them. Maddox put a hand around her arm and led her along the narrow sidewalks and winding streets toward the plaza.

"So what the hell was that about?" she said.

"The kiss? You didn't like it? Felt like you liked it, especially when you grabbed me."

She ground her teeth. "I didn't start it, and I want to know why you did."

"You are a beautiful woman, and Cubans love their women. So unless you want undue attention from every male we meet, you'll have to put up with it from me." He flashed her the biggest smile she'd seen so far.

Her mouth dropped open in disbelief. "What kind of idiotic logic is that?"

"All part of the game, right?" Blue eyes zeroed in on her. "The dress. The act with the officials. It's all a big game to you."

"Not when Walter is missing, it's not."

He nodded, vindicated. "But otherwise it is. Don't you ever worry about what could happen to you if you're caught? And I'm not talking by the law. I'm sure you aren't the only one in your line of work who carries a gun."

She wanted to laugh. She'd faced guns less dangerous than Maddox. "Haven't you heard? Only the good die young."

He gave her a hard look that she ignored. So what if it was a game? Everyone played games. The people who pretended to love their jobs and their lives, when, in reality, they watched their dreams die. The people who lied to themselves day after day, believing love would return. Life was a game with winners and losers, and she had no intention of being a loser.

The alley opened up to a cobbled square lined with aristocratic buildings, graceful archways, and wrought-iron balconies laden with fragrant flowers. White umbrella tables dotted the plaza. People churned around the center, gazing and snapping pictures in the oppressive Havana heat.

And at the far end, the cathedral dominated the square—an ornate marble structure of columns with identical bell towers flanking an imposing front facade. Three massive doors faced the square, but only the middle one was open.

Raven stopped short.

"Nice church," Maddox said.

"Lovely."

She tried to make mental notes of the layout, but the sudden slam of anger and guilt broke her focus. It had been a long time since she'd set foot in a church, not since her mother died. But even before that, it was a place she'd lost hope in. She'd had too many prayers go unanswered. *Doing* was a lot more effective than praying.

She started walking. "The church will close in a few minutes. We need to locate the painting."

They entered the arched center door, and Dax took in the interior. The traditional rectangle floor plan was divided by two rows of towering pillars leading up to a domed cap overhead and an enormous but modestly adorned altar ahead. Dozens of patrons lined the wooden pews.

Out of the corner of his eye, he noticed Raven make the sign of the cross and genuflect before searching for the painting.

His curiosity was piqued as he followed her down an aisle. "Are you Catholic?"

"Used to be," she replied without looking at him.

Used to be? He knew a lot of Catholics. It never went away. "When did you stop?"

"When I was sixteen," she replied.

"What happened when you were sixteen?"

She cast him a quick glare. "Back off, Maddox. My religious beliefs are none of your business."

Now there was a struck nerve if he'd ever seen one. The minute she'd seen this church, she froze up, and he couldn't help but wonder what kind of power this place had over her. "Lose faith, Raven?"

Her icy, hard stare held no mercy. "If you aren't going to help me find this damn painting, you can *leave*." She walked away.

The woman could shut down faster than anyone he'd ever met when she didn't want to deal with something. Like the kid on the sailboard. Like her past. But every once in a while, he'd catch a flash of softness. Just enough to remind him that she was human. Very human. Very female in that dress.

He didn't need color to appreciate the tempting swell of her breasts and long legs that had seduced him in the cab. And the kiss that had gotten away from him. Havana heat had nothing on her. What had he been thinking? She hadn't bought his flimsy excuse, and he couldn't blame her. He hadn't believed it either. He'd wanted to kiss her from the day he met her. The problem was, now he had. He couldn't go back, and he shouldn't go forward.

He turned to search in the opposite direction. A few minutes later, he caught up with Raven standing in front of a small eight-inch-square picture of a young Virgin Mary hanging in the left entry foyer of the church.

Raven lifted her fingers from the painting as he approached.

"Is this the one? It's not signed," Dax said.

"This is the one," she said. "It's Vassalo's early style."

A man's life for this. It didn't seem right, but Dax had to admit, he'd seen people die for less.

Raven drew him into a pew, where they both knelt. She remained quiet and watchful over her clasped hands, and Dax knew she was planning the heist. He hated this so much he couldn't even form a thought around it. Maybe Raven's way of shutting down wasn't such a bad idea.

"My sister would love this church," she said softly.

He gave her an inquiring look, and Raven added, "She's an assistant curator for a museum, specializing in liturgical objects—paintings, statues, altar pieces."

"Your sister is a religious art curator?"

Raven cast him a dark glower. "That's what I just said."

He grinned and shook his head. "I love irony."

Her eyes narrowed, and he was pretty sure the only reason she wasn't telling him to go to hell was because they were sitting in a church.

Instead, she stood up and said, "I want to check the outer perimeter."

He got to his feet. "We aren't taking it now?"

"Later," she said. "After dark, when it's empty."

There was an odd inflection in her voice that he couldn't read. Guilt maybe?

On the way out, she paused long enough to stuff a few bills in the donations box, and Dax smiled.

Definitely guilt.

CHAPTER
12

I'm surprised you're drinking," Maddox said over the remnants of a fried chicken dinner. "What with the upcoming theft and all."

Maddox was becoming a real pain in the ass.

Raven sipped on her second mojito cocktail, contemplating a third, and knowing he was right even if he was just busting on her. She needed to stop, but she couldn't think of a good enough reason to. In fact, she'd like nothing better than to stay right here all night.

She spun her glass. This was so unlike her. It would have been easy to take the painting this afternoon. Small piece, no security, lots of people. No one would have noticed for hours probably. Or maybe they would have. Their artwork collection was modest. She wondered if they had any idea the Vassalo was their single most valuable piece. It always amazed her how trusting churches were, relying on the decency of man to protect them. Didn't they realize there were people like her in the world?

She tilted her head. "Maybe I'll get drunk and let you do this one solo. Think you're up to it?"

Blue eyes narrowed and she grinned, knowing he wouldn't make a fuss in the middle of the crowded garden café wedged between two buildings. It was 8:00 P.M., and the sunset peeking over the rooftops had turned the white walls a soft ivory. Brassy music wafted through the stone archways. Candlelight cast a gentle glow over their table. It was actually kind of nice.

"I think you don't want to do this," he said.

"Don't be ridiculous. I live for this," she deadpanned, and took another big sip.

He watched her for a moment, but she wouldn't meet his gaze. He was too close. Regardless of his vision issues, there were times she believed he could see her better than anyone else could.

"Does it bother you this much every time?"

She glared at him. "I realize this comes as a shock and a disappointment to you, but I don't always steal to get pieces back, Maddox. *Sometimes,* I don't even break a single law."

He put his elbows on the table, his gaze shadowed. "Why the burning desire to return art to its rightful owners? You think your clients are going to care if you rot in jail in a third-world country?"

She traced a design in the condensation on her glass. "It's a challenge."

He shook his head slowly. "Not good enough."

Her eyes met his. Why was he grilling her about this? What did it matter? He would never see her as anything more than a thief, regardless of her reasons. How could she begin to explain to him the debt she owed? That she'd inherited.

"Believe it," she said. "I'm completely shallow and self-serving. It's all about me."

Maddox stared through her. "And that's why you dropped a few bills in the church box? That's why you gave a kid ten bucks for a bag of peanuts worth a buck today? Because you only care about yourself?"

Screw his bad vision. The man had eyes in the back of his head. "Maybe I'm trying to buy my way into heaven." She looked at him over her drink. "Think it'll work?"

He leaned forward with a smile, the hard edges of his face softening in the candlelight between them. "You want to know what I think?"

"No, not really," she said as unease crept over her. She was feeling too good for him to spoil her mood.

"I think you care a whole lot more than you'll ever admit. In fact, I think you're afraid if you stay in one place too long, you might even like it."

Raven blinked at him. Wait, was he saying she was a good person? Is that what she heard? Impossible. She tipped her glass. How much booze was in these things?

She set her drink down and leaned back. "You should ask for a refund on that $9.95 matchbook psychology degree you got."

A slow smile spread across his face. Check that. A slow, sexy smile that had her thinking way too little. A very dangerous thing for a woman whose mind should be elsewhere.

"As long as you can walk away, you think you're safe," he said. "Hate to break this to you, but it doesn't work that way. We're all stuck with people who drive us crazy."

She narrowed her gaze. "You're ruining a perfectly good mojito here, Maddox."

He sat there with a smug grin. *Damn him.* She lifted her chin. "And what about you?"

"What about me?" he asked, his eyebrows rising in amusement.

"You could have stayed on the force if you wanted to. They would have found a place for you. But you left." She waved her hand. "In fact, some people might say you walked away."

His blue eyes hardened above the grin. "I left because I couldn't do my job anymore. You walk away because you're afraid to stay. There's a difference."

"Are you sure about that? Are you sure you didn't leave because of what happened to Nick? Too many reminders?"

The grin faded completely. "I live on Nick's boat. I have enough reminders."

Raven caught the warning in his tone and chose dangerous waters. "Are you staying there for yourself or for him? You think if you live on the boat, Nick lives, too?"

Maddox clenched his jaw, and she knew she had him.

She added, "Maybe if you moved out, the nightmares would stop."

He pulled out his wallet and tossed a few bills on the table. "My dreams aren't about Nick."

"Me?" she said with an innocent smile.

He paused for a split second as his eyes darkened. "Dreams about you wouldn't be nightmares." Then he looked annoyed. "But I could be wrong."

They stepped out of the café and into the summer

heat Havana held. The drinks were working their magic on her, and she didn't argue when Maddox laced his fingers through hers. They strolled the winding streets waiting for night to fall, passing noisy discos, streetwise mulattoes, and hustlers who emerged from the shadows offering everything from cigars to women to taxis.

In a small square, a salsa band played to a crowd of Cubans and tourists primed for the night. Standing on the sidelines, Raven swayed to the saucy beat. It occurred to her that she was really enjoying this city. She might have to stop by again sometime when she wasn't going to pilfer one of its most valuable artworks.

When a young man approached her and asked her to dance, Maddox told him to get lost in no uncertain terms. The man nodded politely and stepped away.

He leaned down and said in her ear, "If you keep moving like that, we're going to have to leave. I'm not getting in a brawl with every guy here."

Raven looked over her shoulder at him in challenge. "Afraid to dance with me, Maddox?"

He stood very still, his eyes fixed on her with unnerving awareness. "Is that what you want?"

She didn't know what she wanted, but she couldn't seem to control the restlessness that had snuck in between drinks. Maybe she wanted more than a dance. Maybe she wanted to see what it was like to sleep with the enemy. She heard herself say, "Why not?"

He hiked their backpack high on his shoulder and pulled her among the other dancers. Raven let out a gasp when he wrapped his hand around her back and yanked her to his chest.

Their eyes locked as they moved together to the lively

rhythm. But Maddox danced to a beat all his own, and
Raven found herself mesmerized by his blue eyes and
hard body. He pulled back and spun her beneath his
hands, then drew her against him with enough sizzle to
make her moan. Hot eyes, hot hands, hot body—all of
which whittled away at the last bit of self-control she had.
Screw the damn painting. Screw the shitty day. This was
what she wanted—to forget.

Song after song, they gyrated and swung with the
frenzied partiers. She lost herself to the sights and
sounds—Maddox in her arms, foreplay on her mind, and
freedom in her soul.

She threw her head back and laughed.

Dax smiled at her carefree laughter ringing above the
music. It was worth the torment of every steamy grind,
and he concentrated on the dance as much as he could.
But he was kidding himself if he thought the feel of her
hips against his didn't affect him. Her high spirits even
more.

For once, her guard was down. Then again, so was
his. Not only that, it'd been far too long since he'd
"danced," so before his better judgment ruined everything, he pulled her close and kissed her. She stopped
swaying. He felt her moan against his lips and took the
invitation to slide his hands down her body to the soft,
bare skin of her thighs.

All kinds of warnings were going off in his head, and
he suppressed them ruthlessly.

Raven responded by molding her body to his. He bid
good-bye to his sanity when she slipped her hands under
his loose shirt. She gently bit his lower lip and ran her
tongue around his mouth. Fingers explored his chest, hips

rubbed against his, and for a moment, he almost forgot they were standing in the middle of fifty people.

He'd never met a woman like her and probably never would again. Such an intriguing mix of fire and ice, and at this moment, he knew perfectly well which one he was playing with.

She smiled at him as she rolled against his growing erection. It wouldn't do any good to try to hide it, and he wrapped his arms around her and kissed her hard and deep. If he was going to burn for this, he was going to enjoy it.

Then he caught movement in the corner of the square as three policemen strolled in. Entrenched instincts surfaced in a flash, and the heat in his belly subsided, replaced by cold, hard reality.

"Time to go," he whispered in her ear.

His words sank into her mind slowly as her eyes focused on him, and her expression turned serious. They left the revelry behind and cut through the streets back toward the church. He inhaled deeply to clear his head. His body was going to take a little longer.

One thing for certain: He was never going to call Raven on a bluff unless he was in a position to follow through. He had no idea what he'd just unleashed; but given the chance, he'd do it again.

But first, there was hell to pay.

Streetlights cast a surreal sheen over the plaza, and at 11:00 P.M. it was still full of laughing, dancing, and partying. If he and Raven played their cards right, no one would even notice them.

She was all business now. Gone was the woman in

flames. Gone was the laughter. He wondered if she even realized the depth of the transformation.

In an alley facing the rear of the church, they covered their street clothes with dark jackets and pants to blend into the night.

Dax reached into the pack and encountered hard steel. Any leftover happy thoughts from the dance vaporized as he pulled out a SIG-Sauer .45 and held it up to Raven. "What is this?"

She looked over for a moment. "I was going to tell you."

"No, you weren't," he said with a shake of his head.

"Okay, I wasn't. Tell me you don't feel better with a gun?"

"I don't," he said, but she was right.

"Fine, then give it to me," she said, and held out her hand.

"*You* can't be trusted." He shoved the gun into his jacket. "Any security systems to worry about?"

"None."

He frowned. "Nothing? With all the artwork they have in there?"

She took out the pick set and slipped it into her pocket. "Ever answer an intrusion alarm at a church?"

"No," he admitted.

She handed him a headset. "We walk in, grab the painting, and leave. Two minutes tops."

"Unless we incur the wrath of God and get struck by lightning," Dax said.

"Right." She handed him the backpack, which he slung over his shoulders. "The small side door is our best bet."

They stood there and looked at each other for a

moment. In the silence, she looked grim and colorless. All that joyous freedom had been crushed like it had never happened. If he hadn't seen it for himself, he might not believe her capable. Somewhere under the cool mask was the real Raven, and for one brief moment, she'd let him in.

Then she brushed by him. "Let's go."

Dax used his body as cover while she picked the lock in a few short minutes and pushed the heavy door inward. They slipped into the sacristy and locked the door behind them. Their eyes quickly adjusted to the pale glow of streetlights through stained-glass saints. Reverent silence settled around them as they made their way across the altar to the back of the church, where the painting hung.

Dax scanned the shadows, but nothing moved. When they reached the foyer, Raven stopped dead in front of the wall.

The painting was gone.

He felt like he'd been sucker punched. "What the hell?"

Raven pressed her bare fingers to the spot under the single nail that once held it. Then she rubbed her fingerprints off with her sleeve. "Maybe they moved it. Look around."

They each took a side of the church and met empty-handed back at the altar.

Raven asked, "Anything?"

The hair on the back of his neck rose. Something was very wrong here. He pulled out the SIG. "It's not here."

"Then where is it?" she said, her voice cracking.

"The police have it."

Dax whipped the gun around to the voice. A lone

priest stood behind the altar, fully robed and watching them. His hair was short, thick, and black with white around the temples. He spoke excellent English, with a thick Cuban accent. "I am Father García."

Dax looked around, but no one else emerged from the shadows. Still, his instincts were screaming to run.

"Maddox, put the gun down," Raven said, her voice low.

He cast her a quick look in disbelief. Did she realize this guy could be an impostor? He asked the man, "Why did they take it?"

The priest shook his head. "They did not tell me."

Raven put her hand on Dax's arm. "You can't pull a gun on a priest."

He frowned at her. "You didn't have any problem pulling one on a cop."

She glowered at him and moved between him and the priest.

The priest studied her. "I saw you here today."

"Reconnaissance," she said simply. "We need that painting to save a man's life. I promise to return it."

The priest raised his hands and dropped them. "I'm sorry. I do not know where it is now. Perhaps I could find out tomorrow."

Loud banging on the church's main door shook the silence. Shouts of *"Abres la puerta! Policia!"* rang out, followed by pounding on both side doors.

Raven glanced over, her eyes wide. They were surrounded.

The pastor said, "I did not call them."

Dax eyed him. "Forgive me if I don't believe you. How do we get out of here? Quietly."

After a few tense moments, the priest sighed. "There is another way." He turned with a flare of robes, and Dax followed, with Raven on his heels. The priest led them through the sacristy and into a small room before stopping in front of a rug. He pulled it aside, revealing a trapdoor. It opened to a ladder and a room below the church.

"The undercroft," the priest explained. "There is a small opening that leads out to the street. It was used many years ago. I do not know if it is still passable."

Dax peered into the well of darkness. If it was a trap, there'd be no way out. "You wouldn't lie to us, would you?"

"Maddox," Raven said with a hiss.

Father García looked over their heads as the banging became more insistent. "I must let them in. Hurry, *por favor.*"

Dax said to Raven, "Go first."

As she descended the ladder, he gave the priest a final look before dropping into the basement. The door closed over their heads with a slam, plunging them into darkness. Raven turned on a flashlight and swept the small, earthen-walled tomb. It was mostly empty and smelled putrid. The floor consisted of matted cardboard and black slime. Battered wooden crates were stacked haphazardly. A chalky waterline ringed the walls, but she didn't see a doorway anywhere.

"I knew it," he murmured. "We've been set up."

"He wouldn't do that to us," Raven said from behind him.

"He might for a painting worth millions," he reminded

her. "And did it ever occur to you that he might not be a priest at all?"

"He is," she said simply, as if that made it so.

Footsteps hammered the floor above. Loud voices rose as Father García talked to the police. Standing on the ladder, Dax groped around the ceiling for some way to seal the opening but found none.

"If they come through, I'll tell them I was working alone," he told her in a hushed voice. "You find a place to hide. Maybe you can get out later."

She flashed the light behind the debris along the perimeter. "Sure. No problem. Over my dead body."

Boots rattled the floorboards inches from his head. "You might want to rephrase that."

Her flashlight settled on a spot to his right. "Found it."

He jumped down from the ladder and helped her push two pallets aside to reveal a tiny one-foot-by-two-foot alcove. Raven shoved against the back panel, and it swung open. She flashed her light through the other side, then glanced at him with a grimace. "Pray it doesn't rain."

They tossed the backpack out first and shimmied through the tight opening one at a time into the street sewer. Cold, sticky waste came up to his knees.

Dax reached through and dragged a pallet back in place and wedged the door shut tight behind them. Raven shone her light down both ends of the tunnel, which appeared to be identical. Luminescent eyes peered back at them from one end.

"Rats. Crap," Raven said, and headed in the opposite direction. "This way."

They half walked, half dragged themselves along

Havana's underbelly. Just when he thought they'd be down there forever, a vertical well appeared above them. He scaled the ladder first and lifted the manhole cover enough to check their location. Middle of a quiet street. It wouldn't get any better than that.

"Please tell me it's clear," Raven said below him.

"Even if it wasn't, I'm not going back down there." He slid the metal cover aside and pulled himself up. Raven quickly followed. They replaced the cover and sprinted to the nearest alley.

He yanked off his jacket. "We have a problem."

"I know." She peeled off her overclothes and tugged the dress back into place. "They knew we were coming, and they knew what we wanted."

"Maybe someone recognized you today."

She paused to glare at him. "You think I'm some kind of notorious international criminal? Trust me, I'm not that big."

He stripped off his filthy pants and kicked them aside. "It's what you do for a living, Raven. You said it yourself."

"Go to hell, Maddox," she said, hurt evident in her voice. "I wasn't the one who tipped them off."

A low rumble of thunder filled the sticky air, and the first raindrops began to fall. *Perfect,* Dax thought.

He said, "Then who did? Who knew we were here?"

"You, me, and Paulie."

"Your boss?"

"Haven't talked to him since we lost Walter in Miami." She picked up the pack and stood in front of him. "What about *your* friend?"

"No."

Raven shook her head and looked away. "It doesn't matter. The bottom line is that we don't have the painting."

"No, the bottom line is they know who we are. We need to get back to the boat," he said. The skies opened, and the downpour drenched them as they ran.

CHAPTER
13

Forty minutes later, a taxi dropped them along the dark road outside Marina Tarara. Warm rain soaked Raven to the skin, rinsing away most of the sewer stench. Having left her ruined shoes in Havana, she walked barefoot next to Maddox.

Maybe he was right. Maybe she had been recognized. She couldn't deny it was a possibility. She'd done jobs all over the world. Even though she'd never been caught, she had to be on someone's radar.

When they neared the dock within sight of the boat, Maddox guided her under a dark overhang of the bait shop building. A sheet of rain fell from the roof like a curtain. He leaned close to her, but his mind was elsewhere as he peered around the corner at the dock. His body felt tense, warm, and rain-slicked beneath her hands. The gun was pressed between them. At least she thought it was the gun.

"Trouble?" she whispered.

"Waiting to see if anyone is on the boat," he said quietly.

She leaned around the corner. The boat was completely dark. "How can you see anything?"

"I have excellent night vision. One of the benefits of losing my color sight." Then he cocked his head to listen to the male voices coming down the path behind him.

Before she could say anything, Maddox pushed her against the wall and lifted her bare thigh with one hand. The other hand cupped her breast through the thin, wet fabric as he wedged himself between her legs. His kiss was deep and rough.

She gripped his biceps, and just like that, she was swept into his storm. Her heart pounded in her ears, louder than the rain. She knew she should hold back, show some scrap of dignity, but her body wasn't listening. Right now—when everything else had gone to hell—he felt like the only solid thing she could hold on to. She wanted the careless freedom of the dance, that one blinding moment of faith.

The laughter of men rang out as they slowed. They chatted to each other, sounding slightly drunk before moving on. Slowly, she realized why Maddox had taken her so fast and hard, and the solid ground she'd latched on to dissolved.

Seconds later, Maddox pulled back and looked around the corner, his expression grim. Not a hint of passion. It had all been just another diversion. A game. And he could play it as well as she could.

She shoved against him, but he didn't budge.

Maddox said, "They aren't gone yet. Don't move."

He held her firm, his fingers burning the sensitive skin of her inner thigh. He kept his head turned away from her as he watched and waited. Lightning flashed behind him, illuminating his face. Then his gaze dropped to hers, focused and held. Heat resurrected in an instant.

He eased his grip slightly and slid his fingers along her skin a fraction as he watched her reaction. The tiny caress shot through her with enough intensity to bring her to her knees. She bit her lower lip to stop from moaning as he traced up her leg. Pressure built in her belly, betraying her with a whimper.

Oh damn, this is bad. Wrong place, wrong time, wrong man. The touch went straight to her center, and she was gone. Maddox's eyes narrowed. He knew it, too, which was even worse.

"Stop playing," she said breathlessly.

He leaned in and moved his cheek against hers. "Does it feel like I'm playing?"

She closed her eyes. It wasn't the gun pressed against her. "No."

He kissed her once more, and she dug her fingers into his flesh. *More.*

He pulled away, his face drawn. "Damn." His heated gaze lingered for a moment before he looked away. "We can't stay here."

They boarded the boat, and while Maddox checked the darkened rooms, she listened to the radio's police frequencies. Rain drummed on the deck above.

"Anything?" he asked, coming up from the berths.

"Lots of chatter from Havana. They are looking for a couple of tourists in the city," she told him. "We're safe for now."

He stared out the door for a moment before saying, "I'm going to make sure no one has messed with anything topside." Then he looked her up and down.

"As much as I like that dress, you might want to change into something dry."

He disappeared out the door, and she looked at the fabric plastered to her body. The dress that had felt so good to dance in was now beyond saving. A shame, really. She hadn't danced in a very long time. Why was that? Oh, right. No one had stuck around long enough to ask her. Or maybe it was because she never stuck around long enough to be asked.

She wrinkled her nose. Stupid matchbox degree. She walked down the stairs to the master suite and peeled off the dress. Finding a dance partner was the least of her worries.

What happened at the church tonight? What had she done wrong? She'd never had a job go this bad before.

Wait, she had. Last time she ran into Maddox. With a frustrated growl, she wadded up the dress and tossed it in the bottom of the shower. Well, he wasn't going to stop her this time.

She hadn't gotten anything off the spot where the painting had hung, so it must have been lifted quickly. The priest mentioned that he might be able to find out where the police had taken the painting. So if the good padre wasn't locked up somewhere by tomorrow morning, she could contact him for help. Even then . . .

She sat on the bed and put her head in her hands. What was she doing? How could she possibly ask a priest to help her and risk his life, too? How had this become so wrong?

Then she heard the engines rumble to life, and her head came up.

"Maddox?" she hollered as the boat lurched. She

hastily yanked a shirt over her head and pulled on some shorts before running up the stairs. By the time she reached the back door, the marina was fading into the distance.

Dammit. He'd lied to her—again.

Driving rain stung her skin and soaked her dry clothes in seconds. She scrambled up the ladder to find him at the controls, facing the black ocean ahead. They had just cleared the mouth of the harbor.

"What are you doing?" she yelled over the engines.

He spared her a quick glance. "Leaving while we still can. It's only a matter of time before they shut down the marinas."

"We didn't get the painting," she reminded him, even as panic rose in her throat.

His voice was sharp and firm, and flashes of lightning lit his stern expression. "This isn't the U.S., Raven. And I, for one, don't want to see how the Cuban judicial system works."

"The painting is probably in a storage facility. I have enough money to bribe the officials—"

He interrupted her, growing furious. "Do you understand the gravity of the situation here?"

He pointed toward the shore. "They are *looking* for us. They are going to search every boat in every marina until they find us. At this point, I don't think a bribe is going to work."

She held on as the boat breached bigger waves. His demeanor was unyielding, and she knew short of her jumping ship, he wasn't going to stop the boat. Defeat crept over her. Didn't he understand they couldn't return empty-handed? They hadn't come all this way to quit now.

She gripped the railing with all her might and watched the marina lights fade into the distance. As much as she hated him for leaving, Maddox was probably right about the painting being a loss. Even if she could return to the island, there was no time to locate it. But that didn't mean she was giving up on Walter. She'd find another way to get him back safely. She had to. Failure was not an option.

"Next time we discuss it first," she yelled, just to make sure he understood that she wasn't happy about his executive decision. She ignored the stern look he gave her.

"Hold on," he said. Then he killed all the lights on the boat and opened up the throttle. The Hatteras surged forward over the incoming surf. She couldn't see a thing in front of them. They were running blind.

"How long before we have the Cuban Coast Guard after us?" she shouted.

"Anytime now. Let's hope that money you stuffed in the church box gets us into international waters."

Exhausted and drenched, Dax dropped anchor a half mile off Key West in the bleak darkness. Raven had finally gone below after enduring pelting downpours and near-zero visibility with him. It had been a crappy ride back. He needed a shower, dry clothes, six hours of sleep, and a beer. Not necessarily in that order.

He peeled off his soaked shirt, threw it over the rail to drip dry, and descended the ladder. He was about to go in when he noticed Raven standing in the cockpit shrouded in shadow. In the gray drizzle, she stared forlornly across the straits toward Cuba.

"What do we do now?" she asked. "We can't save Walter without that painting."

There was an edge of desperation in her voice that caught him off guard. This was the real Raven talking. No games. No thrill-seeking. Just one woman grasping at hope.

He shook his head wearily. "I don't know. Maybe we can cut another deal or slip the kidnapper a fake."

"There's not enough time," Raven said. "We're supposed to have it today. He's going to call me, and I have nothing."

"I'm sorry," he said, and he meant it. This was not the way it was supposed to go down.

Dax rubbed the back of his neck. He didn't have near enough energy for this conversation. "Can we talk about this after a couple of hours' sleep?"

"I promised Bigley." She ran both her hands through her wet hair. "And you promised Nick."

He frowned. "I never promised Nick anything."

She looked at him, eyes assessing. "Yes, you did. That's why you're selling your soul, isn't it? You were a good cop, Maddox. Don't tell me you're enjoying this. Every time you break a law, it hurts."

"Raven, let's get some sleep. Then we'll figure out what to do," he said, too drained to go another round with her.

Raven wrapped her arms around her belly and stared over the sea. Rainwater trickled down her skin and from the tips of her hair, but she didn't seem to notice or care. "Not tired."

He gritted his teeth in frustration. "You planning on swimming back to Cuba?"

"Maybe. All I know is that I don't want to sleep. I can't."

His last straw broke. He wasn't in any mood to wait for her to burn herself out. He was done. He needed to go inside and get dry and forget this lousy day. "Then what *do* you want?"

Her head turned slowly toward him. Water dripped from her eyelashes. She looked at him like she was seeing him for the first time. Soft, sensual hunger swept over her face, and Dax could feel the pull from where he stood.

"You."

Of all the things he thought she was going to say, that wasn't one of them. Perhaps it was because he was already primed, but his body went into ready mode in three seconds flat. He hissed at the potent mix of pain and pleasure. Obviously, he wasn't as tired as he thought.

"I need *you*."

He barely heard her words through the rain. She looked more vulnerable than he'd ever seen her, and the urge to soothe and protect gripped him powerfully. He didn't remember covering the distance between them. All he could see was the desire in her face.

Thunder boomed in the distance and vibrated through his already charged body as he filled his hands with her. He wrapped his hand around the back of her neck and guided her up to his mouth. The kiss was long and slow, full of heat and need. She answered with reckless abandon, sinking her fingers into his skin and sipping the rain from between their lips.

Her hands explored his shoulders and chest, every touch and caress going straight to his groin. He didn't think he could get any harder, but she might prove him wrong. When she leaned down and licked water off a nipple, he clenched his teeth for self-control.

He pulled her to face him and slipped his fingers under her tank, up over her rib cage, and skimmed the impossibly tender undersides of her breasts. Raven rolled her head back and moaned when he ran his thumbs across her taut nipples. Lightning lit her face, unguarded and consumed by the moment.

He made her feel like that. She didn't do this for other men; she wouldn't be vulnerable for anyone. He knew that to his soul. Realization shifted to a possessiveness that he acknowledged with a growl.

He rolled her tank top over her head, exposing her breasts. Full, round, and peaked just for him. He kissed her throat and skin, soft against his stubbled face. Her long body flowed under his hands from shoulders to hips, arching against his mouth with every kiss.

Warm rain poured down, racing across the ocean with a deafening racket. Lightning tracked across the sky, and thunder boomed overhead. With a thread of clarity, he realized the last thing he wanted was to get struck by lightning before he had a chance to make love to her.

"We should go in—"

"No," she whispered. "Here."

When she pushed his shorts down over his thighs and released his erection to the moist air, he didn't give a damn where they were. Raven wanted sex here and now, and he wasn't the man to tell her no.

Oblivious to the elements, Raven worked her way down his chest and stomach, nipping and kissing. The wind picked up, and the boat rocked beneath his feet. He swore softly when her tongue licked his length, and her fingers dug into his ass. He closed his eyes and reveled in the staggering sensations, her technique as smooth and sure as everything else she did.

In a flash he was too close to the edge, and he reached for her. As she stood up, he shoved her shorts down her long, smooth legs until they pooled around her feet. He cupped her with one hand and she gasped as lightning struck the water and lit up the sky.

Dax slipped his fingers deep between her legs, and Raven leaned into him, eyes closed tightly. He caressed her, working his thumb across her clit. Within seconds, she started squirming, and he wrapped an arm around her waist to hold her tight. Her entire body tensed, and the climax rose until her strangled cry drowned out the downpour.

For a moment he held her, balancing them both as the boat rode the storm's chop. The footing was slick and slippery with rainwater and seawater, and as much as he wanted to grant her wish, he couldn't see them rolling against the sides of the boat. The metal ladder was out of the question, and hanging her over the railing in a storm probably wasn't wise either.

He breathed in her ear. "We should go inside. Better traction."

"Not yet," she whispered, and squeezed his erection in her hands. "We aren't done. Tell me you have a condom."

"Back pocket," he rasped, close to losing his mind as she traced him with her fingertips.

"I knew you were a Boy Scout," she said, and reached down to retrieve the condom. "Against the wall."

He let the shorts slide down his legs and kicked them off. Then pulled her with him beneath the overhang until his back hit the cabin. "I think that's my line."

"We can play cops and robbers later." She pushed down on his shoulders. "I might even let you cuff me."

Handcuffs. Like he needed added incentive. Dax grinned and slid down the wall, taking her with him. She gasped when they hit the floor together in a tangle of legs. Then he pulled her onto his lap and kissed her hard enough to silence any words. She positioned her hips against his, grinding his aching erection between them until he was numb in his need.

He sucked air when she sheathed him in the condom, unrolling it with the excruciating unhurried pace of a woman who'd already had an orgasm. And that was all he could take.

He gripped her by the waist and lifted her, watching her expression change as he guided her onto his erection. Lightning lit up her face, eyes heavy, lips parted. He let loose a growl when she settled down onto the base.

For a moment, she didn't move, her face tense.

"You okay?" he asked.

She nodded quickly. "Best moment of my day."

"Mine, too," he said. Shit, best moment of his year.

Then she rolled forward and kissed his lips. She flexed her legs and rose nearly all the way up, then slid back down with a patience he didn't think she possessed. He gripped her hips, drawing her up and down again, pushing the rhythm faster.

Raven threw her head back, and Dax could feel her on the edge of another climax. He lifted his hips to meet her, driving them both off the deck. The boat pitched, adding another element to his already overloaded senses. Pressure built in his groin, painful in its intensity. Her delicate muscles gripped him in orgasm, and he lost control. Wild passion poured through his veins as the pace became more frenzied.

And then the world exploded behind his eyes as he pulled her around him one last time. Release ripped through him with enough force to make him yell aloud before slipping into a mindless, timeless, satisfying haze.

The storm had passed by the time he came back to his senses. Raven was wrapped in his arms, her hair splayed across his chest. Dawn was breaking in front of them.

He kissed the top of her head. "Bedtime, lady."

She made a muffled sound of disapproval. He grinned and felt his cock thicken. A few seconds later, Raven noticed, too, and lifted her head, a sinful look on her face. She smiled wide and trailed her fingers down his belly. "Just for the record. Neither one of us made it fifteen minutes."

Raven studied Maddox, all relaxed and sexy as he slept sprawled across the bed next to her. He had long dark eyelashes that she hadn't noticed before. And lips that were as incredible-looking as they felt against every part of her body. His hair was still damp from the rain. He'd been just what she needed to unwind, to forget.

It was only sex, she told herself for the hundredth time. That's all it could ever be. But she knew already it was different. For some reason, he had the ability to strip her of the distance she was usually able to maintain with men. It was as if she lost herself when she was swept up in his heat. That was a bad thing. She brushed the hair from his forehead. She'd need to be more careful around him.

Raven slipped out from under the sheet and padded naked through the boat to her cell phone. She curled up in a chair and checked her messages. Twelve from Paulie, three from Bigley, none from the kidnapper. So far, so good.

Unfortunately, time was running out. There had to be something she could offer the kidnapper. Money maybe, another piece of artwork . . .

She stilled. Bigley's Vassalo. The one in his vault that started it all. The companion piece to the painting they'd already stolen for the kidnapper and worth far more than the small one in the Cuban church.

Relief eased into her. That was Walter's ticket. All she had to do was convince the kidnapper. And get Bigley's painting to Miami—fast. That would be the tricky part.

She glanced back to make sure Maddox wasn't following her before dialing Paulie's number. He answered with a groggy "Raven. About time you checked in. Do you know how many messages I've left on your voice mail?"

"I told you I'd call when I got back. Patience, grasshopper."

"Don't play the patience card with me," he said, working himself into alertness. "You didn't get thirty-two calls from Bigley. He's ready to hop a plane and come down here personally."

Might not be a bad idea, she thought. *And bring the Vassalo.*

Paulie yawned. "Just tell me you got the painting."

She closed her eyes at the failure that radiated through her. "There was a problem."

"I knew it. Have you noticed that nothing in this whole fucking mess has been easy?"

She laid her head back against the chair. "I noticed."

"So what happened?"

How did she explain to him that she'd had it right there in front of her and didn't steal it? How could she be so good at what she did and screw up this badly?

"The police ambushed us," she finally said. "They knew we were there for the painting. Almost didn't get out of Havana."

There was a pause. "How could they know you were going to get the painting?"

"No idea. Unless someone's watching us."

"Who could be watching you? Who else cares? The cops?"

She let that sink in. They could have motive—Yarrow's attack, stealing the painting in Richmond, Walter's kidnapping, entering Cuba illegally. Take your pick.

"Maybe U.S. authorities tipped off the Cubans," Paulie added.

She closed her eyes. Had Maddox confided in his cop friend where they were or what they were doing? She had to remember that no matter what, she couldn't trust him. His loyalties were engrained from fifteen years of service, and a few rounds of great sex weren't going to change that.

"Or," Paulie said, "the police recognized you."

She narrowed her eyes. "You really think my picture is plastered all over the world?"

"Maybe."

Lovely. "Thanks for the vote of confidence, Paulie."

"Sorry. So what now?"

She took a breath. "I have something else the kidnapper might want instead, but I'll need to clear it with Bigley first."

"Good. Call the man. Maybe he'll stop bugging me."

She was already dreading that conversation. Better to wait until Bigley was awake and in his office. "If he calls you again, tell him I'll talk to him soon."

"Got it."

"And do me a favor," she added. "Recheck all our communications. See if there are any leaks anywhere."

"Right-o."

She said good-bye and flipped the phone closed. It might work. She could only hope.

Dawn stripped the carpet through the slats of the windows and lit up the photos on the wall. Raven reached out and touched the picture of Nick and Maddox.

The first emotions came through clearly, almost protective toward the rookie. Then friendship, followed by sorrow. Regret. Frustration. And finally it turned really dark and painful. She caught herself and pulled back before it got any worse. It was buried deep, it was very bad, and she wasn't going there.

Her gaze trailed down to the photo of his family. She didn't even have to touch it to know there was love. The way they stood by each other, comfortable and relaxed. Admiration. Respect. Tolerance. Unlike her family.

She doubted Maddox's mother would be weak enough to die of a broken heart or to give up on life even when she had teenage daughters to raise. And she doubted his father would have let her.

That's what happens when you stick around too long. Next thing you know, you care, you believe, you trust. You sacrifice everything for love. Then it all falls apart, and you're left with nothing.

An old wound opened up, and Raven clenched her fists until the pain subsided and was once again locked out of harm's way. Her eyes ached with the sudden emotional overload, but there would be no tears. They were a weakness she could not afford. Just like love.

CHAPTER
14

They are back in the U.S. So much for your plan to get rid of them. Now what?"

Fauss listened at his desk while he scoured the Cuban news sites. Nothing. No arrests of two Americans trying to steal a priceless national treasure. He'd given the Cuban officials everything they needed. How could they have let them escape?

"It's not a problem," he said.

A sharp laugh rang out on the other end of the phone. "Right. Now you have to revise the model. You hate when that happens."

Fauss clenched his jaw at the blatant disrespect. Someday, his son would appreciate the value of predictive modeling. "The model is flawless. The contingency event is already in motion. I'll simply give the Miami authorities a head start."

His son huffed. "You better make it a good one if you want to stop Raven. I told you she was the best."

Fauss glowered at the screen. *He* was the best. He

was the one who'd spent the last twenty years plotting the perfect revenge. He was the one who always planned, minimized the risks, did the research. Hours upon hours of analysis had gone into this final job. One woman was not going to destroy that.

"Don't worry. She won't get out of this one. None of them will."

Raven woke up alone in bed. Sunshine brightened the small suite, and the boat rocked gently. So peaceful. She rolled on her belly and slid her hand across the sheets with a heartfelt sigh. Amazing what a little mind-blowing sex could do for a girl.

And then she looked at the clock. It read 10:32 A.M.

Raven shot out of bed and grabbed her cell phone off the dresser. No messages from the kidnapper. Thank God. Then she remembered that she was supposed to have called Bigley first thing this morning.

She held the phone for a minute, trying to figure out how to start the conversation. How to explain to Bigley that she'd failed yet again. How to confess that she hadn't really called in the cops in the first place.

"Crap." She needed a cup of coffee for this.

She pulled on a robe, shoved the phone in the pocket, and headed for the galley. When she turned the corner, she nearly fell over.

Maddox was standing in front of the stove wearing only shorts that showed off muscular thighs, a compact ass, and a broad back that was as powerful as it was beautiful. His hair still glistened from a morning shower, and he was clean-shaven, the stubble that had ravaged her skin last night gone. He turned to her with a spatula in his hand, and her heart nearly stopped.

He was the sexiest thing she'd ever seen in her entire life.

"Morning," he said, his voice low.

She licked her lips and came up behind him. "You can cook?"

He frowned, looked at the stove, and turned back to her. "It's just pancakes and bacon."

He could cook. She untied the sash of her robe. "Take off your clothes."

His eyebrows rose. "'Scuse me?"

The robe slipped from her shoulders and fell to the floor. His gaze traveled over her and darkened. He reached around, turned off the stove, and tossed the spatula on the counter.

"We're having cold pancakes for breakfast," he murmured against her mouth before he kissed her and crushed her against the refrigerator door. Already, he was hard and ready. The man was amazing.

She ran her palms over the corded muscles of his shoulders, steely biceps, and thick forearms before skimming over his broad back. He hissed softly when she traced the lines of his tight abs to the flat planes of his deep chest. Smooth skin over muscle and bone, his heat warmed her hands. She could get used to this.

He grazed her throat lightly and worked his way down to her breasts, which were painfully taut, and he had only just begun. His lips, his hands, and his passion were everywhere. A man who wasn't afraid to explore, to experiment with infinite patience and impressive technique. He surprised her at every turn. It didn't happen often, and she was going to enjoy this while she could. Bigley could wait fifteen minutes.

Maddox kissed her breasts, and she moaned. He dipped his head lower, nuzzling her belly and working his way down. She shoved her fingers into his hair and uttered a hushed "Oh" when he pushed her legs apart and touched her. Just a flick of his tongue, and she was gone. The refrigerator door was smooth and cool against her back; a sharp contrast to the heat building inside her.

Her belly tightened with every caress of his tongue, and pressure coiled inside. She reached one hand over her head to grip the top of the door for support and braced herself for the ride. A sweet calm rolled across her as the tension crested, then broke, shattering her body and mind. For a few seconds, she allowed the ecstasy to dominate.

By the time he was standing again, she'd rallied her senses. While he sheathed himself in a condom, she wrapped her arms around his neck and kissed him with a desperation that surprised even her. She wanted to lose herself in the warmth of his face against hers, the smell of soap and man, and the power of his desire.

He lifted her off the floor, and she wrapped her legs around him. Slowly, he eased her down over his erection, and she held her breath as she took him. He filled her with a growl that resonated through her bones. The rhythm was fast and hard, his body straining, and she realized he was already as lost as she was.

The climax was upon her before she could gain control of it. She dug her fingers into his back as it shook her body. Maddox let out a guttural shout and drove into her, his head thrown back in release.

He was so beautiful, just like this. Making love to her. Because of her. It gave her more satisfaction than she . . .

She shook her head. *Don't do that, Raven.*

He let her feet settle back to the floor and leaned against her, lightly kissing her shoulder. She rested her head against his chest to catch her breath, her heart pumping. Who needed coffee?

An annoying chirping broke the silence, and he tensed under her hands. She closed her eyes. Damn reality. Neither of them moved until the second ring.

"My cell. Sorry," he said by way of apology before leaving her on unsteady legs.

He retrieved the cell phone from a basket and glanced at the incoming number. She knew it couldn't be good by the way his lips thinned.

"Morning, Harry. What's up?"

Raven picked up her robe as she watched him go perfectly still while he listened. Slow seconds ticked by.

"How long?" he asked, his voice tight.

She clutched the robe to her chest, letting her fingers pull his essence and strength from it. Still, the cold descended over her as worst-case scenarios started to parade through her head. There were a surprising number of them.

His eyes shifted to her. "No, I haven't seen her since I left Miami."

She couldn't breathe as he turned his back to her, nodding his head at whatever Harry was telling him. He was lying about her. Why?

"If I hear from her, I'll let you know," he finally said. He ended with "See you tomorrow" and hung up the phone. For a moment, he looked straight ahead.

See you tomorrow?

"What happened?" she asked.

He tossed the phone back into the basket and turned to her, his expression bleak. "Miami-Dade PD found Walter Abbott in a bike locker at Government Center Station this morning."

Her heart stopped as she waited for the inevitable crash.

Maddox added, "He'd been dead for at least twenty-four hours."

Dax stood inside the screen door watching Raven at the back of the boat staring out toward the Key West shoreline. She'd changed into a lightweight tunic and low-rise pants that molded to her tense body in the breeze.

She hadn't said a word for two hours.

No tears. No screams. No emotion at all over Walter's murder. He didn't have a clue what was going on inside her head, but it couldn't be good. He realized how much she'd loosened up over the past few days. But now she'd completely shut down and become, once again, the cool, calculating thief he thought he knew. It bothered him more than he cared to admit.

He should have turned this over to Miami-Dade PD in the beginning. Maybe Walter would have had a chance. Damned if he did. Damned if he didn't. There were no easy choices these days. A year ago, he thought he had his life all figured out. Five more years on the force, and he'd retire and drive a fishing boat all day. The job was the job, and he knew where he belonged in it.

Then, in one split second, it all fell apart. Quitting

seemed like the only option. He thought by taking matters into his own hands, he couldn't do worse than anyone else. So much for that theory. Now he had to go back to where it all started. He was not looking forward to spending the next twenty-four hours in a police station, on the wrong side of the desk.

He pushed the cabin door open and walked outside. Sun warmed the deck floor under his feet. Waves, driven by a light breeze, lapped the boat's hull. It would have been a perfect day if an innocent man hadn't been murdered.

Dax crossed his arms and leaned against the ladder. "Harry wants me to come in and give a statement. I think you should come with me. We can leave out the part about stealing the painting and Cuba. The stuff that can get us incarcerated for life. But we need to tell them about the kidnapping. Maybe they can put that together with the forensics and come up with a lead."

No reaction. Big surprise there.

He added, "We have to get our stories straight."

She blinked but didn't respond, her stance rigid and closed.

"Don't make me drag you in," he said with renewed conviction.

She turned then, slowly, deliberately, and in her eyes he saw something he recognized only too well: the thirst for revenge.

"You can try," she replied coolly.

She was about to walk again, leave without looking back.

"You were working with Abbott. Sooner or later, they're going to come looking for you as part of his murder investigation," he warned her.

"I'll deal with it then. Besides, I'm sure your story will be fine. You know as much as I do. *Maybe more.*"

He noted the emphasis on the last two words. "I told you everything I knew about the killer, Raven."

She took a few breaths, working to cover the pain he knew was there. She couldn't fool him. He'd seen the other side of her wall.

"I'm not blaming you," she said.

He shoved his hands in his pockets. "No, you're blaming yourself, and you're trying to figure how to fix it."

"I know how to fix it," she said firmly.

Damn. She was going to track down the murderer herself. And it was hell to admit there was nothing he could do to stop her except beat her to him.

Dax said, "If you want to get this guy, you're going to have to wait in line."

She eyed him like the enemy. It would be a race to the death. "He never planned on delivering Walter. We would have stolen another painting for a killer. And another . . ."

"We couldn't have known that—"

She cut in. "I think it's safe to say our business together is finished, Maddox. How long until we get back to the marina?"

Just like that. Like there was nothing between them. Hard to believe this was the same woman who'd taken him to heaven all morning. The woman who said she wanted him.

Fine. He could shut down, too. "A few hours."

She nodded, her gaze fixed on land.

The boat's phone rang, and Dax stepped inside to pick up the extension in the salon. "Yeah?"

"Finally," Paulie said, sounding frantic. "You want to tell me what's the point of having a cell phone if you don't answer it?"

Dax glanced up as Raven walked in and stood in front of him. "What's up, Paulie?"

"What's up? Have you been watching the TV? They found Walter's body. He's dead. D-E-A-D. And now they are looking for Raven. Her picture is up on the local news."

Dax picked up the remote to his satellite TV. "What channel?"

Paulie told him, and Dax flicked to the station. A reporter was at Government Center Station, in front of the bike storage lockers.

"The man found dead has been identified as Walter Abbott, an art dealer from New York City who was here on business for an art recovery firm called the Antiquities Preservation Institute. A woman known as Susan Carrey is wanted for questioning. They were last seen together at the Miami Luxus Hotel five days ago." Raven's image flashed on the screen as she and Walter walked past a surveillance camera during the auction.

"Are you watching this?" Paulie said, his voice getting more high-pitched. "It's only a matter of time before they come looking for us, Dax. You know what they do to guys like me in prison? I'm going to spend my days trying to convince Bubba that I don't want to be his girlfriend."

"I'll call you back," Dax said, and hung up.

Raven was still watching the TV, her expression stoic and unreadable. The wall was firmly in place.

Dax told her, "I'm going to find out what they have on you. Pick up the extension downstairs if you want."

Without a word, she nodded and went down to the lower deck as he rang Harry's cell.

When he answered, Dax said, "What the fuck, Harry? You couldn't have told me about the APB on Raven?"

"*You* said you hadn't seen her since Miami," he came back. "Where is she?"

"I don't know."

"Christ, Dax. Don't pull that shit on me. Do you have any idea how much trouble I could be in here? I ran her through the system. How long before someone figures that out? And imagine their surprise when they find my pretty mug on the surveillance tapes from Government Station? Fuck. I have two more years till retirement. I could lose everything."

Dax blew out a breath to release his anger. He couldn't blame Harry. He had kids, a wife, and a career to think about. "Sorry."

"Yeah, I'm sure you are," Harry said, calming down. "But this is getting ugly. Your girl is the only lead right now."

Dax said, "All they have is a working relationship between her and Walter."

"Thanks to an anonymous tip, they have more than that."

Dax stilled. "A tip? When?"

"Got it sometime last night. Ask your girlfriend where her red scarf is. The one she wore at the hotel."

"Why?"

"It was the murder weapon."

Dax could only imagine what Raven was thinking on the other line. "There are a lot of red scarves out there, Harry."

"Not designer ones like this. Plus I hear there's DNA that doesn't belong to the murder victim. One long hair. You want to guess who it'll belong to?"

Shit.

"And wait till they get a load of her career choice," Harry added.

Dax's mind was racing. "Any idea where the tip came from?"

"None. It went directly to Miami-Dade. All I'm telling you is what I've heard. Right now, it's local, but if anyone puts this together with the other shit you've been doing, the Feds are coming in."

Time, Dax thought. They needed time. "Have they linked her to me?"

"Not yet, but it won't take long. You were at the hotel. You'll pop up on the radar soon enough. And if they catch you on video at Government Center . . ."

"How long?"

"Twenty-four hours tops before they're on your tail."

The whole thing was unraveling. Dax said, "Hang tight. We'll find him."

"I wish I could believe that."

"We're close," Dax lied.

"That's not what I'm talking about. Are you sure you can trust this woman?"

"I'm sure," Dax said firmly. He had to trust her. He was in too deep not to.

There was a pause. "You know, if you turned her in, all this would end. You could tell them you've been watching her, tracking her movements, gathering evidence. You'd be clear."

Dax gripped the phone. "And the real killer would still

be loose. Is that what you want? Her to take the fall for
the guy who really popped Walter and Nick?"

Harry swore on the other end. "You slept with her,
didn't you?"

"That makes no difference."

"I knew it. She's going to take you down."

"If I go down, it'll be my choice," Dax told him. "I'm
not stopping until we find this guy."

"You know what that means," Harry said.

"Yes." He understood exactly what that meant, but he
wasn't giving up. Not on Raven. Not on himself.

Harry took a deep breath. "Fine. I'll start working
on my I-don't-know-shit speech for the Internal Affairs
boys. But just so you know, if it comes down to her or
you, I'm turning her over."

There was nothing he could say to that. If Harry did
that, Dax would go, too. He was as much a part of this as
she was. "Do what you have to, Harry."

"And, Dax?"

"Yeah?"

"Don't call me again." Harry disconnected.

Dax tossed the phone in the cradle and headed down the
stairs. Raven was hanging up the extension when he reached
the master suite. Her suitcase was open on the bed.

"Going somewhere?" Dax said, blocking the doorway
with his body.

She looked at him, and there was an emptiness in her
eyes that made his chest tighten.

"The bastard set me up," she said as she threw her
clothes into the case. "He killed Walter with my scarf.
I didn't realize it was missing from my room. How could
I not notice? God, I didn't—"

He took a step toward her as she started to fall apart, but she put her hands up. "Don't. I'm fine. I need to . . . to—"

The strain of trying to hold herself together etched her face, and he decided to hell with it, and pulled her into his arms. She fought him at first with angry elbows and hands, but he wouldn't let go. Finally, she gave it up and leaned into him with a muffled cry of rage.

"Where did I screw up, Maddox?"

He closed his eyes. "You didn't. I don't know what happened, but it wasn't us."

He knew she wouldn't believe him, but he didn't have anything else to offer her. There weren't any words that could make this better. Only action. And justice. That's what he held on to.

After a few minutes, the tension returned, and she eased out of his grip. He watched her gather herself with a deep inhale.

"I have to find him," she said.

"*We*," Dax corrected her, "need to regroup. We've been running flat out for days, playing by this guy's rules. I think it's about time we start playing by our own."

She shook her head. "You have to get Harry off the hook."

"Harry can take care of himself," he said. "Besides, I'm your alibi."

Her eyes narrowed. "You think? Once they see us together on surveillance tapes, your word won't mean squat."

"You can't do this without me," he said.

She lifted her chin. "And why not?"

He leveled his gaze at her so she would know that

there was no way in hell she was getting rid of him. "Because I won't let you."

Fear filled her eyes, and the wall crumbled enough for him to see the truth. Her voice was very quiet. "I don't want to take you down with me. Please don't make me do that."

"You won't." He picked up the phone and handed it to her. "Tell Paulie to get his ass down here."

CHAPTER
15

Raven left Dax outside to tie up the boat at a Key West marina. She walked down to the lower level and into the master bathroom. Once inside, she locked the door and slid down the door with her cell phone dialing.

Jillian answered, "Hello."

"Hey," Raven said.

There was a long hesitation.

"Who died?"

Raven frowned. "What?"

"You *never* call me."

"I have too called you," Raven said with the sudden indignation of a sister wronged.

"No, I always call you. What happened?"

Fury blossomed painfully from the acknowledgment alone. She could barely say the words. "Walter Abbott was murdered."

Jillian responded with a sympathetic "How awful. The poor man. How—" Another pause. "Wait. Weren't you supposed to go to Miami with him?"

"We did."

There was a pause while Jill processed the obvious. "Oh God, are you in danger?"

Raven rubbed her forehead. Danger? Where did she begin? "We were supposed to pick up a Vassalo at the auction. Simple job. Then everything went to hell. He was kidnapped and . . . I lost him."

"Oh damn," Jillian said. "I'm sorry, hon. Did they catch the murderer?"

Raven said, "No. In fact, we don't even have a name. It's not going well, actually."

"We?"

"Me, Paulie, and Maddox."

"Maddox? Does he work for API?"

"Not quite. He's an ex-cop."

There was a gasp on the other end. "Oh my God. You are working with a former police officer?"

Raven looked up at the ceiling in the tiny cubicle of a bathroom. "Ironic, huh?"

"I don't think ironic begins to cover this one. How— Never mind. I don't think I want to know how this happened. I'm just glad that you brought in the proper authorities."

Only because I had no choice, Raven thought. But now that he was here, she was grateful. Even if it was only for a little while. Even if he didn't realize how much trouble she could bring him.

Jillian asked, "Does he know what you do?"

"He knows. Actually, that's why Walter was kidnapped— for the ransom." She dropped her head on her knees. "Because I'm a th—recovery specialist. I could get the painting."

There was a moment of silent comfort on the other end. "Oh."

Raven smiled and shook her head at the weighty reply. Jillian would never say a bad word about anyone, never judge. It was one of the many reasons Raven loved her.

Jillian asked, "Is there anything I can do?"

"You want to help me track down a killer?"

Jillian gasped. "Oh God, *no*. And you aren't going to do that either. Don't even think about it. Let the police handle this."

The words *wanted for questioning* came to mind. "Trust me when I say I'm on my own."

"But you have Maddox."

Raven cast a glance at the bathroom door. "Right."

"That wasn't a convincing 'right,' Raven. *Promise* me you'll work with him on this."

She hated lying to her sister, but sometimes, a lie was the least painful way to go all around. "Promise."

"Okay, then," her sister said, sounding relieved because she really believed that Raven would always tell her the truth. Jillian's heart was too big for her body. A trusting lamb in the world of wolves, and Raven was about to hand her one big, bad wolf to worry about.

Raven said, "Jill, you need to be careful."

"Why?"

"Because the killer knows me. And if he knows me, he might know about you, too."

Jillian said, "But you use an alias. How would they connect us? We've always been so careful."

You got me, Raven admitted. "I'm just saying, watch out for anything or anyone unusual."

Jillian gave a short laugh. "And what do I *do* if I find someone or something unusual?"

"You call me," Raven said firmly. "I'm the only person you can trust. You have to remember that."

Jill sighed. "We have to work on this paranoia issue you have. Honestly, I wish you would relax. I'm not totally helpless."

Raven closed her eyes, torn between wanting to tell her sister just how ugly the real world could be and not wanting to slaughter the lamb.

"I'll call you later," Raven said, feeling worse than before the conversation.

"No, you won't."

Raven frowned. "I will so."

"Will not."

Raven narrowed her eyes. *Sisters.*

Jillian said, "Love you."

"You, too."

Raven hung up and stared at the pink shell design on the walls. "Damn."

She had spent a great deal of time and energy creating levels of identities between her and her family ties. Careful to make sure that no one came close to the one person she cared most about. But this killer had ways of knowing things he shouldn't. There was something personal about this entire mess, and that was the thought she kept coming back to.

Paulie showed up around five o'clock, and after an hour of spazzing and venting had finally calmed down enough to eat the Big Bob's fish-and-chips dinner he'd brought for them. On the table sat sodas, the two notes from the kidnapper, and a blank pad of paper. The TV local news was on mute ten feet away.

Raven glanced at the door for the hundredth time in case anyone walking along the pier came looking for her. And soon, for them.

How so much could fall apart so fast was beyond her. Walter's murder. The disaster in Cuba. Her scarf. It wouldn't be long before Bigley and API would be under investigation. Paulie was already stressed to the max. And then there was Dax.

She slid him a glance while he sat beside her, elbows on the table. He was serious and calm, in control. She closed her eyes at the stab of pain. Did he realize what happened to ex-cops in prison? Of course he did. Had he even thought that far ahead? Probably. And he was still willing to risk everything. For her? Hopefully not. She could take care of herself. She'd made a career out of it.

"So what do we know about this guy?" Paulie asked, pen poised.

"Besides the fact that he's a lying, murdering son of a bitch?" Raven said.

"Yeah, besides that."

Reluctantly, she picked up the first ransom note and felt the influx of Walter's emotional turmoil. She focused on the task at hand, not the death. He'd been scared but calm. Then she reread it word by word. "It's addressed to Raven, not the name I registered in the hotel under. And he says we sought *him* out."

Dax nodded and leaned against her to take a look. She welcomed his warmth and strength even as she tried to pretend she didn't need it. Like the embrace in the bedroom when she'd nearly fallen apart. He wouldn't let go until she'd surrendered. She didn't want to admit how much she needed that one moment of comfort.

"'This time it will end differently,'" Dax read on. "*This time.* It's as if he thinks we've dealt with him before."

She shook her head. "We weren't even in the same state until a few days ago. And just once last year."

Paulie pointed at each of them with the pen. "Maybe you dealt with him separately. Like you arrested him, Dax? Or you stole from him, Raven?"

Dax shook his head. "The only contact I had with him was during the robbery six months ago."

He looked to Raven, and she shrugged. "If he was moving stolen artwork, our paths may have crossed."

"Ever team up with another partner?" Dax asked.

She raised an eyebrow at the multiple implications of his question and the cool edge to his voice. "I always work alone."

Paulie made an ahem sound, and Raven added, "Or with Paulie."

Dax held her gaze for a moment, and she caught the flash of heat that passed over his face. "I guess that rules that out."

Paulie drew a little box on the sheet and filled it with text. Then he handed Raven the second note. She took it, and immediately felt the difference in Walter. He was truly afraid. Terrified. He probably knew he was going to die. Her heart broke.

"Raven?" Dax asked.

She turned to him before she could pull herself out of Walter's emotions. Blue eyes narrowed in concern, and she set the paper on the table. "I'm fine."

Dax and Paulie exchanged a glance before Dax

said, "This one isn't addressed to either one of us, only 'children.'"

"Which could mean he's older," Paulie pointed out.

"Or a jerk," Raven said.

Dax's mouth curved. "Jerk gets my vote. Here he says something about not forgiving us 'so quickly,' like we have had a past with him. Doesn't make sense."

"Unless he believes we did. Maybe he's mistaken us for a different couple," Raven said. "Ever date another female thief?"

"Not that I know of." Dax grinned slightly.

Paulie watched them both for a minute, then shook his head as if they'd both lost their minds. "And what about this part? 'Your father would be so proud.'" Paulie looked up. "Whose father?"

Raven stilled. In all the chaos, she'd forgotten about that.

Dax sat back on the sofa beside her, and said, "Mine was a patrol officer in Chicago. He probably made a few enemies along the way, but I can't imagine anyone going to this much trouble for a uniform."

Paulie turned to Raven. "What about your dad?"

She had so hoped it was Dax's father and not hers. But why would it be? Of course his father would be a good man. Dax was.

"He's a salesman in New York," she said simply. *Hell,* she didn't want to do this. "Before that, he was a thief."

Paulie's eyes grew huge. "No shit? I didn't know that."

She could feel Dax's gaze on her, but she couldn't bring herself to look at him. "Small-time stuff. He quit long ago."

"Wow," Paulie said. "That explains a lot about you." Then he saw her scowl, and added, "I mean, why you are so good, you know?" Then he wisely changed the subject. "Was your mom a thief, too?"

Raven smiled at that. "Hardly. She was going to be a Catholic nun before she married my father. She died when I was sixteen."

"Sorry," Paulie said.

"Is it possible your father might know this guy?" Dax asked.

"Maybe, I don't know. I haven't spoken to him in twenty years," Raven said with a growing feeling of dread. What if her father was involved? Could this get any worse?

"We need to talk to him," Dax said.

Her father's identity would lead them to Jillian, and considering this killer appeared to be psychic, she wanted to make sure that didn't happen. "I'll call him myself."

Dax didn't look convinced. "So if you haven't had any contact with him, how do you know he quit stealing?"

"My sister told me."

Paulie's jaw dropped. "And a sister, too? This is so cool. I've learned more about you in the past three minutes than I have in the past three years."

She gave him a withering look. "And I want to keep it that way. I've spent a lot of time building a persona that doesn't include them. I don't want them involved in this."

"If someone digs deep enough, they're going to surface," Dax pointed out.

"Let's hope not," she said, shrugging off the chill despite the heat. "Can we get back to the killer?"

Paulie looked over his notes. "So besides the letters,

we got the runaround at the Metromover. This guy sure had that figured out, didn't he?" He gazed at them. "He had to know that system inside and out. He's at least been to Miami."

"He also robbed the place in Ouray," Dax noted. "Maybe he's operating out of southern Florida."

Raven said, "He could be anywhere. Hell, he could be in Cuba."

"And what happened in Cuba?" Paulie asked. "I rechecked all the communications, cleared the boat before you left and everything. No one's tapping in. So how did they know you were there?"

Maddox said, "We think they may have recognized Raven when we cased the church."

She raised her hands in frustration. "I'm telling you, I'm not that big."

"They had to know which painting we were going for before we got there. Who knew that besides us?" Dax asked.

"The killer," she said.

Paulie pointed his pen at her. "Now, see? That makes no sense at all."

Dax stared at her for a moment, and she could tell he was thinking the same thing. *They knew we were coming, and they knew what we wanted.*

"If he turns us in, he doesn't get his painting," Dax said.

"I know." She rubbed her temples.

"Moving on," Paulie said. "Miami-Dade PD got a tip about Raven and Walter. That we know came from the killer. And you figure he took your scarf from the hotel room? And the hair could have been from a hairbrush."

"The DNA is going to be the problem," Dax said. "Even if it was planted, it's still part of the crime scene." He looked at her. "Got a DNA profile on record anywhere?"

"No."

Dax looked relieved. "Then forensics can't make a match unless they catch you."

Harry's words came back to her. *If you turn her in, all this goes away.* He was right. Everything tied back to her.

"And then he strangled Walter with the scarf," Paulie said. "What a sicko."

"He planned to kill Walter all along," Raven said, anger lacing her words. "It wouldn't have mattered how many Vassalos we got for him. If I'd only noticed the missing scarf—"

Dax interrupted. "Even if you'd noticed it was gone, there's nothing you could have done about it."

Paulie tapped the pen on the table. "Maybe he had something against Walter."

Raven shook her head. "I can't imagine Walter was anything more than an innocent victim. What did you find on Santo Vassalo?"

"Almost forgot," Paulie said, brightening. He pulled some papers out of his case. "Vassalo the painter was very successful. Born an only child to a wealthy family in Venice around 1860. Had a slew of sponsors and enjoyed considerable recognition and celebrity."

"Pretty nice life," Dax said.

"You'd think," Paulie replied. "However, Vassalo the man was a mess, and here's where it gets interesting. He married Maria in 1889 and had three kids. But apparently, Mrs. Vassalo wasn't as impressed by his technique as everyone else because she took herself a lover. In 1905, the two of them murdered Santo Vassalo, sold off his collection of paintings, hightailed it out of Venice for parts unknown, and lived happily ever after. The Vassalo family was furious. They spent years trying to locate the missing paintings, but they didn't surface for ages."

Raven frowned at Paulie when he suddenly grinned.

"And?"

"And I have a theory." He pointed to Raven and Dax. "He thinks you two are his wife and lover reincarnated."

Raven slid a glance to Dax, who was looking at Paulie like he'd lost his mind.

"Uh—," she started.

He raised a hand. "Wait. Think about it. He wants his Vassalos back, and he's making you two get them. It's payback."

"It's nuts," Raven pointed out.

"Well, *he's* nuts," Paulie said, waving both his arms wide. "Why else would he want *all* the Vassalos for himself?"

"Because they're worth a fortune?" Dax said, looking more amused by the minute.

Paulie's expression dropped marginally, and he shrugged. "Well, yeah, but you gotta admit, it's a good theory."

"Except that I don't think it's the Vassalos he wants," Raven said.

Dax and Paulie turned to her.

She tapped the tabletop. "Walter was killed before we had the second painting, possibly before we even left for

Havana. Why would he do that? If he kills Walter, we won't get the painting for him."

"If he doesn't want the paintings, then what does he want?" Dax said.

More than the paintings, Raven realized. He wanted something more personal. "Us?"

Dax asked. "So what's the connection between us?"

She realized it was a long shot, but she couldn't shake the certainty. "I don't know."

Paulie smiled. "The reincarnation theory is looking better and better, isn't it?"

Raven and Dax shook their heads in unison.

"Fine," Paulie said. "Well, that's it. He's a damn smart thief who might or might not operate near Miami. He knows you both and at least one of your fathers. He's killed two people and framed Raven for one murder. And he wants Vassalos." Paulie tossed down his pen. "Folks, we need a miracle, because this is just a big pile of crap."

A miracle, Raven thought. "Or another Vassalo."

Paulie snorted. "Yeah, right. You got a couple mil lying around?"

She took a breath. "We have one."

"One what?" Dax said. "A painting?"

"Bigley got it a few weeks ago," she said. "It's a new discovery. Not even on the books yet."

Dax's gaze lingered on her, and he didn't look pleased.

"I was going to tell you," she said to him.

Paulie rolled his eyes. "You guys don't communicate at all, do you?"

"If we can convince Bigley to make it public, the

killer might contact us," she said as the plan began to form.

"Bait," Paulie said, bobbing his head in approval. "Awesome idea."

"Unless he doesn't want the painting," Dax pointed out.

"He wants us," she said, knowing in her heart that was true. "How can he turn down the chance at a painting and the two of us?"

Paulie leaned back and crossed his arms. "The problem's gonna be convincing Bigley to go along. He's pretty upset right now between Walter's murder and Raven's being under suspicion. I'm not sure he's going to want to take any more chances unless it's part of a real investigation."

Dax didn't say anything. They both knew what a "real investigation" would mean at this point.

"Heads up, people," Paulie said suddenly, and used the remote to unmute the TV.

A female reporter was standing in front of the Miami Luxus Hotel with Raven's photo on the other half of the screen. "The woman has now been identified as Raven Callahan, a recovery specialist who works for the Antiquities Preservation Institute in New York City. She is being considered a suspect in the death of the New York buyer found murdered this morning as well as a robbery assault on another art dealer at the hotel. If you have any information on this woman, contact the police at the number below."

"Crap," Paulie said. His shaved head started to sweat. "If they put my picture up there, my mom is going to freak."

"They can't do anything to you," Raven said, hoping she sounded more certain than she felt. She looked at Dax, who was watching the screen. He wasn't going to be so lucky.

She leaned forward. "Paulie, call Bigley on a secure line. Tell him the plan. No discussion. We need that Vassalo. Ask him to make the painting public knowledge as soon as possible. Let him know we're coming up to get it."

He frowned. "What if the killer follows us to New York?"

She stood up and looked outside. "Counting on it."

CHAPTER
16

Dax felt a whole lot better with a few hours between them and the Florida state line. Not that distance would save them from the Feds if they decided to pursue. By 4:00 A.M., I-95 had become a monotony of exits and gray road in a truck that wasn't designed for cross-country travel.

Paulie was snoring on the floor in the back. Raven slept in the passenger seat, wearing sunglasses and a hood pulled over her head so no one would recognize her. He wondered if that was the real reason or if it was because she was trying to hide from him. She'd had a rough day, although she would never admit it.

The woman was an island. She'd pushed everyone as far away from her as she could and still do the work she loved. He remembered the battle when he'd tried to hold her on the boat. Was she fighting him or herself? Who comforted Raven when things went bad?

He tightened his grip on the wheel. They had to find the killer. If they didn't, Raven would take the fall for

Abbott's death. Dax wasn't going to let that happen. She was getting his protection, whether or not she wanted it. If that meant chasing her down, tying her up, and keeping her under lock and key, he'd do it. And it would probably come to that.

She had one foot out the door, ready to leave at the first sign of roots. It was easier for her to run than to trust. Regardless of what she said, he knew the first chance she got, she'd bolt. She probably didn't even realize it. It was just who she was. He didn't have a clue how to change that.

But she wasn't the only one with commitment issues. Harry wasn't going to be too happy when Dax didn't show up, and he couldn't risk another phone call to explain why. There was no way he was walking into a police station now that Raven was a prime suspect.

He'd chosen this road the moment he'd quit his job. He had known then and there that he'd do whatever it took to find Nick's killer. There was no going back. He'd been a good cop. He'd done his job and, most days, he'd even liked it. One mistake, one blinding moment of bad judgment wiped away fifteen years, leaving him with nothing but nightmares.

Sorry, Harry.

Raven stirred slowly and lifted her head to look out the window. "Savannah? Again? Weren't we just here?"

He smiled. "Seems like only yesterday."

"I'm pretty sure it was. I'll take over at the next exit," she said, stretching her long body in the seat. Dax watched with appreciation as the tunic stretched over her breasts, and leg muscles flexed beneath the light pants. A body built for distraction.

She arched an eyebrow when she noticed him staring at her. Just like that, he was hard. If Paulie hadn't been in the truck with them, he'd have seriously considered pulling over and playing cops and robbers for a while.

Instead, he concentrated on the road before they got into an accident. At the next exit, he parked at a service station and killed the engine. At this hour, there were mostly semis and early risers. A good time to use the facilities, get some food, and gas up under the cover of night.

His thoughts were interrupted when Raven said, "Why are you here?"

Dax frowned at her. "Thought we already covered this."

"No, I mean why did he drag you into this?" She looked at him thoughtfully. "I'm here because he wanted a painting stolen. But you? Why bring a former cop into the picture?"

He'd been thinking about that, too. "The only reasonable explanation is that I caught him during the robbery. But I didn't get a good look at him."

"What if he doesn't know that? He thinks you can ID him. So he puts us together because he wants to get rid of both of us at once."

Dax twisted in the seat to face her. "The man is a two-time murderer. If he wanted us out of the picture, he could have killed us by now."

"Unless he doesn't want us dead," she said, looking disgusted. "Maybe he just wants us to suffer."

"Then he's doing a hell of a job," Dax muttered. "Did you contact your father?"

Her lips thinned. "Not yet. I will."

He heard the reluctance in her voice. "He's a possible lead, Raven."

She removed the sunglasses, and smoky eyes stared back at him. The strain was there, beneath the beauty.

"I honestly don't know if he'll even help me. We don't talk. We don't see each other."

"You're his daughter," Dax said. "That doesn't change."

She gave a short laugh. "My family isn't like yours. It's not normal, and it never will be."

He heard the shame and the yearning. He reached out and ran his fingers through her thick, silky hair. "What makes you think my family is normal?"

She blinked. "Because you are."

His fingers stilled. He almost said, *I think you are, too,* and stopped himself when he remembered how she had acted in the church and with the priest, her father a thief and her mother a saint, and the guilt-ridden dance between right and wrong. On the other hand, he wasn't doing much better these days. If she only knew just how screwed up he was.

"I'm glad you think so because we need to stop at my sister's in Baltimore on the way through. She's the family scrapbooker. I'm going to grab some of my father's albums while the kids are in school and she and Robert are at work."

Raven's forehead furrowed. "What if the killer is following us? We could lead him right to your sister."

Dax warmed at her concern. "He already knows about my family, Raven. If he wanted them, he would have gone after them already."

Her voice rose. "What about the police? What if they come to her house while we're there?"

"We're okay until this goes to the Feds. Besides, we won't be there long, I promise."

"I don't like it, Dax," she said.

He lifted an eyebrow. It was the first time she'd called him anything other than Maddox. "I don't like any of this, but there might be a lead in there somewhere."

She gave a long sigh. "Is your sister a cop, too?"

"No, she's a physical therapist, and her husband is a lawyer."

Raven leveled her gaze at him. "That might come in handy."

"Let's hope not." He took the keys out of the ignition and pocketed them. He leaned over the seat and yelled at Paulie. "Wake up, bud. Pit stop."

Raven got back to the truck first and tossed her bag in the back. She'd cleaned up and changed into black capri pants and a white terry sweatshirt with a hood. Sandals and dark sunglasses completed the look of a woman who didn't want to be recognized.

She slipped into the driver's side and checked to make sure Paulie and Dax weren't back. It was now or never. She found her cell phone and punched in a phone number she hadn't called in ages, but had never managed to fully purge from her long-term memory.

"Hello?"

Raven paused for a moment, concentrating on all the reasons why she was doing this. "It's Raven."

Murphy Talbot took a few seconds to reply. "Rebecca,"

he said, his Irish accent heavy. "This is . . . It's good to hear from you."

"It's Raven now," she said, recovering from the sudden shock of hearing her birth name.

"Yes, of course. What can I do for you?"

She squeezed her eyes shut and rubbed her chest. "I need your help."

"I heard about Walter Abbott's death and the police. Are you safe?"

"How do you know about Walter?" she asked.

"Jillian told me. You should call her. She worries."

"Right," she said. Wait till the cops show up at her door. "Have you had any visits from the local authorities?"

"Not yet. It's that bad?"

"Yeah," she admitted. "We're . . . I'm trying to track down the thief who killed Walter." She hesitated. "I thought you might—"

"I'll do anything."

She realized her fingers were turning white, and she unclenched her fists. Then she told him about the letters and what they knew so far.

"We're looking for a man who is hoarding Santo Vassalo paintings. His works have been systematically disappearing over the past ten years. I think it's the same thief."

"Now that's something. I don't run in those circles anymore, you understand, but I'll see what I can do."

"I appreciate it," she said.

"Anytime."

There was an awkward silence that Raven didn't know how to fill with anything other than a million questions.

Why did you leave us? Why did you let your wife die?
What was so damn important that you couldn't stick
around? What did we do to deserve that? All that old
anger rose in her throat and threatened to take control.

She managed a quick "I'll call you tomorrow."

"Right. Right. G'bye, Raven."

She hung up and dropped her head on the steering
wheel, feeling exhausted, and the day had just started. In
twenty years, you'd think she would have found a way
to deal with her abandonment issues, but it wasn't looking like it. How Jillian had managed to forgive him was
beyond her. How she'd emerged from the fallout was
nothing less than miraculous.

For four years, they'd watched their mother silently
fade away, withdrawing into a smaller and smaller world.
Having two daughters who needed her wasn't even
enough to keep her from eventually starving herself to
death. Raven would walk by her bedroom every morning, too afraid to look inside to see the shell that had once
been her mother and hating her for it. At fourteen, Raven
had been forced to become the mother—forging her
mother's signature to pay the bills, making up excuses
why her mother couldn't make the parent-teacher con-
ferences, never having anyone to cry to when fourteen
wasn't big enough to deal with it all.

No amount of begging could make her mother believe
in life again. All in the name of love. Never would Raven
put herself in a situation where her entire existence
revolved around one man.

She closed her eyes. Especially one man named David
Maddox. Unfortunately, leaving was going to be the hard

part, and the longer she waited, the worse it would be. It would hurt, but it wouldn't kill her.

She glanced at the empty ignition.

How long would it take to hot-wire the truck? A couple of minutes. She could drive away and turn herself in at the nearest police station, confess to everything.

Maybe then the killer would be happy with her head and let everyone else off the hook. If she left now, she would probably be saving lives. Besides, what other options did they have? They were officially fugitives, they had no leads, and Bigley's painting was a very long shot.

Raven ran her hands along the steering wheel, sensing Dax's fresh emotions. Maybe just one more for the road.

She closed her eyes and concentrated. Breathing deep, she inhaled his thoughts. Some were so hot and carnal, she moaned. Some were tender enough to make her cry. The guilt-ridden and frustrated thoughts, she could relate to. And then, concern and intimacy. She stilled, sinking into those fragments. He was worried for her safety, but there was more. He... She swallowed. He felt... love.

She released the wheel.

For a moment, she let the panic radiate across her chest.

How did this happen? She'd been so careful, kept her distance. She didn't want him to love her. Didn't he realize she was all wrong for him? What if she did to him what her father had done...

"You shouldn't have stayed so long," she said to herself. Layer by layer, she pulled the shield back around her. Her head cleared and focused. It was time to leave. She ducked under the dashboard and reached for the ignition wires. Her fingers froze when the driver's side door opened.

Luckily—or not—she recognized the pants.

"Car trouble, lady?"

She winced and sat upright, with Dax's big frame blocking the opening. Oh crap. This wouldn't be pretty.

He leaned in. "What? Can't come up with a good explanation?"

"I'm thinking," she said.

"I'm sure you are." He closed the door, walked around the truck to the passenger side, slid in, and tossed a brown bag that smelled like donuts on her lap.

"Keep this up, and I'm going to stop feeding you," he said, looking quite pissed.

"Planning to handcuff me to the steering wheel?" she asked, trying to lighten the mood.

His gaze locked on hers. "If I handcuff you to anything, it'll be me. And don't think I haven't considered it."

Handcuffed to Dax. Her heart skipped a beat just thinking about it. She took a sip of the coffee he handed her and licked her lips. "Maybe later?"

"You're trying to distract me," he said, a cup of orange juice poised near his mouth. "And although I'm willing to take you up on the offer at the first opportunity, it won't work. I know what you were doing."

She studied his weary face. "Maybe I was doing the best thing for everyone. Something I know you don't have the—" She paused. "Heart to do."

He squinted. "Why don't I like where this is heading?"

She took a deep breath and looked out the window. "Harry was right, you know. If you turned me in now, all this would end. I could tell them I acted alone, and they wouldn't have enough on you or Harry or API to do anything."

For a minute, he didn't respond to that. Or maybe he was mulling it over, considering it. It hurt, but she wouldn't blame him if he did. She wasn't her father. She'd do the right thing.

"You think I'd go for that?" he finally said softly after an interminable silence.

Raven spared him a glance and sucked in a quick breath at the fierce look on his face. Guess that was her answer. "I knew you'd be like this. What if this doesn't work, Dax?"

"We aren't giving up." He tossed the empty cup in the trash and leaned back to close his eyes. "Don't ever mention it again."

They reached the Baltimore city limits at midday after a long, hard, straight run up the East Coast. Dax rolled his head, careful to keep his eyes on the Beltway traffic. He was cramped and tired and cranky, and he sure as hell wasn't looking forward to breaking into his sister's house.

As he drove through the immaculate homes of the affluent Bolton Hill streets, his mood grew blacker. Sculpted landscapes, majestic columns, brick facades— the epitome of American success. By the time he parked the truck one street over under the shade of maple trees, he was officially disgusted with himself.

He glanced back at Paulie, who was sacked out again. "Does that kid do anything besides sleep?"

"Growing boy," Raven said, watching him intently. "Are you all right?"

He rubbed his eyes. "Just tired."

When he opened his eyes, she had leaned over to kiss him. He slipped his palm around her head and pulled her to him. The kiss ebbed and flowed, at times gentle, at times rough when his emotions got the better of him. Slowly, the tension in his muscles eased, redirected in passion.

Raven finally broke the connection to look at him. "I know you don't want to do this."

He ran a thumb across her soft lips. "I don't, but we need those albums. Let's get it over with."

She sat back in her seat like she'd been shot. "Why do I have to go? She's *your* sister."

He grinned in understanding at the sudden terror in her eyes. "You're afraid of the suburbs."

"Am not," she said, but she didn't look any less uneasy.

"Good, because I really need your hot little fingers."

One eyebrow arched in interest. "Just my fingers?"

"I'll get to the rest of you later," he said, and pulled on a baseball cap. "Speaking of later, looks like we're staying in a hotel somewhere. We can't go to your place or Paulie's."

She hesitated for a moment before saying, "I have a safe house in Jersey City."

"A safe house," he repeated, all the humor fading. "You have a safe house. When were you going to tell me?"

She narrowed her eyes. "I just did."

Only because it was necessary, he thought. And then he understood why. Because she had planned to use it for herself once she finally got rid of him. He shook his head. Why did he even bother?

He wrenched the door open. "Let's go break and enter."

CHAPTER
17

"Nice place," Raven murmured to herself as she walked the rear perimeter of the two-story brick Colonial. Dax was a few steps behind her, playing lookout, while she found the easiest point of entry. The doors were solid and too heavy to kick in. That left windows.

"Any dogs?" Raven asked him.

"Ian's allergic," he said, his voice tight.

She scanned the first-floor windows five feet above the ground. Without a ladder, it was impossible to reach them. On the other hand, it also meant this house had a big-ass basement. And most basements in old houses had big-ass windows.

Sure enough, she found one sunk into a wide drain well behind a hedge. The original wood frame gave with a quick kick, and she slipped inside. Dax came in behind her muttering something she was sure she didn't want to hear.

They made their way through the boxes and miscellany people stored to the stairs that led up to the kitchen.

It wasn't locked, and Raven cautiously opened the door, looking for motion detectors. There was one in the corner of the breakfast nook. She pushed the door open very slowly until she noticed the security system panel two feet away.

"It's not armed," she told Dax as she stepped into the kitchen.

"Christ," he said in obvious disgust.

"You'd be surprised how many people only use their security systems at night."

He walked ahead of her through the kitchen into the family room. Raven tagged along behind him, feeling like an alien in this bastion of normalcy. White cabinets contrasted with black granite countertops and shining copper pots that hung over a big island. Flowers in vases, toys in the corners, thick rugs, and a warm, lived-in feel that nearly smothered her.

She was very careful not to touch anything.

The short hallway between the kitchen and the front of the house was lined with framed photographs—black-and-white candid pictures of the family. Raven stopped in her tracks. She recognized that hard-edged, austere style of photography. Dax had taken these. And they were good, capturing the inner joy of the kids and the love of the parents.

She stared at the happy faces, and it occurred to her that she didn't own a single picture of Jillian. Of course, there was a perfectly logical reason why. She needed to keep her distance. It was one of the sacrifices she made to do her job. The sharp pang of melancholy caught her off guard, and she shook it off and moved on.

She entered the family room, and amid the overstuffed furniture and traditional decor, Dax stood by a built-in library pulling out photo albums. One by one, he opened them until he found what he was looking for.

Raven peered over his shoulder at the pictures of his father in uniform, regal and proud. She felt the change in Dax when he slapped the pages closed and handed it to her. His face was emotionless. He'd done the same thing in the car, and she'd been unable to control the swell of compassion she'd felt for him.

But a kiss wasn't going to make his pain go away.

While he pulled two more out and handed them to her, she scanned the other albums, her gaze dropping to the one marked "David."

Suddenly, the front door was flung open and a small herd of children crashed through. Raven took a step back and looked around for an exit. Heavily draped windows flanked the built-in shelves. She was about to slip behind the drapes when a blond-haired, blue-eyed, two-foot-tall boy shrieked and hurtled himself at Dax with an exuberant "Unc-o David!"

Dax picked him up and hung him over his shoulder. "Hey, Ian. How you been?"

"Dood," Ian said, then locked on Raven. "Hi."

"Hi," she said and thought, *I have to get the hell out of here*.

Two more children entered the room. One was a dark-haired girl about six years old and the other, a lanky older boy. Their faces lit up when they saw Dax, and a minute later, he was covered in kids.

A woman appeared in the archway and cast Raven a surprised look. Petite and slim with shoulder-length blond hair, she was the perfect image of a working mom. Then she stepped in, parted the kids, and greeted Dax with a big hug.

"David," she said. "You didn't call me to tell me you were coming. I'd have been here for you."

He gave her a warm smile. "I just stopped on my way through. We're working on a case, and I need to be in Boston tonight."

Raven listened in confusion. *A case?*

He checked his watch. "In fact, we really need to get going."

"You just got here," his sister said, and held out her hand to Raven. "Hi. I'm Deirdre."

"Laurie," Raven said smoothly. "Nice to meet you."

"Do you work with David in the department?" she asked.

Police department? "I'm more of an independent consultant," Raven said, and looked at Dax. He stared back in warning. What the hell? Hadn't he told her he wasn't a cop anymore?

"I see," Deirdre said with a nod. "Do you work together often?"

"This is our first time," she said, her gaze locked on Dax's.

"I'm Ian," the little boy said.

Raven smiled down at him. "So I heard."

"William and Heather," Deirdre said, hugging her two older kids. Then she shooed them along. "Go start your homework."

Ian planted himself next to Raven, looking up at her expectantly. She said, "David is right. We really should be going. We have a late appointment."

Deirdre gave her brother an exasperated look. "Can you at least stop by on the way back?"

"I don't know yet," he said. "If I can, I'll call."

She frowned. "Hey, how did you get in here anyway?"

Raven could see Dax's body tense.

"You have a broken window in your basement. You better have someone fix it. And bars would be a good idea. And arming your security system when you are out would be a great idea."

She rolled her eyes. "Good God, you sound like Dad. Yes, yes, I'll do all that." She glanced at Raven for sympathy. "It was nice meeting you. I hope to see you again."

Not on your life. "Me, too."

Dax said, "I'm going to borrow a few family albums, if you don't mind. The department is doing an article on legacies."

"Oh sure," she said with a smile. "Dad will love that."

"I know," Dax said.

While he hugged his sister, Raven slipped Dax's album from the wall and underneath the others. They said their good-byes and strolled down the front walk before Deirdre noticed they weren't parked near the house.

Paulie was still asleep in the back when they climbed into the truck. Raven put the albums under the seat, and Dax slid into the driver's side. The strain on his face said it all. And no wonder. He'd just lied through his teeth to cover for them.

"You think she bought it?" she asked.

"No." He pulled onto the street.

"You haven't told your family you aren't a cop anymore, have you?"

His silent profile was her answer.

"Why not?"

"You know how you have your secrets?" he started.

"Screw that," she said, furious that he would turn this around. "This is important. This is your family. They love you. Why wouldn't you tell them?"

His jaw muscle clenched. "Take a look in the album sometime."

"So your father was a cop, so what?"

"You should understand better than anyone."

She frowned. "What?"

"You followed in your father's footsteps, too." And then he looked at her, and she caught the full brunt of what he was saying. "And you still are."

She admitted, "Even if by some miracle we find this guy, my career is over. My picture has been plastered all over the law enforcement channels."

He looked straight ahead, his expression resolute. "That won't stop you. Nothing will."

Dax hung his head in the shower and let the water pummel his neck. He hoped Raven's safe house had a lot of hot water, because he wasn't going anywhere. Maybe while he was in here, he'd figure out how to apologize to her.

He'd been pissed, and he'd taken it out on her. From the silence she'd worn all the way to Jersey, he knew he'd cut her deep.

The worst part was that he meant it, just not in the way it came out. He wanted her to stop stealing. Not because it was illegal. Not because she could get locked up in some godforsaken prison for the rest of her life. He wanted her to stop because there was more to life than the thrill of the chase and waking up every morning in a different place.

But mostly, he just wanted her.

And he wasn't going to get her.

That's the part that made him crazy.

He finished his shower and toweled off. The small bathroom had steamed up, and he ran a hand across the mirror. The face that looked back at him was gray and unfamiliar.

The moment they found the killer, the other foot was going to step out the door and she'd be gone, taking with her the only color he could recall. He had already forgotten how blue the ocean was and the glory of a Florida sunset. But he remembered everything about Raven—the rich black hair and bewitching pale blue eyes, lips, full and pink, and smooth golden skin. He held on to the image, burning it into his memory.

He'd never forget the look on her face when his sister and the kids had shown up. She'd been ready to run. He was surprised she'd even played along as well as she had; but then again, it was all a game. What would it take to convince Raven to live a normal life? One where she wouldn't be running from the good guys, the bad guys, and herself?

Probably handcuffs. Not that he had a problem with that, but she might.

He pulled on a pair of shorts and opened the door that connected the bathroom to the guest bedroom. Paulie was hunched in front of a computer. Two monitors displayed a split view from cameras fixed on the entrances, every hallway and room, and the interior of a two-car garage that now hid the delivery truck and a new blue Honda Accord that was already here.

The town house itself was in the middle of two hundred identical units in a gated community minutes from Manhattan. It was the most innocuous place he could think of.

Paulie looked over his shoulder and shoved a potato chip into his mouth. He was wearing a Pink Floyd T-shirt and boxer shorts. "Hey."

"How's it going?" Dax asked while he stopped to look at the screens.

"So far, so good. No one's snooping around, at least not here. Bigs said the police have already been to API asking questions about Walter and Raven. We won't be visiting there anytime soon."

"Did you ask him about using the painting for bait?"

Paulie nodded. "Yeah. He's making the public announcement first thing in the morning. It's in his vault, so we just need to figure out a plan to get it."

Dax clapped him on the shoulder. "Good job."

Paulie said, "There's one more thing. I've been monitoring Miami news."

Dax stilled. "DNA results?"

"No," Paulie said and frowned. "Well, maybe, I don't know actually. But you've been ID'd."

His stomach clenched. *Harry.*

"We got problems, don't we?" Paulie asked, looking older than his years.

"It could be worse," Dax told him.

"Yeah, right," Paulie said with a snort. "Nice try. You think this guy knows about me?"

"He might."

Paulie shrugged. "That's fine. I can take care of myself."

He really liked Paulie. "How old are you?"

Paulie's forehead wrinkled. "Twenty-six. Why?"

Same age as Nick. "Nothing."

Movement on one of the monitors caught Dax's attention. Raven, dressed in a thin tank top and knit pants, stepped up to the kitchen island covered with cartons of takeout.

She flipped the page of a photo album from his sister's house. Her fingers tentatively traced the newspaper article titles.

"You've been working with Raven for three years?"

Paulie nodded. "About that."

"She's a good agent," he stated.

"The best API has," Paulie said. "Probably one of the best there is. Her recovery rate is nearly perfect. She's brought back stuff we thought was gone forever. She never gives up."

"She takes a lot of risks."

Paulie hitched his shoulder. "Her methods can be a little dicey, but she's good enough to pull it off."

Until the day she doesn't. "Why does she do it?"

"No idea," Paulie said. "I'm not even sure she likes art that much. I think it's more the principle. All I know is that she wouldn't be happy doing anything else."

Not what Dax wanted to hear. Regardless of what she'd said in the truck, he had no doubt that Raven would find a way to work again once this was all over.

"Call me up if you see or hear anything," Dax told Paulie. Then he descended the stairs, and nearly lost a step at the full impact of seeing Raven in such a domestic setting. Dinner on the counter, wine at the ready—it was like his secret fantasy. And it would remain a secret unless he wanted Raven to kill him in his sleep.

So he didn't say anything as he pulled up a stool and took a glass of Chianti from her. She clinked the rims. "To not having a SWAT team crash through the door tonight."

He laughed, a day's full of stress washing away. "That would worry me coming from any other woman."

"But not me," she said dryly, taking a sip of her wine.

"You aren't like other women, Raven."

"I know," she said with a little grin.

He looked around at the town house's furnishings. Everything in the room could have come out of an IKEA catalog and probably had. The furniture looked like it'd never been used, the carpet spotless, and there wasn't a personal item in sight.

"How many other safe houses does API keep?" he asked her.

"API doesn't keep safe houses. This is mine."

That was another surprise, although by now he should be used to them.

She added, "No one knows about it except Paulie. He wired it for me."

Dax couldn't help but smile. "I guess that makes me special."

"That makes you hard to get rid of." Raven ran her finger around the rim of the glass, and Dax realized she actually looked relaxed for the first time in a long time. And why wouldn't she be? She was back in her element, in control and surrounded by the safety net she'd built for herself.

She flipped another page. "Your father had quite a career. Commendations. Medals. Remarkable legacy to live up to."

Dax stared at her over his glass at the ominous change of topic.

She glanced up at him. "Sooner or later, they are going to find out you left the force."

"I'm sure they already have," he said. "Paulie just told me I've been identified in the Miami media. Everyone knows now."

Her gaze held for a few seconds. "Your family will support you no matter what."

Doubtful. He didn't even want to consider what his family was thinking right about now, but the phrase "Where did we go wrong?" probably topped the list. He just hoped they weren't dragged into the investigation. That would just about kill his parents.

A few seconds of silence stretched between them before he asked Raven, "Why did you stop talking to your father?"

She finished her wine and slid the glass aside. "He abandoned my mother, my sister, and me with no warning, and we didn't hear from him again until after my mother died."

Dax had to give her credit. She didn't miss a beat. She could have been reciting the grocery list. "Did he ever tell you why he left?"

"No. I didn't ask, don't care."

What would make a man abandon his wife and kids? Even though Dax had seen it happen plenty of times on the streets, personally it was unthinkable. "So how did you end up in his line of work?"

Her fingers paused on the page, and her expression darkened. "I'm not like him. I recover stolen artworks. I give them to their rightful owners. There's a difference."

And then he got it. The fire in her soul, the anger in her heart. "How many stolen pieces does it take to repay your father's sins?"

"That's not why I do it," she said crisply.

"You don't owe anyone anything, Raven. This is your life. You can do whatever you want with it."

She gave him a hard look. "Maybe you should be worrying about your own future, Dax. What happens when you go to renew your captain's license next time and flunk the color sight eye test? What then?"

His jaw tightened. "I have plans."

"No, you don't," she said with maddening certainty. "Why didn't you stay on the force? They would have found a job for you."

How the hell did this conversation turn on him so fast? "Because sitting behind a desk all day entering traffic citations into a computer isn't a job."

"Maybe not like your father's, but it's still honorable," she said. Raven shoved the album toward him. "You shouldn't have quit."

"And you should," he said. "Before it's too late."

A flash of disappointment crossed her face so fast, he almost missed it. "It's already too late."

He doubted that. "Really? So what are your plans? A couple of kids and a house in the suburbs?"

She didn't reply right away, and he realized he'd stepped into unwelcome territory. Unforgivable territory.

"I don't think you want to know what my future plans are," she said quietly. They stared at each other, knowing full well what she meant. Then she got up and headed for the stairs.

One foot out the door, and she was gone.

Dax drained his wine and set the glass down. That hadn't gone well. He'd skipped the apology part and gone straight for total alienation. He should know better than to corner Raven. Whatever her future was, it didn't include him, and he couldn't change that. Or her. And he didn't want to. He just wanted . . . more than he was going to get.

The bedroom door slammed upstairs. And it looked like he was sleeping alone tonight.

"They're in town. I thought you said you had them in Florida. What happens if they figure this out?"

Fauss stared at the model, the phone gripped tightly in his hand. They were supposed to have stayed in Florida, hiding until the cops could catch them. This completely skewed the model. It would take all night to recalculate the adjustment.

"Where are they now?"

"New York City area. How could they know where we are?"

"Perhaps they don't," Fauss said, studying the boxes on the model. Why would Raven return? His gaze fell to one box—Jillian. Yes, she would return to protect her sister. But David Maddox was another story.

"What would draw Maddox here?"

"How should I know? You're the one with all the answers. You told me he was going to turn her in. He never did, and he's obviously not going to."

Fauss bristled. "I haven't had time to fully explore his outcomes. Unfortunately, you dragged him into this late."

"It's not my fault he's decided to play hero. And by the way, Yarrow is awake."

"So?"

"So *you* dragged him into this, too."

"I had no choice. There was an 82 percent chance that Yarrow would accept Raven's counteroffer on the painting. I couldn't allow that to happen. Besides, he can't identify me. I was in disguise. As far as the police are concerned, it was a random robbery."

"And what if they tie you to it anyway?"

"Then I'll take care of Yarrow myself. What else do you have for me?" Fauss said, trying to regain control of the situation. He needed more data if he was going to work out the next outcome.

"Nothing."

"Something new happened," Fauss pressed. "Someone must have set a new event in motion."

There was a short pause. "Bigley is going to announce the discovery of his Vassalo tomorrow morning."

Fauss worked the new variable into the equation. This was not a random event. Thomas Bigley had a specific reason for revealing the Vassalo at this time. But why? Why announce the painting when API was under investigation? It had to bear significance.

Unless . . .

"They are going to use the Vassalo to lure us out," he said. "They think we want it."

"So let them deliver it. We can always use another Vassalo."

"Agreed. If we play along, we can still execute the plan and eliminate them ourselves."

"Are you going to catch them stealing it?"

Fauss started adjusting the model to accommodate a new event. "No. Too many variables I can't contain from here. The only certainty of success is if we control the situation ourselves. I'm going to need your help."

"You always do."

Fauss frowned. "The plan is nearly complete. Do not get insolent now."

There was a moment of silence on the other end. "I wouldn't think of it. I just want this over with." He hung up.

Fauss set down the phone and turned his full attention to the model. Children were so impatient.

CHAPTER
18

The ceiling overhead was dark and gray and too close to his face. Dax tested his restraints and resigned himself when they held fast. A low whimper beside him sent a shot of fear to his heart.

"Who's there?"

A groan was his answer.

Nick's face appeared in his line of vision. He was wearing Paulie's Pink Floyd T-shirt. No blood. "Hey, Senior. You're all set."

Dax shook his head. "Set for what?"

"Your eyes are fine. You're good to go."

"But everything is gray."

A woman cried out, and Dax winced at her pain in his head. "Who is that? Who are you working on?"

Nick grinned. "She'll be fine. We just need to fix her hands."

A soulful "no-ooo" rose from the woman. Terror worked its way into his body, his heart beating louder in his head. *Raven.*

"Leave her alone!" Dax yelled out.

No reaction at all from Nick. What was wrong with him? Why was he letting them hurt her?

Panic set in. "Nick, stop them."

He grinned. "Can't. I'm not the one who started this."

"Dammit, Nick. Do something." It was a plea, not an order.

Then Raven cried out again, and Nick disappeared from sight. Dax was on his own. He twisted, fighting with the restraints. He needed to save her. Her screams filled his ears, and he closed his eyes, setting his entire focus on getting off the gurney so he could rescue her.

Somewhere in the back of his mind, he felt her cries starting to fade, and he thrashed violently to break free.

"Stop it," he yelled. "There's nothing wrong with her!"

"She's almost done," Nick said.

And with that, she slipped from his mind. Dax struggled to find her, grasping at the fragments of memories. Anger set in, consuming everything else. He threw his head back and yelled, "No!"

When he opened his eyes, he realized he'd fallen off the couch in the living room of Raven's safe house. The digital clock on the wall flashed 11:33 P.M. No sign of Raven, and for that he was grateful.

He leaned against the sofa and put his head in his hands. Thank God. It was only a nightmare. The absolute terror he'd felt subsided slowly, leaving behind a bad feeling he couldn't shake. A dream analyst would have a field day with him.

A series of sharp tapping sounds drew his head up. He got to his feet and listened to the noises coming from the basement level. He slipped his Glock from under the pillow and made his way down the stairway. Sliding along the wall, he cleared the first corner.

Tap-tap in quick succession and then a *kerplunk* broke the hard-thumping baseline of Heart's "Barracuda" rocking in the background. Either their intruder really needed a pool game fix, or someone else was still up.

Dax came around the doorway with his gun drawn.

Raven was leaning over the table, pool stick poised for a shot, when she saw him. Other than the pool table, some workout equipment in the far end, and a Sirius satellite radio mounted on the wall, the room was empty.

She looked at the weapon, then made a perfect stop shot on the three ball in the side pocket. Dax let out a breath and lowered the weapon.

"Most guys don't pull out the guns until *after* they lose," she said, chalking up for another shot.

He set the gun on the radio shelf and stepped into the pool table light while she dropped the six ball with a smooth, sure stroke. She only had two balls left, and he'd bet she'd cleared the rest of them without missing.

"You always shoot pool at midnight?" he asked.

"Couldn't sleep." She glanced up and froze when she saw his face. Her expression turned serious, then troubled. "It happened again. Another nightmare."

He narrowed his eyes. How did she do that? "Just a dream."

She held his gaze for a moment before sinking the five in the corner pocket. The cue ball slid back and lined up in position for the eight. "Barracuda" wailed out as Raven made her way around the table across from him to line up the next shot. "Want to talk about it?"

He didn't think she'd appreciate the symbolism of losing her hands. Then she bent forward, opening the camisole and giving him an eyeful of magnificent breasts, and he almost forgot what they were talking about.

"Not really. Where'd you learn to shoot?"

She dropped the final ball. "Jill and I used to play against each other for hours. She's actually better than I am. It wasn't until I got into the real world that I learned being a girl on a pool table had its advantages."

He could imagine the number of men she'd left drooling on the green felt.

"But I still prefer to play solo," she said, setting the stick against the head of the table. She gave him her full attention, and his body tightened in response. It was an automatic reaction he could neither deny nor control.

"Sounds unnaturally dull for you."

She retrieved the triangle frame and loaded it with balls that she arranged in the rack. "It's relaxing. So shut up and break."

He pulled a stick off the wall, rolled the cue ball into position, and broke the rack. Balls scattered, and a high ball dropped.

He walked around the table. "How about we make this a little interesting?"

He lined up the sixteen and missed wide right.

"After that shot, what do I have to lose?" she said with a wide grin. "What's the wager?"

He leaned on his stick and took in her slightly tousled hair and midnight eyes. "Fifteen minutes."

It did him a world of good to see those eyes widen in interest. He was hard in a flash.

"Fifteen minutes of what?" she asked, her voice husky.

"Of whatever the winner wants. No negotiation. No discussion. And no saying *no*."

She licked her lips. He was getting harder by the minute. At this rate, he'd never finish the game.

"Barracuda" finished and "Born in the U.S.A." started up.

"Deal," she said, and proceeded to drop four balls in a row before missing a tough bank shot.

He grinned at her obvious disappointment. She really wanted those fifteen minutes. It would almost be worth losing just to see what she had in mind, but he had his own fifteen minutes to think about.

He ran the table.

She'd been had. She couldn't believe it.

Triumphant and without a word, Dax took her stick and put it in the wall rack. His bare back muscles flexed, and she could already see his erection pushing against his trunks. A tremble ran through her. She was his for the next fifteen minutes. Blood was already racing to key spots around her body.

Dax stopped in front of the Sirius box and changed the station from classic rock to the smooth groove of Sade.

At 12:12 A.M., he finally came to her. Breath held, she waited for the slow seduction his intensity promised. Every fiber of her being was focused on him when he stopped inches from her, anticipation riveting her in place.

He held out a hand. "Dance with me."

She blinked, expecting something that involved removing clothing. She cut a glance to the Sirius box and the intimately seductive beat coming from it.

"Afraid to dance with me, Raven?"

She looked back at the expectation in his face. A slow dance—heart to heart, soul to soul, two bodies moving as one. And suddenly she was nervous. This was no longer a game, and there was nowhere to run.

She tried for humor. "What? No sex?"

A flicker of disappointment passed. "No negotiation."

Then he slipped a hand around her waist and pulled her into his arms. She settled against him, fitting perfectly as he wrapped her hand in his and led her into the dance. He smelled like soap and heat, and she nestled against him.

They moved with the music. She relaxed more with every turn, following him. She could hear the beating of his heart, feel his steady breathing, sense the growing desire rising in his warmth.

His shoulders rolled beneath her hands, his erection pressed against her belly, and he was all hers. There wasn't another place on earth she'd rather be at this moment. He could draw from her torturous anticipation one minute, then terrifying vulnerability the next, leaving her wondering what lay around the next corner.

She tightened her grip, and he responded by caressing the back of her neck with his fingers. Unhurried and with amazing tenderness, his hands slid across her skin. Steamy heat built between the one thin layer of fabric separating them.

It was only 12:15 A.M. She wanted him so badly, and he hadn't even kissed her yet. What was he waiting for? She shifted her weight and pressed her hip against his erection.

"Easy," he whispered in her ear.

She bit her tongue. She would not break. It was only fifteen minutes. She'd survive. Probably.

Dax didn't change his tempo as he traced the hollow in her back from top to bottom. She shivered at the trail he left behind. The ache between her legs was becoming unbearable.

By 12:19 A.M., she was positive that she was going to spontaneously combust. The song had changed, and the Stones were singing "Angie." Sweat trickled between her breasts, fueled by Dax's body heat and slow caresses.

At 12:22 A.M., Dax kissed her lips, never missing a step. He delved into her mouth, patiently, thoroughly. She moaned, more from the sexual outlet than anything else. Desperation won over pride and she kissed him hard. No change. The man was killing her.

Exactly one minute later, he slid a hand between their bodies and under the waistband of her pajama bottoms. His fingers found her, swollen and needy.

By 12:25, she was climaxing, barely standing on her feet and unable to move. Dax held her tightly so she wouldn't fall.

At 12:26 he had her naked, balanced on the edge of the pool table. His mouth worked down her body with the same leisurely pace he'd kept up for the past fourteen minutes.

One second past 12:27, he entered her. She wrapped her legs around him and marveled at the raw need in his face. Eyes closed, expression tense, she realized how much it had cost him to hold back. Thrust for thrust, she stayed with him until they were both spent and gasping for breath on the table.

She was ruined for foreplay for the rest of her adult life.

Fifteen minutes he'd spent holding her, worshipping her. His time, and that's what he'd chosen to do with it.

She closed her eyes with the realization that she was in serious trouble. Because she wanted to turn the clock back and start over again. And again. She wanted more than fifteen minutes. More than just tonight. This was by far her most dangerous job, and one she was going to have a hard time walking away from without significant carnage.

Dax gave a low growl of contentment, and she kissed his soaked neck. "Nice shooting."

A smile pressed against her skin. "Nice rack."

Raven bolted out of bed with the certainty that something was horribly wrong. The clock read 5:02 A.M. Security alarms were silent. Dax lay sleeping in the bed.

She hurried down the hallway, past a snoring Paulie, and glanced into the control room. All quiet on the monitors. She padded down the stairs and checked the rest of the town house. Everything looked fine. So why was her heart in her throat? Why were her hands sweating?

Raven stopped and willed her brain to focus. Her cell phone light flashed on the kitchen counter, and she picked it up. No new messages.

She stared at the date. Tuesday.

Tuesday, and Jillian hadn't called last night.

"Oh God," she said, and dialed Jill's number.

"What are you doing?" Dax asked from behind her.

The phone rang away while she turned to face him. "I'm calling my sister."

He rubbed his neck. "A little early, don't you think?"

"She's not answering."

"She might be in bed like the rest of the world."

"Light sleeper. She should answer."

He crossed his arms over his chest. "Maybe she's sleeping somewhere else tonight."

Raven shook her head. "Not Jill."

The answering machine picked up, and the greeting played. Raven could barely hear herself talk over her pounding heartbeat. "It's me. Pick up."

Nothing.

"Raven, what's wrong?" Dax asked, sounding more alert and concerned. But she couldn't tell him that her greatest fear had come true.

"Jillian, if you are there, answer the phone."

She could hear the panic building in her own voice. After a long silence, she added, "When you get this message, call my cell."

She hung up, the overwhelming feeling of terror stealing her breath. With shaky hands, she dialed Jillian's cell phone. It went to voice mail after five rings.

"Hell." Raven sat down on the stool and put her head in her hand. What had she done? She should have protected Jillian better. Somehow—

Dax took her by the arms and forced her to look at him. "Raven, what is wrong?"

She gazed into his eyes. "He took her."

CHAPTER
19

Jillian's apartment was neat, feminine, and empty at six o'clock in the morning. Dax took in the elegantly upholstered furniture, floral fabric, and plump throw pillows. A large, richly detailed poster with the words "The Unicorn in Captivity" dominated one wall, and a small upright piano took up the other.

Everything in its place. No sign of struggle. Suitcase in the closet. Food in the fridge. Fresh flowers on the table. Dax tried to imagine Raven with fresh flowers, but all he could envision was a vase full of dead stems.

"She didn't sleep in her bed last night," Raven reported after she came out of the bedroom. "And I can't find her purse or wallet."

Since he'd met her, Dax had never seen so much fear in her eyes. All the dangers they'd faced, and yet the cool facade was shattered with a couple of phone calls. He couldn't figure out how she could be so certain something had happened to her sister, let alone that the kidnapper had taken her.

"She could be at work already."

Raven picked up the phone and reviewed the previous incoming phone numbers. "She leaves at 8:30 A.M. every morning, without fail."

Raven put the phone back and played the messages. There was one hang-up from 5:00 P.M. last night and her own message this morning.

Dax said, "Are you sure Jill wasn't seeing someone?"

"She would have told me." Raven skimmed her fingers along the counter to an empty in-box tray beside a neat stack of opened bills. "No mail. She didn't come home after work. He must have grabbed her then."

Dax watched her walk through the apartment, touching everything—the TV, the couch, the door handles. What was she doing? It was as if she was willing the answers to come to her.

Raven stopped in the middle of the room and ran her fingers through her hair, pulling it away from her strained face. "This is my fault."

Dax said, "You don't know that."

She paced the small living room with her arms tightly crossed. "He knows everything about me. Everything. And now he has Jillian. It's the only explanation."

"That's an awfully long shot."

She turned to him with irritation. "Jillian calls me every Monday night to ask if I want to go to dinner with her and my father. She hasn't missed a call in years. Until last night."

Dax squinted. All this for one missed phone call? "Raven—"

"You don't know my sister," she cut him off sharply, her voice rising. "Jill walks the same line every day. She doesn't like surprises, she's the antithesis of impulsive, and being late is not an option."

Raven stood there vibrating with worry and energy. The woman had nerves of steel. She wouldn't worry for nothing.

"Have you tried contacting your father?"

Raven's eyes registered the connection, and she pulled out her cell phone. From the lack of emotion in her face, no one answered. She pocketed the phone and walked past him. "Let's check his place. There's nothing here."

Thanks to the persistent trembling of her fingers, it took Raven longer than usual to pick the lock on the third-story apartment. No one answered their knock, and a quick walk through the cramped and cluttered one-bedroom flat confirmed that Murphy Talbot wasn't home.

She surveyed her father's very humble abode. The furniture had seen better days, but the place was comfortable. Utilitarian kitchen, tiny bathroom, living room, and bedroom. Not a single piece of artwork anywhere.

While Dax checked the rooms, she stopped at one corner of the living room that had been converted into an office. An old oak desk faced a wall covered with corkboard and photos. Raven counted a dozen pictures of her mother when she was young and happy with ready smiles. Before she let herself wither away waiting for a man who was never coming back for her.

Raven wasn't prepared for the depth and breadth of sorrow and anger that seized her. Why had her father returned at all? He'd waited until after her mother died to make his grand entrance back into the family, supposedly to take care of his teenage girls. As if he had the right.

She scanned the other pictures—of her and Jillian at various ages from infancy to adulthood. Photos Raven didn't even remember taking. In fact, every family photo she could imagine was on this wall.

Emotion lodged in her throat. She was old enough to remember what it was like before he left and destroyed the family. It had been safe and warm. And then everything fell apart. She wished . . . She shook her head. Those days were gone, lost in the pain of the past.

It was the present that worried the hell out of her.

Dax came up behind her. "Same thing here. No struggle. No mail from yesterday. You might be right."

"I know I am."

He scanned the photos. "This your family?"

"Used to be."

Dax leaned closer to one photo of two young girls on swings. "Jillian and Rebecca, May 1981." He turned to her. "Who's Rebecca?"

"It's my given name."

He narrowed his gaze. "I knew it. You picked Raven."

"Rebecca doesn't exactly strike fear in the hearts of men," she said, and pulled up the chair to sit down. Dax leaned on the desk beside her. Intense blue eyes peered back at her full of determination and compassion. "We'll find them."

"Yes, we will," she said, with a conviction that ran to her soul. No matter how painful it was. If there was a time to use this God-given curse of hers, it was now. With a deep breath, she braced herself and booted up the computer.

"I'll search his computer. Why don't you start on the paper files," she said to Dax. "He was checking around on the Vassalos for me. He might have found something."

"You think your father got too close?"

She was relieved to see the PC wasn't password-protected. "Maybe." The desktop screen appeared.

Dax said, "Perhaps they were kidnapped in exchange for more Vassalos?"

Her hands paused over the keyboard. "The Vassalos are a ruse. They have to be."

Dax opened the file drawer and started flipping through the folders. "So what's the ransom?"

She steeled herself against the certain emotions attached to the mouse and placed her hand over it. To her relief, there was only surface warmth. She scanned the directories—spreadsheets, letters, games. Nothing jumped out at her.

"I'm not sure there's going to be a ransom this time."

"That would be bad." There was no humor in his voice. He read the contents of one folder and put it back. "I'm beginning to think this is bigger than you and me."

Raven accessed her father's e-mail and waited while incoming mail loaded. She froze when she saw the Sent address on one e-mail: Thomas Bigley.

She opened it, and read in disbelief.

Dax looked at the screen. "Find something?"

The note was from Bigley giving her father an update on Raven's situation, including the fact that he would be outing the Vassalo they found last month.

They found.

Dax leaned over her shoulder and read the e-mail. "What is this, Raven?"

She did a search on Bigley's address and found dozens of e-mails dating back years.

"I don't understand," she said. "They didn't . . .

couldn't have known each other. Bigley would have told me."

Dax scanned the notes along with her. "Looks like they have a pretty close friendship. They e-mail at least once a week."

Mostly about her. Bigley telling her father of her latest successes, the artifacts she'd saved, snippets of her exploits. How could this be? Betrayal waged in. Bigley never once mentioned this to her, never asked her permission. How could he have lied to her all these years? The more e-mails she read, the angrier she became. She had trusted Bigley. How could she have not seen this?

"Now this is interesting," Dax said, breaking her thoughts.

He unfolded a yellowed newspaper article on the desk. The headline read "Art Dealer Shot in Attempted Robbery."

"Says here Thomas Bigley was shot by a man attempting to rob his Yonkers gallery after hours," Dax recapped. "He subdued the robber, Clayton Fauss, before the authorities arrived." He looked at her. "Did he ever mention this to you?"

"Never." Just another secret Bigley had kept from her.

Dax pulled out another article. "This is the sentencing. Fauss pleaded not guilty, was convicted, and given ten years for attempted murder and attempted robbery."

Raven looked at the two articles, trying to make sense of all the shit that had just hit the fan. "Why would my father have this?"

Dax got real quiet, and she looked at him with dread. He pointed to one line in the article. "Fauss claimed he had a partner, an accomplice who was also in on the botched burglary. Bigley insisted Fauss acted alone. No name was released, but the man in question was cleared when his wife provided an alibi."

A feeling of apprehension crawled across her. "You think my father was there."

Dax asked, "Isn't this around the time he left?"

She checked the date. Twenty years ago. Exactly the time. Oh God. What had her father gotten himself into? What had he done all those years ago? And Bigley. Was he involved, too?

She realized there was only one way to find out.

Her fingers trembled as she took the clipping from Dax and opened her senses. Snippets of memories—a dark room full of art, partitions falling, Bigley's face, angry shouts, a single loud pop, blood on his hands. Anguish rolled through her, followed by regret, pain, and shame. Pangs of heart-wrenching loneliness and loss, still so fresh and raw . . .

She shut down with a groan and dropped her head into her hands. How could this happen?

The present came back to her, and she was aware of Dax kneeling beside her. He swiveled the chair around and wrapped his arms around her. She leaned into him, but no matter how hard she tried, the feelings of shame and misery lingered.

"My father was there," she said. "He and Bigley were involved. They did something very wrong. Something my father regretted."

"Raven." Dax pressed his head to hers. "What just happened?"

She froze at the realization of what she'd just revealed to him. But there was no alarm in his voice, only concern.

She buried her face in his shoulder and clutched his shirt, not wanting to say the words that would change everything between them. Would he understand if she told him? Or would he see her as a freak? A threat? Either way, it was time to tell him the truth. He deserved it. No more lies. Not today.

Please don't turn away, she thought with growing dread. *I need you.*

She breathed. "I have a sixth sense. A type of psychic ability called *psychometry*. I get impressions from touching, through my fingers—emotions, sounds, scents, images, thoughts."

Raven waited for that to sink in, afraid to move, afraid to look at his face. But she felt the subtle change in his body as he tensed under her hands.

A few moments later, he pulled away from her, and the fear that had simmered in the back of her mind loomed large. Even though he tried to hide it, she could see the wariness in his eyes.

"That's how you authenticate art," he said. "That's why you were touching the Vassalo at the auction."

She nodded, pressing her back to the chair as his serious cop face returned. She glanced at the door with the overwhelming desire to run.

Dax stood up and shoved his hands in his pockets. "What about people?"

Her chest squeezed painfully. There it was.

She shouldn't have told him. He didn't and wouldn't understand. Wouldn't trust her with the secrets that lurked deep in his own heart. Regardless of all they'd been through together . . . Why would she think they could be anything more than just two people with a common goal? She would always be alone. It was simply safer.

"It only works on objects," she said, careful to mask the disappointment, and turned back to the folder on the desk.

He stood behind her while she sifted through the newspaper clippings. Uncomfortable silence stretched between them, and she ignored it. She'd made a mistake, and she'd find a way to live with it. Right now, she had a job to do. Jillian's life depended on her.

Raven read through each clipping and handed them to Dax, but they didn't offer up any new clues. The last item was an envelope with a return address of Marcy Correctional Facility, postmarked May 23, 1993. The year her mother died.

She slipped the two-page letter from the envelope and started reading.

> *Dear Murphy...I now understand the error of my ways...May you and God forgive me for what I tried to do...Thank goodness you stopped me...Bless you and your family...Sincerely yours...Clayton Fauss.*

Her father had held this letter many times, his imprint unmistakable along the edges. But those weren't the impressions making her shudder. She pressed her fingers to the handwritten text. Her father's residual feelings of relief faded, and a darkness overshadowed the emotional vacuum. Without warning, monstrous anger, hatred, and revenge raged and sliced through her mind. Numbers and calculations merged and shifted. Acute focus and twisted intelligence. Determination, day upon day. He would never stop until...until...

"Raven?"

She inhaled at the sound of Dax's voice and disconnected from the past. Her heart pounded in her ears, and her stomach rolled. She braced her hands on the desk for support and fought the urge to vomit.

She'd found the killer.

"It's an apology to my father from Fauss," she said aloud once she'd regained control of her stomach. "Nice letter, but it's a lie. All of it. He never forgave them for whatever it was they did to him."

"You think your father bought the apology?"

"Yes, he did. He wanted to." She handed Dax the letter. "Meanwhile, Fauss was plotting against my father, even then."

Dax scanned the note, serious and focused. "You're sure this is our man?"

She nodded. "No doubt about it. But I don't know how it ties together with the Vassalos and why we're all involved."

"I have a feeling we're going to find out very soon," Dax said. He was holding the newspaper article and the letter side by side.

"Why do you say that?"

Dax looked grim. "Because tomorrow is the twenty-year anniversary of the robbery."

He paused, and slowly met her gaze. "I think we really need to find your sister and father before midnight tonight."

"I checked like you asked me to. Looks like Bigley's gone, too. According to Gilmore, he never showed up for

work this morning," Paulie told them when they entered
the computer center of the safe house. "Gilmore said he'd
help any way he could, so I asked him to check Big's
place and give me a call back."

"Who's Gilmore?" Dax asked.

"Bigley's private secretary," Paulie told him. "So, this
is bad, right?"

"More than you can imagine," Raven said. She pulled
up a chair and tossed the folder on the desk in front of
Paulie.

Dax leaned against the table, crossed his arms, and
kept his eyes on her. She hadn't said much since they left
her father's place. Closed up tight. Part of it was concern
for her sister and maybe even her father. But part of it
was him, and there wasn't anything he could do about
that.

Had he been an open book all this time? If she could
get so much off a letter or newspaper clipping or authenticate an old painting, how much could she get off his
boat? Or his personal belongings? It was unnerving to
realize she might know parts of him that he didn't want
to acknowledge, let alone share.

Paulie flipped through the contents of the folder. "I
can't believe your father and this nutcase were partners
twenty years ago. That blows my mind. Did you ever
meet Fauss?"

Raven's expression was weary. "Not that I remember.
What did you get on him?"

Paulie said, "A lot actually. Nothing about the robbery
on the Net since it was so long ago. But I can confirm that
Fauss spent ten years in Marcy. A model inmate. Earned
an actuarial certificate and a degree in criminology

through the Prison Ed Program. Nice to know he put our taxpayer dollars to good use. Highly intelligent man with a built-in calculator in his head. No wonder he knows exactly what we'll do next."

"That would fit our profile," Dax said. "Any idea where he is now?"

Paulie showed them a MapQuest Web page of Albany with a big star on the east side. "Right here. He's currently living in an apartment in Albany and consulting independently as an actuarial criminologist."

Dax frowned. This was too easy. "You have an address?"

Paulie raised his hands. "Yeah, surprised the hell out of me, too. If this is our guy, he's not hiding anything. No alias. Doesn't even have an unlisted phone number. In fact"—he opened a file, and a picture popped up—"we got a photo."

Clayton Fauss's dark eyes peered out from under thick eyebrows. His nose was narrow and long, much like his face. His gray-streaked black hair was pulled back into a ponytail.

"Recognize him?" Dax asked Raven.

She studied the photo and shook her head. "No. Did you try to call him, Paulie?"

"Twice. Answering machine picked up both times."

Dax asked, "Any family? Anyone he might be staying with?"

"Not that I could find. He divorced shortly after he went to prison. His ex-wife moved out of state, and I lose her after that. He never remarried."

"We could take a trip to Albany," Dax suggested to

Raven. "Even if his place is empty, you could use your ability to find something."

Paulie looked at him, then at Raven, who was glaring back at Dax. "What ability?"

Dax raised an eyebrow in her direction. What the hell? Paulie didn't know? He figured everyone in the whole world knew except him. Her potent glare didn't subside. Or maybe not. It occurred to him that Raven barely volunteered any information about herself to anyone, let alone something as personal as this. Maybe she shared this one only with people she trusted.

Like him.

Shit.

"Her gift for acquisitions," he said, his gaze locked with hers. A flicker of relief passed over her face before icy cool returned.

Paulie shrugged. "Whatever. You're looking at three hours' driving time each way, so if you're going to do it, you better start now."

Raven stood up and paced the small room. "It'll cost us six hours, and we don't know if we'll find anything. He's here, in the city somewhere."

Dax looked at Paulie. "Does he own any properties besides his apartment?"

Paulie shook his head. "Nothing popped up when I checked, but I only have limited access to property records. There's no guarantee I'll get a hit if the purchase was recent. And if it's been leased or rented, I won't get anything at all."

Raven rubbed her forehead. "We're missing something. Why is he going to all this trouble? If he wanted revenge on my father and Bigley, why didn't he just go after them? Why bring us into it? Why screw around with the paintings at all?"

"If this is the guy who's been stealing all the Vassalos over the past ten years, then he's got almost the entire collection. We're talking a hundred mil here," Paulie said. "How could he turn down the chance of having you guys help him out? Two thieves are better than one."

"He's not in it for the money," Raven said with conviction. "Greed and revenge are two different things. He's using the paintings for revenge. The question is, how?"

Dax thought through the past few days, and a grim reality surfaced. He looked at Raven. "Maybe he's trying to pin the robberies on your father . . . and you. You told me your father doesn't steal anymore. What better revenge than to frame him for the theft of every Vassalo over the past ten years? And you helped. You stole one for Fauss. If he can prove that, you'll fry, too."

Raven frowned. "What about Bigley? Why is he involved? And Walter? And Jillian? Or you, for that matter."

Dax admitted, "I don't know, but I'm sure Fauss has it all figured out."

"So we find the Vassalos, we find everyone, right?" Paulie said. "I mean, if he's going to blame the heists on Murphy, then he has to link Murphy and Raven with all those Vassalos. Show possession. He'll have to make sure there's a connection in order for the cops to make a case."

"Exactly," Dax said.

Raven became very still. "Paulie, check to see if my father or I have any property holdings in New York State."

"Oh crap." Paulie's eyes widened and he swung his chair around to start typing. "It'll take me a few hours."

Dax said, "You better run a check on Bigley, you, me, and Jillian, too."

"Got it," he said. "I hate to tell you, but this is going to take most of the day."

"Give us what you have as you get it," Dax said, pushing off the table. "We'll check each location ourselves."

Raven's cell phone rang. She unclipped it from her hip and checked the screen.

Her eyes cut to Dax. "Blocked caller."

CHAPTER
20

Raven hit speakerphone and answered. "Hello?"

"Hello, Raven." The voice was soft and sent a shiver down her spine as it filled the room. "It's been a long time."

Dax mouthed silently, *Ask his name.*

She nodded and said, "Who is this?"

Fauss laughed. "You don't remember me. That's a shame. We had so much fun together. I used to push you on the swing in your backyard."

She blinked at the fragment of a memory that wafted by and was gone, leaving behind a layer of queasiness. "Where are they?"

"You were always bright, Raven. In fact, you have been the most surprising element of all. Very tenacious. I've had to adjust you many times."

"Where are they?" she said again, this time anger getting the better of her.

"I have them. They're fine, for now."

Tenuous relief eased the tension in her shoulders. "What do you want?"

"Thomas Bigley's Vassalo."

A confused look crossed Dax's face, and she knew what he was thinking. How did Fauss know about the painting in Bigley's office? It hadn't been made public yet.

"Where and when?" she asked.

"Gorman Park, Washington Heights, tonight. Eleven sharp," he replied. "Just you and Mr. Maddox. If I see anyone else, your loved ones will die."

"You won't get the painting until I see them alive," she said, working hard to hold her voice steady.

"Of course." He hung up.

She hit *69, but the phone couldn't connect to the number he'd just called from. Bastard. She closed the cell phone. "It's a trap."

"No kidding?" Paulie said. "Does he think we're idiots?"

"He thinks we're desperate. And he's right," Raven said. She looked at Dax. "He knows about Bigley's painting. How?"

"He has inside info," Dax said. He paused a moment, then added, "Or he's the one who sent it to Bigley in the first place."

She pointed at him. "Bingo. He sends it to my father or Bigley. They chat, then surprise, surprise, the companion piece shows up at an auction in Miami a few weeks later, providing the perfect opportunity to validate this new piece."

"What are the odds of that?" Dax asked.

She smirked. "Astronomical. He knew Bigley would bite."

"Then he sent the painting to auction, too," Dax said.

Paulie squinted like he was barely hanging on to the conversation. "Okay, but why sell it in Miami? Why not use Christie's right here in New York? It's closer to Bigley."

"Because I'm in Florida," Dax said. "He drew me in."

Raven added, "You saw him during the robbery. All you have to do is testify it wasn't me or my father who stole that Vassalo from the Lowrys that night. It would be enough to raise doubt and ruin his whole scheme."

"So he made sure we'd have to steal the auction painting together to implicate us both," Dax said, following her lead.

Paulie scratched his head. "Yeah, but Yarrow won that piece. What if you'd won it instead? You wouldn't have had to steal it."

"I don't know," she admitted. "But everything else fits."

"And what about that rat race at the Metromover?" Paulie added. "What? Was that just for jollies?"

"It got us on the surveillance tapes," Dax said. "And placed us in the vicinity where Walter's body was found."

Paulie said, "And Cuba?"

"A trap." Dax looked at Raven. "You were right. He must have tipped off the Cuban authorities. He wanted us caught. And now he knows we're here."

"Damn," Raven said. "He does. He didn't even ask if we were close. He didn't have to."

Paulie looked totally bewildered. "Whoa, wait a minute. Are you saying this guy set this entire thing up from the beginning? Why?"

Raven stared at Dax. "To make sure my father spends the rest of his days in prison for the biggest string of art thefts in history. To implicate and ruin Bigley and his reputation. To get rid of the only cop who lived to see him."

"And the only woman who would never stop tracking him down," Dax said, his eyes locked on hers. "What about Jill?"

Raven felt sick. "I have a feeling..." She couldn't say it. She couldn't say that Jill was collateral damage like Walter. "She's in big trouble."

"Holy shit," Paulie said, clearly impressed. "That's what I call revenge."

Dax said, "Now all we have to do is prove it. Because if we don't, it's going to work."

Dax lowered his binoculars. "All these places are occupied. Fauss wouldn't be using any of them."

Raven nodded silent agreement. One of Bigley's storage facilities—a warehouse in Tarrytown—sat fifty feet from the Honda. The white block building gleamed in the sunlight. Delivery trucks came and went. Employee cars sat in the parking lot. Fauss wasn't here. Where was he? Where was Jillian? Bigley and her father?

This was the third place she and Dax had checked today, and all they'd gotten out of it was six hours of wasted daylight.

"Paulie didn't get any more hits?" he asked.

She adjusted her sunglasses. "No, and his search is almost completed. He checked every source he had. Fauss must have rented a place in my father's name. We got nothing."

Dax slammed his fist on the steering wheel, and Raven lifted an eyebrow. "And here I thought you were taking this all so well."

He wore the stress of the day on his face. "I don't need to tell you how this is going to end if we don't find this guy."

She wasn't giving up. She couldn't. If that meant walking into a trap tonight, she'd do it. "There's still time."

They sat for a few minutes in silence, then Dax said, "I'm sorry."

"A little premature, don't you think?"

"About earlier. You caught me off guard with the psychometry thing."

Hell. She didn't want to deal with this one. Not now. Not ever. "Forget it. It's fine."

"No, it's not. It's a part of who you are. You didn't choose to have it, but you have to live with it." He took a breath. "When I thought about all the times you backed off. Now I know why." He turned to her. "I'm sure you've found things you wish you hadn't."

She froze at his astute observation. "All the time."

His eyes stayed on hers. "Walter's notes and his jacket. You must have felt his fear. And the insanity in Fauss's letter."

She sat in disbelief. He got it. He'd thought about it, into how she must feel. No man had ever done that for her. Not that she'd confided her secret often, but the few times she had were complete disasters.

"Right," she said softly.

"Is there any way to block it when you want to?" he asked.

She looked down at her fingers. "I've learned to control it somewhat, but if the emotions are strong . . ." *I'm screwed,* she wanted to say. "It's a little more difficult."

He reached out and took her hand, brought it to his lips and kissed her fingertips. The warmth radiated down her arm into a part of her chest she thought would be cold forever. She withdrew her hand, and the moment of panic at how close he was passed.

She smiled. "Thanks."

He nodded and said, "Let's check the buildings in back."

They drove around to the rear of the property. Across the road sat a residential neighborhood. Neat houses stood proud among stately oaks and maples. Flower-lined walkways and big porches beckoned. Kids ran across green lawns, and the guilt that had followed her from Baltimore became more than it was worth carrying.

"I took your photo album from your sister's house," she heard herself say out loud.

"You what?"

She sighed and turned to face him. "I wanted to . . ." How could she say this and not tell him how curious she'd been about him and his past? And how much she wanted a glimpse into his life? "See what your job was like. You did a lot of good in fifteen years. You should be proud. Your family is. I felt it on every page. Every newspaper clipping, every photo."

For a moment, he just looked at her as if he couldn't believe she was telling him the truth.

"I wouldn't joke about this," she said.

He said, "It was just a job."

"But you loved it," she stated.

He pulled the car onto the shoulder of the road facing two small buildings behind Bigley's primary storage facility. "I used to."

Used to?

"You lose faith, Dax?"

He picked up the binoculars to take a look. "Something like that."

She didn't believe him. A man like Dax didn't quit unless he had a damn good reason. Screw the eyesight. Screw the legacy.

"What really happened that night with Nick?"

Dax lowered the binoculars slowly but kept his gaze out the window. The longer he was silent, the worse she realized it was. She thought at first he might not tell her. That she hadn't earned his trust.

When he finally spoke, his voice was rough. "The call came in at the end of our shift, and Nick was in a hurry to finish up because he had a date. When we got inside, he wanted to split up to cover the house faster. He took the upstairs, and I cleared the downstairs."

His voice got quieter. "I was hit from behind. I went down and passed out for a few minutes. Woke up when I heard the gunshot. My vision was double, but I saw the burglar run out of the house. I found Nick halfway up the stairs. He was lying on his stomach with a single shot to the back."

He paused, and she braced herself. Whatever it was, she needed to know. Wanted to know. To be a part of it.

"He wasn't moving. Wasn't breathing. And when I rolled him over, he had a hole the size of New Jersey in his chest," Dax said, staring straight ahead. "The cop part of me knew he was dead and told me to go after the killer.

But I didn't. Nick was just a kid. So I stuck my hand in his chest and tried to get his heart moving."

She listened, frozen in the horror of what he'd been through.

A bleak smile touched his lips. "Didn't work, of course. Too much damage." He stopped. "That's when I realized that my service revolver was gone."

Raven covered her mouth. *Oh no.*

"Fauss killed Nick with my gun," Dax said.

Time stood still between them, the tragedy of the past lingering in silence. She wanted to hold Dax and take the past away. But mostly she wanted to kill Fauss for murdering Nick and leaving Dax to pay for it.

"You didn't leave the force because of the legacy or the eyesight, did you?" she said.

He looked at her, and the pain . . . The threat of tears burned in her eyes. "I'm so sorry, Dax."

"We broke protocol. I was the senior officer. I should have stayed with Nick. I knew it even though the department cleared me. Everyone knew it."

She shook her head. "Dax, it wasn't your fault—"

"You always protect your partner." His gaze hardened as he said the words. "Always."

She thought of Jillian and Paulie and all the other people she loved and protected, and understood.

"I kept waiting for Homicide to catch the killer. Waiting for justice," he said, looking away. "Didn't happen. The only way I could get involved in the investigation was to quit, so I did."

He blamed himself for Nick's death. Carried that responsibility and regret every minute of every day. All the torment she felt over Walter and the others at this moment, the crushing guilt, the helplessness—Dax was way ahead of her.

"How do you do it? How do you live with that?" she asked, because she really didn't know.

He turned to her, his eyes dark. "You find the bastard yourself."

Realization dawned. She hadn't seen the vengeance before. Maybe it was because she was so wrapped up in her own guilt that she'd been willing to overlook it. But it was there now in his stillness. And it scared her because she suddenly realized he had nothing to lose and no future. He'd done just enough to support himself while he looked for the killer and no more.

"And then what?" she asked.

He turned away and peered at the buildings through the binoculars. "We have to find him first."

A frightening understanding gripped her. "You can't just take justice into your own hands, Dax. You have to believe in the system."

He didn't look at her. "That's quite a statement considering you're living proof the system doesn't work."

She winced. She deserved that, and, honestly, she couldn't argue with him. There were criminal laws and there were her laws. Hers tended to be far more lenient and completely self-serving. How could she tell him to follow the system when she made up her own? He risked his life to protect citizens from people like her.

But the reality of the situation was that she couldn't kill Fauss, even after everything he'd done. As much as she'd like to see him dead, there would be consequences, and she wasn't going to let him steal her future. Or Dax's.

She tried another tack. "We're partners, remember. You don't move without me."

Dax chuckled. "Right."

He didn't believe her. He didn't think she'd stick around to follow through on her statement. And why would he? What had she done to prove she'd be there for him? For any of them? Whether she liked it or not, she was part of a team. It was the only way this would work.

"We need to meet Fauss tonight," she said.

Dax dropped the binoculars in an instant and turned to her. "He won't be there, but I'll guarantee all of NYPD will be. Walking into an ambush isn't going to help, and it's not going to find Fauss."

She glared at him in frustration. "Then what the hell do you suggest, Dax? Because we've got exactly six hours before Fauss destroys the people I love."

Dax tapped his fingers on the wheel, deep in thought. "Maybe we've been dealing with this guy the wrong way. Maybe what we need to do is think like him instead of the way normal people think."

"You don't want to go where this guy thinks. It's not pretty," she muttered.

Dax frowned. "I'll bet. But you know him better than any of us."

Then they both froze at the sound of sirens coming up the road behind them. *Oh God no,* she thought. *Not now.* If the police picked them up now, Jill and the others wouldn't have a chance.

Dax reached for the ignition, and Raven reached for the door handle. Two police cars, lights flashing, cruised by them without slowing down. She exhaled as the sirens faded in the distance.

Dax started the car, pulled out, and headed in the opposite direction to pick up Route 9 south.

"Okay, you win," she said after her heartbeat returned to normal. "So how do we start thinking like Fauss?"

Dax cast her a surprised look at her quick change of heart and nodded. "He's spent a good part of the last twenty years plotting revenge. All so he could get your father and the paintings in one place. I can't believe that place wouldn't have some significance to him. Maybe somewhere they went when they worked together."

She searched her memory. "Twenty years ago, my family was living in a small bungalow in the Bronx, but the house was demolished to make room for a new development. Most of the neighborhood is unrecognizable now. Other than that, I have no idea where my father and Fauss would have hung out."

"Raven," Dax said slowly. "Where did the newspaper article say Bigley's art gallery was located?"

She studied his profile. "Yonkers, but it's no longer on his property list."

"Yes." Dax turned to her with a glint of hope in his eyes. "But is it still standing?"

CHAPTER
21

Jillian watched the shadows of a madman moving around the interior of the vault she was held captive in and finally admitted that she was in major trouble.

Which meant that Raven was right. Again.

Don't trust anyone but me.

Jillian sighed in resignation. *Got it. Got it now. Thanks.*

Unfortunately, those words of wisdom were a little too late to save her and her father from being abducted at gunpoint during their Monday night dinner date. Jillian had felt so useless. All she could think of was, what would her sister do? Raven would have executed something spectacular that involved lightning-quick reflexes, and Clayton Fauss would be behind bars by now.

But Jillian didn't have those skills, never thought she'd need them. So here they were—she and Raven's boss, Thomas Bigley—locked up tight inside a basement vault in Yonkers. Who knew where her father was or if he was even alive?

She leaned back against the cold wall. It was a low walk-in vault, about the size of her bedroom, with cement ceiling, walls, and floor. Long, narrow built-in map drawers lined one wall—all empty. One bare light-bulb illuminated the interior containing a pair of folding chairs and a couple of blankets. That was it. What it lacked, of course, was air vents. It was funny how you never noticed them until you didn't have them.

For the past day, she and Thomas had taken turns trying to find a way out, but the only exit was through the massive door at the end. And the solid six-inch-thick steel wasn't moving from this side. Clayton Fauss had made as sure of that as he had everything else.

She used her psychic vision to study the shadows of the past that moved around the room, concentrating on the way the light and dark shifted around the person when he came within a foot or so of an object. In this case, the map drawers that had been used to store paintings.

Fauss spent time in here, anticipating and plotting. His hands were clear on the drawer pulls, but everything else was blurred. If he'd put his nose close to the surface, she'd be able to see his face. As it was, the only clues she had that it was Fauss were opportunity and the darkness that shrouded every action.

She hated the dark and the evil it represented to her psychic mind. And there was so much hovering around this man that it nearly consumed him.

He was going to kill her.

She knew that the moment he'd smiled in victory the first time he slammed the vault door. The only thing she didn't know was when. He'd come back twice to let them use the bathroom and feed them. How long would he keep them alive before the evil prevailed? Would he continue to feed people he planned to murder?

A dark shadow passed by her.

Yes, he would.

She had tried to talk to him and even to beg for their release, but there was no reasoning with a man whose mind had been ravaged by anger and revenge.

Jillian inhaled precious air. How many more hours did they have before it ran out? She had no idea. Of all the ways she'd imagined dying, this wasn't even in the top ten.

If she ever got out of here, she was going to change her life. Take her sick days. Venture out of the city. Hell, venture out of Manhattan. Live life. Take chances. Like Raven. She wanted to be Raven for a while. Feel the freedom and adventure, where every day was a battle for life or death.

Actually, the death part wasn't that appealing. Maybe she'd start slow and work her way up.

Thomas Bigley huffed in despair and sat down in the chair facing her.

"I can't do anything with the door," he said, running his hands through his gray hair. "The worst part is that I coded the combination myself."

Jillian looked at him. "You did?"

He sighed. "I installed this vault twenty-five years ago."

She said, "You owned this building?"

"It was my first gallery," he admitted.

"What happened between you and my father and Clayton Fauss?" she asked. "Why is he doing this to us?"

Thomas put his head in his hands. "He was your father's partner." He looked up at her, his eyes tired. "They stole artwork together. I was working late one night when they broke in here. I guess I surprised them. Clayton wanted to kill me."

Jillian stilled. Her instincts were right.

He continued. "Your father didn't agree. When Fauss fired, Murphy tackled him. Luckily, the shot went wild, and it only wounded me. Your father knocked Fauss out before he could get off another shot."

She listened in disbelief. Her father had never mentioned this to her. She thought she knew him. She thought he trusted her. Why wouldn't he tell her this?

Thomas leaned back in his chair. "And that's when we made our fatal mistake. I cut a deal with Murphy. Since he saved my life, I would forget he was ever here. I'd blame the break-in and shooting on Fauss."

Jillian's jaw dropped open. "Oh no."

"At the time, I felt it only fair. Your father would never harm anyone. He's a good man." Thomas took a deep breath. "So Fauss went to jail alone. And your father gave up crime and moved away."

Her heart started to race. "That's why he left?"

"He was scared. He was afraid you and your family would end up paying for his crimes."

Her father had never told her why he left. She never asked, too afraid of what the reason might be. When you're eight years old, you figure everything bad is your fault. It was just easier to pretend it never happened.

Thomas said, "About five years later, we started getting letters from Fauss saying that he'd found God. All these years. We thought he'd forgiven us. That it was over."

"And Dad figured it was okay to come back," Jillian murmured, still a little shell-shocked from the bomb that had just been dropped on her.

Thomas nodded his head. "Yes. He missed you very much. You have no idea."

She blinked back the tears for the man who'd tried so hard to fix the past. There was no fixing something that was done. There was no fixing lies.

"I'm so sorry you're here, my dear," Thomas said, looking at her with sadness. "So very sorry."

He knew Fauss was going to kill them, too, and he didn't even have psychic abilities.

"His insanity isn't your fault," Jillian said. "Besides, Raven will find us."

Thomas groaned. "Lord, I hope not. She's as much a target as we are."

Jillian looked at the steel door. "She's pretty much our only hope right now."

The old three-story factory sat half a block away in a rough section of Yonkers, flanked by apartment buildings and barbed-wire parking lots. The stone arch entry and door were unlit, outlined only by the glow of a full moon. Each floor had a row of four front windows, all boarded up.

The street was quiet at 11:00 P.M., and Dax hoped it stayed that way. This was their last chance. They'd just passed the time they had agreed to meet Fauss, and he could tell that Raven was internalizing a lot of stress.

They studied the monitors as night-vision cameras focused on the building, searching for a sign of life. In the past hour, no one had entered or left. It appeared to be abandoned.

"They have to be in there," she said.

Paulie zoomed the camera in closer. "We're only getting one view from here. I'd say it's safe to rule out any side entry since the other buildings butt up to it. Can't tell you what the back looks like."

"Doesn't matter. I'm going through the front door," Raven said.

"And you don't make a move on Fauss until I'm in position inside," Dax reminded her. "We don't know how many people he has working for him."

She looked at him. Really looked at him. Partners. She'd said it in the car. Maybe this time she meant it. It was probably more than he should hope for.

"We are *all* sticking to the plan," she said firmly.

She wasn't talking about herself when she said it. Six months of frustration were already building in his gut, and Nick's face kept surfacing in his mind. This would be his only opportunity to get Fauss to admit to Nick's murder. Dax would follow the plan to protect Raven and the hostages. But he wasn't leaving without justice.

"I still don't know why we have to do this," Paulie said. "It'd be a lot safer to call the cops in."

"Too dangerous for the others." Raven lifted her T-shirt and adjusted the wire taped to her stomach. "Besides, the only way to clear us is to get a confession from Fauss. Otherwise, we have nothing."

Paulie gave Dax a worried look. "You really think he's going to talk?"

"He's been plotting this night for twenty years. He won't pass up the chance to gloat," Dax said.

"And Raven will be safe?" Paulie said.

"Hey, I'm right here," she cut in with a huff. "You just make sure this thing records. We won't get a second chance."

Paulie waved her off. "Please. You think I'm going to be outclassed by an actuary? No freakin' way. So what happens once you get the confession?"

Dax put the communications earpiece in and tucked the box in the pocket of his jacket. "As soon as Raven gives the word, I'll move in and take him down."

"Then we find Jillian, Bigley, and my father," Raven said.

"Think he'll give them up?" Paulie asked.

"He will," Dax said. Both Raven and Paulie looked at him, but he didn't elaborate. "*Then* you can call in the troops."

"So, this sounds easy enough," Paulie said, clapping his hands together.

Raven kept her gaze on Dax. "No matter what you hear or what happens, Paulie, stay put."

Dax stared back at her. "If it all goes to shit, call the police and get out of here."

Paulie frowned. "Crap. I forget that nothing is easy with you guys."

"Have a little faith." Raven gave him a quick hug before she and Dax exited the truck into the side street.

"You head around the back," Raven said to Dax. "I'll give you a few minutes to get inside."

"Paulie, did you copy Raven on that?" Dax said into his comm.

"Loud and clear."

"Good. Turn down the volume for a minute."

Raven squinted at him in the moonlight.

"What?" Paulie asked.

Dax reached out and pulled Raven to him. She wrapped her arms around his neck. The kiss was long and slow and desperate. A moan rose. He wasn't sure if it was him or her, and he didn't care. He just wanted to hold on to this moment.

"Oh," he heard Paulie say before his earpiece went quiet.

"Be careful," he murmured against her lips.

"You, too," she said.

"I wish there was another way to do this."

She shook her head. "He's got us wrapped up tight. We don't get him on tape, we're screwed."

Dax took a deep breath and tried to convince himself that she was right. She could take care of herself. She'd be safe. He'd make sure of it.

"Dax?"

"Yeah?"

"Wait for me," she said softly, still gripping him tight.

Did she mean once they got inside or something else? He couldn't tell from her expression, and he didn't want to ask. There was a debt he needed to repay. If they didn't get the confession, if this went to hell, he was going to make sure Clayton Fauss didn't walk away this time.

He couldn't promise to wait for her, but he would protect her with his life. He would give her the chance to start over—with or without him. "You aren't alone."

Unease flashed in her eyes. He knew it went against

her nature to be part of a team. He could only hope, this one time, she'd play nice.

Raven stepped back out of his arms, took one long look at him, and headed down the street. Dax watched her until she disappeared around the corner. Then he turned and sprinted in the other direction. "Paulie? You back?"

"Right here."

"Keep the cameras on her as long as you can."

"Got it. You sure she'll be okay? She's walking in there unarmed."

Paulie sounded worried.

"You have my word," Dax vowed.

"Okay," Paulie said. "Let's rock and roll. I'm patching her broadcast into your comm now. We are recording."

CHAPTER
22

Raven walked up to the front door and, after a quick look around, picked the lock. Her adrenaline kicked in as the door swung on its hinges with a low groan. A thick smell of dust, dirt, and neglect preceded the visual. She stepped in and waited for her eyes to adjust.

"I'm inside," she whispered for the team's sake.

The greeting area had seen better days. The walls were battered, and chunks of plaster covered the floors. Old ceiling lights swung from bare wires. Anything of value had been removed long ago.

She moved silently through the front room and into the interior. In the center of the structure, a large atrium rose the full three-story height up to a skylight. Industrial railings lined each balcony. A pair of metal staircases, one perched on either side of the balconies, led to the upper floors. Freestanding wall partitions broke up the first-floor plan—some upright, some toppled. The exterior walls were lined with deep alcoves. Crates and other junk littered the entire space.

"We have a logistical nightmare. Lots of hiding places," she said in a barely audible whisper that she hoped Dax picked up.

She stood still for several long minutes, but nothing moved. If Fauss had any friends, they weren't showing themselves. It would really suck if she got shot before she even had a chance to face him. She mentally logged as much of the floor plan as she could. Dax should be inside by now, but she couldn't see him, and chances were he couldn't see her either.

She took a moment to calm the surge of emotions she felt every time she thought of him. He could take care of himself, she reminded herself for the hundredth time. He would be fine. At least he had a gun.

Wait for me.

She'd meant it. She was worried that he'd do something they would both regret in the name of vengeance. Yes, she wanted Fauss, too; but she wanted him alive. So he could pay for everything he'd done. She wasn't so sure Dax felt the same way, and that was what scared her. Maybe if she could get Fauss to admit to killing Nick, Dax would have his redemption. She wanted more than anything to ease his pain and purge the nightmares from his sleep. Give him something to live for.

A new resolve settled over her as she turned toward a meager light coming from the left rear corner. She navigated the distance, careful not to disturb anything. It was so quiet, she began to have doubts that Fauss was here at all.

Then she heard voices in the back.

She moved to the edge of a makeshift room, roughly enclosed within partitions and crates. A priceless collection of Vassalos were hung carelessly on the wall and stacked on the floor. A single fluorescent ceiling fixture hung crookedly overhead.

Beneath it, Fauss sat at his laptop behind a battered desk. Her father was on the right side of the desk, handcuffed in a chair.

"Clayton, this is madness. We're talking twenty years," her father was saying. "It's ancient history."

Fauss didn't gaze up from his computer. "I wasted ten years of my life in prison because of you. It might be ancient history to you, but it isn't to me."

Murphy sighed in disgust. "For God's sake, listen to yourself. You're not making sense."

Fauss looked up then. "It makes perfect sense. Did you forget that I did all the work? I found the jobs. I planned the robberies, and you . . . you were too busy spending your nights in the bars. And then you betrayed *me*? Who did you think you were dealing with? Some idiot?"

"I was young—," her father said.

Fauss cut him off. "You were old enough to have a family."

Her father scowled. "They knew nothing of this."

"They do now," Fauss said, turning back to his laptop. "Everyone will know when I'm done."

Raven closed her eyes. Jesus, this guy was nuts. She hoped to hell Paulie was picking up their conversation.

She deflected a brief moment of fear. If she failed . . . *No.* If she had a problem, Dax would be there. She knew that without a doubt. But having a weapon would make this so much easier.

She rounded the corner and headed straight for Fauss.

His head snapped up, and his eyes focused on her with more annoyance than surprise. The photo she'd seen of him couldn't convey the soulless black eyes or the madness of his appearance.

"I hear you've been looking for me, Fauss," she said, stopping ten feet from the desk.

Her father's gaze swung to her, and his eyes widened. Then he frowned. He wasn't happy to see her. Big surprise. *Jig's up, Pop.*

Fauss stood up slowly, towering six feet easily and holding a semiautomatic gun in his hand. "If you kill me, you'll never find them."

She raised her hands. "You can put the gun down. I'm unarmed."

His expression darkened in distrust. "Then why are you here?"

"For a trade. My life for theirs."

"No!" her father shouted and stood up to face her. "I won't allow it."

She gave him a stern look. "Sit down, Dad. You had your chance. This is between me and Fauss now."

He shook his head, looking far older than she remembered. She swept the emotional wave aside. Didn't need to be dealing with that right now.

"No," he replied firmly. "You shouldn't be here."

"I didn't get a choice."

Fauss came around the desk and roughly shoved her father down into his chair. An unexpected wave of anger shot through her. She took a step closer to draw Fauss's attention. "Let's deal. I'm here in good faith."

A corner of his mouth rose. "You have no faith. You trust no one. You only believe in your own abilities."

"Your point?"

His eyes narrowed. "Where is Mr. Maddox?"

"I got rid of him. He wanted to call in the cops, and I didn't agree," she said, and waited for him to process that.

Fauss sank into thought before replying, "I see. And what of your associate, Paulie?"

"Do you really think I'd endanger him? He's just a kid."

His expression eased in agreement. "Of course not. You would come alone."

She breathed tenuous relief. He had bitten. Now all she had to do was reel him in. "So do we have a deal?"

Then he raised the gun. "I'm afraid not."

She expected as much. Now he felt he had nothing to lose. Time to talk. "Planning to kill us all, Fauss? Seems like a waste of a perfectly good plan."

Something flashed in his eyes, and she could see she'd piqued his interest.

"I mean, no one will know, right?" she added. "They'll just find us all dead, except for maybe Dad here." She swept a hand toward her father.

"Gotta leave him alive to take the fall," she said. "But who's going to believe him? Who's going to believe that a genius set all this up?"

She let Fauss absorb that before surveying the paintings on the walls. "Look at all these."

She walked toward the paintings.

"*Little Boy*," she said stopping in front of one. "From a New York museum, I believe." She turned to Fauss.

"In the original frame, no less. Not many thieves could pull that off."

He cracked a smile.

She moved to the next. "*Blue Café*. Private collection." She reached out and stroked the frame with her fingertips. Fresh hatred and bitterness slammed through her with such force that she nearly lost her composure. She fought for control of her emotions. Something was wrong. Very wrong. This wasn't Fauss.

There was someone else.

She stepped back, masking her shock. If she mentioned another thief, Fauss would freak out and probably kill them all on the spot. But there was another person involved; she was sure of it.

"Very nice," she said. "You've been collecting these for twenty years?"

"Ten actually," Fauss said with obvious pride. "I spent the prior ten years working on the model."

She nodded and continued to stroll the room as though she were at an art show. "Which is brilliant, by the way. I had a devil of a time figuring it out. You sent the Vassalo to Bigley and staged the auction in Miami to set the plan in motion. Sent us to Havana to get caught. Murdered Walter so he couldn't ID you."

She looked at him. "Am I right?"

He smiled. "How did you like the touch with the scarf? I took it as a contingency."

A tremor of hatred ran through her. "Frame me for his murder and hand me over to the cops. What I don't get is why you sent us to Virginia for Yarrow's painting."

Fauss grinned and reached over to spin the laptop screen to face her. He pressed a few keys, and a green video played showing her and Dax carrying the Vassalo out of Yarrow's storage unit.

He had them on tape. Her heart sank.

"Yarrow was working for you all along," she said. "You were the seller and the buyer. Then you took Yarrow out of the picture so we'd have to get the painting. The nail in the coffin."

His eyebrows rose. "Very good."

"Even if you let us go and we talked, no one would believe us," she said. "The evidence is overwhelming. Why kill everyone?"

He looked at her as if she were an idiot. "It's the only acceptable outcome. The only way the model can terminate."

Her father shook his head. "Good lord, Clayton. I always knew you were crazy."

Fauss's face turned red as he rounded on her father. "I didn't start this. You did. You and Bigley. You lied, and you left me to pay."

"I couldn't let you kill him," her father said.

"He could identify us," Fauss shouted.

"That was the risk we took, Clayton."

"There is no risk!"

Raven watched as Fauss breathed deeply and battled his inner demons. The burst of reckless emotion told her more than she wanted to know. He was not in control of himself, and since he was the one holding the gun, that made him very dangerous.

She had enough confession to clear them, but she wanted one more thing. Nick's killer. For Dax and for justice.

"What about the cop you killed last year in Miami? At the Lowry house. Was he also an unacceptable risk?"

Fauss turned to her, blinking as he regained his grasp on sanity. He opened his mouth to reply, then looked at something behind her.

For a moment, she was afraid Dax had made his move. But when she spun around, it was much worse.

Paulie walked toward her, looking pale and scared.

"I told you to stay in the truck," she said, knowing the plan was blown.

He grimaced. "Sorry, but you got outranked by Smith & Wesson."

Then a hand grabbed his shoulder from behind and drew him sideways.

Raven stilled when she saw Fauss's accomplice, the one whose anger riddled the Vassalos she'd touched. All the pieces fell into place.

"Gilmore," she said.

He grinned, pressing the gun to the back of Paulie's head. "Raven."

CHAPTER
23

Damn," Dax said softly.

He watched from his vantage point as a man walked Paulie through the building at gunpoint. Thanks to a challenging entry through a rear window, he hadn't been able to get into position fast enough to cut them off before they reached Raven and her father. And he couldn't risk hitting Paulie.

There was no warning that Paulie had trouble. Just radio silence, which Dax took as worry. Never assume.

The gunman looked younger than Paulie, small-framed and unassuming. Who was he? One of Fauss's men? Dax hoped there weren't any more of them hiding in the labyrinth of walls and rooms and floors. How many people would Fauss have trusted with his plan? Dax was betting not many.

The bad news was that if Paulie had been forced from the truck, chances were good they weren't recording anymore. Chances were also good that Paulie didn't get a call off to the local police department. Of course, the *really* bad news was that now there were two gunmen to worry about. In fact, it was pretty much all bad.

Dax moved closer to the corner where they had all converged so he could see their exact positions. Gilmore was using Paulie as a shield. Fauss had Raven covered. And her father was handcuffed. If Dax shot Gilmore, Fauss would kill Raven. If he shot Fauss, Gilmore would kill Paulie.

All bad.

He slid closer and heard Raven speaking.

"You bastard, Gilmore," she said, obviously furious. "I knew Bigley should have canned you."

The young man laughed at her. "Why would he? He trusted me. I was his right-hand man. Everyone bought the act—hook, line, and sinker—including you. How's it feel to be suckered?"

"You knew Walter was going to die," she said. "You made our hotel reservations knowing that."

Gilmore shrugged. "You're *all* going to die."

Dax moved a few feet to the right, trying to get a bead on Gilmore. If he could get a good shot off, maybe he could take them one after the other.

Fauss stepped forward. "What are you doing, Gilmore?"

"They were recording your conversation," Gilmore told him. "She's wearing a wire. And they aren't alone." He turned toward the atrium and yelled, "Come out, Maddox!"

Dax froze.

Raven said, "He's not here. I got rid of him."

Gilmore just grinned and shouted, "Maddox, come out, or I'll start shooting people."

Dax held his position, tempted to take the shot. Adrenaline rushed his muscles. If he didn't do it now, they'd all die.

Then Raven turned and looked in his general direction. He could tell by the expression on her face that she knew he was ready. She'd understand if he shot and missed. She would want him to take the chance. But he couldn't.

If he hit her or Paulie or her father . . . Nothing was worth that. Dax lowered the gun. He stepped out from his cover and walked into the room with his hands up. Raven closed her eyes when she saw him, realizing as he did that they were screwed.

Fauss looked at her in disbelief. "You lied."

Gilmore snorted. "Didn't your model tell you that, Dad?"

Dax studied Gilmore and Fauss, side by side. Fauss was a big man, but his son . . . The shadow of an escaping man flashed in his mind. They weren't dealing with one killer. They were dealing with two.

Gilmore shoved his weapon into Paulie's skull. "Toss the gun on the floor, Maddox."

Dax dropped it a few feet away, and Raven's gaze followed. He knew she was trying to figure out how to get her hands on it. Their eyes locked, and Dax felt the squeeze of his heart. It wasn't going to end this way. It couldn't. Not after all they'd been through.

He'd been so wrapped up in revenge, in making sure he got justice . . . He'd never told her he loved her.

Raven took in the dire situation. No one was coming to their rescue. They had one last chance, and she was the only person who could pull it off. But it was hell saying good-bye. Raven gave Dax one last look just in case her plan didn't work. He frowned in silent question, and she turned away.

Trying to appear surprised, she said to Gilmore, "Fauss is your father?"

"Why else do you think I'd work for that old fart Bigley?" Gilmore said. "And put up with you."

"Not when you're such a good thief," Raven said. "Must have killed you to watch me bring in all the good stuff. Enough to notify the scavengers about my every move? That last guy almost killed me, you know."

Fauss cut in, "That's impossible. My son knows that would have ruined the model."

Raven gave him a little smile. "He doesn't care. He didn't spend twenty years perfecting this plan. He didn't sit in a jail cell, contemplating revenge. He's only here for the money."

"Money? What money?" Fauss said, confused.

"Look around you," she said. "You think he's going to let you leave millions of dollars' worth of paintings for the cops to find? Just so you can have closure?"

Fauss was looking more unstable by the moment. "He knows how important this is to me."

"More important than *he* is to you," she said, her voice strangely calm. "Did you ever ask him what *he* wanted?"

Fauss's blank expression told her he'd never even considered it. She hitched her head toward the laptop. "Tell me, Fauss. Did you ever think to put him in your model? He's in a position to be a bigger threat than any of us."

The horror on Fauss's face said it all. The man didn't trust his own son. She almost felt sorry for Gilmore.

Dax gave her a warning look and said, "Raven."

I know what I'm doing, she wanted to tell him. *Just trust me this once. I'm going to make it right for everyone.*

Gilmore stepped away from Paulie and pointed his gun at her. "Shut up, you bitch."

She stared into his eyes. The pupils were huge and black, and as soulless as Fauss's. Killer's eyes. Any pity she had for him vanished.

Fauss gave Gilmore a suspicious look. "Is this true?"

Gilmore practically snarled. "I just saved your ass, and that's all you think about? That damn model?"

His father pursed his lips tightly. "She's right. I should have factored you in."

The gun in Gilmore's hand started shaking, and his face turned red from humiliation and fury. "I did everything you asked me to. I've listened to you yak about the damn plan every day for the last ten years of my life. You spent more quality time with *it* than you did with me. How can you treat me like one of them?"

"He doesn't respect you," Murphy said to Gilmore. He stood tall. "In all the letters he wrote to me, he never once mentioned you. You didn't exist."

Raven looked at him in disbelief. Her father was trying to draw the attention away from her. Why?

Fauss turned to Murphy. "He couldn't be revealed. I needed him for the plan."

Raven glanced at Gilmore, who had gone very still and tense. The hatred she'd felt on the painting was clear on his face, but Fauss seemed oblivious to it. It was like watching the calm before the deadly storm.

Murphy peered around Fauss to Gilmore. "I'll bet he won't even let you have one painting for all your sacrifice. Ask him yourself."

Fauss spun toward Gilmore, his eyes wide. "You *can't* have any of them. It'll ruin the model."

"Fuck the model!" Gilmore yelled and shot the laptop, blowing it off the desk. Pieces scattered across the floor.

Raven took a step back, closer to the wall. Like her, Dax was watching and waiting for the fallout.

Fauss rounded on his son and roared, "How dare you! How dare you do that to me, you worthless—"

He reached for Gilmore's throat, and a muffled gunshot ended his words. Fauss slumped forward.

Now or never. Raven grabbed *Blue Café* off the wall and flung it toward the ceiling light. The fluorescent tubes exploded in a blinding flash and everything went dark.

Dax went low as Gilmore started shooting indiscriminately, and everyone scattered in the sudden darkness. Blindly, Dax grabbed a stunned Paulie and threw him to the ground.

Dax whispered, "Stay down," and scrambled to where he'd left his gun.

Raven's voice rang out from the atrium behind him. "You missed me, Gilmore. You're still second-string."

Dax hissed. That woman had a death wish. He would have yelled for her to wait, but he didn't dare give away his position until he had his gun. None of them were getting out of here alive without it.

A body hurtled by him in the darkness.

Gilmore.

Dax reached out to grab him a second too late. Gunfire narrowly missed him as he dove for cover.

Raven called out from above, luring Gilmore away from their location, and Dax heard him run up the stairs.

A flashlight bobbed across the room, and Paulie shone it on Dax's face. "You okay?"

Okay was relative. Dax grabbed the light from him and flashed it on the floor. "I need to find my weapon. Get Murphy out of here."

"Gilmore blocked all the exits."

"Find a way out, Paulie. Are we still recording?" He retrieved his gun from under a pile of debris.

"Not in the truck." Paulie handed him a thick metal pen. "But I have a backup. Got the whole thing on digital voice recorder."

God bless geeks.

More gunshots rang out overhead, and Dax's heart seized up. He shoved the pen recorder in his pocket as he got to his feet. He tossed the flashlight back to Paulie and ran for the stairs. "Go!"

Raven hit the landing of the third floor and realized she was out of stairs. Moonlight through the glass skylight gave the space an eerie glow. If there was access to the roof, it was hiding in the dark corners.

It was the end of the line and as far away as she was going to get Gilmore from the others. The only way down was the set of stairs on the other side of the atrium. It was a long ways away, and, unfortunately, this level didn't have as much cover as the others.

Gilmore's approaching footsteps galvanized her, and she raced toward the back of the building before ducking behind a structural column.

The footsteps slowed on the stairs. No doubt Gilmore was enjoying this cat-and-mouse game, especially since he had the gun. She was good, but she wasn't faster than a speeding bullet.

As he stepped on the landing, Raven scanned the shadows for anything that she could use as a weapon. A short but hefty length of steel conduit was the only thing within reach.

The silence was deadly, and the metal cold in her hands. Her heart pounded in her ears as she eased her head around the corner of the column. Gilmore was thirty feet away and moving in her direction.

She gripped the bar. She'd get one shot. When a piece of glass crackled behind her, Raven spun around and hurled the pipe at him. She took off at a dead run without sticking around to see the outcome.

He fired wide, and the pipe clanked to the floor. She ran hard around the open atrium. If she could make it to the other set of stairs—

She felt the bullet rip through her thigh at the same time she heard the gunshot. Her leg gave out, and she stumbled to the floor. Burning pain ricocheted up the back of her leg as she tried to crawl to cover. She had reached the outside wall when she heard Gilmore's voice.

"Stop right there."

She grabbed her leg in agony and sat with her back to the wall. Warm blood dripped between her fingers, and everything slowed. She felt the cool concrete beneath her, smelled the dust, heard her heartbeat. This was it.

All the adventures she'd had. All the times she'd cheated death. To die at the hands of this little shit . . .

Gilmore was smiling when she looked up.

Yours is not the last face I want to see before I die, she thought suddenly, panic setting in. Not because she was about to die. But because Dax would never know how much she loved him.

Gilmore chuckled. "No snappy comebacks, Raven? No final words? Not even to beg for mercy?"

She would for the others. "You can end this now if you give yourself up, Gilmore."

He laughed. "You'd love that. But I'm not stupid like my father."

"He was wrong to treat you the way he did," she said, going for sympathy. "The courts would take that into consideration."

"You don't get it, do you?" Gilmore replied. "You think I was going to let him pull this off? That I'd walk out of here without those paintings?"

Then it all made sense. "You're going to pin him for all this again."

Gilmore grinned. "Sweet, huh? Killed by his own model?"

So much for sympathy. There was no saving Gilmore. Nothing she could say would stop him. He was going to kill her, and all she could think of was how Dax was going to handle it when he found her dead. Well, nearly all.

Gilmore aimed his gun at her. "Of course, now I have to finish the job. You're first."

She winced. What were the chances that he'd used all his bullets? Not good. That only happened in the movies.

"Just so you know," she said, gritting her teeth, "I'll be waiting for you when you die."

Silhouetted in the moonlight, he smiled. "Then you'll be waiting a long time."

"Not necessarily."

Raven jumped at the voice and the simultaneous gunshot. Gilmore spun around violently and dropped to the floor with a groan. It took her a moment to process what had happened.

She let out a long exhale of relief when Dax walked up and kicked Gilmore's gun aside. He looked at her in deep concern as he covered Gilmore. "Are you okay?"

She gave him a little smile. "Fine. Nice shooting."

"We'll discuss the whole team concept later," he told her. Then he turned to Gilmore. "Get up."

"I'm shot," he said, rolling on the floor.

"Get up, or I'll shoot you again."

Gilmore struggled to his feet, holding his shoulder.

Raven blinked at the cold anger in Dax's voice. He seemed so fierce in the gray glow of the moon. Why? They were done. They just needed to wait for the cops to show up.

"You killed Nick," Dax said. "It wasn't Fauss. It was you."

Oh God. Raven sucked in a breath. *Oh God.*

Gilmore snorted. "Took you long enough."

"I found you, didn't I?" Dax said.

"You didn't," he said, and pointed to Raven. "She did. *You* were happy driving a boat all day and taking pictures of fish."

Raven dragged herself to her feet, using the wall for support. "Shut up, Gilmore."

He looked at her. "The only reason he's here is because my father was fucking paranoid. He didn't believe me when I told him they had nothing on me. No physical evidence, no eyewitnesses. Nothing to pin me for shooting a cop."

"You just admitted it to us," she said.

He huffed. "Right, and they're going to believe you?"

"Don't need our word." Dax reached into his pocket and took out a mini-voice recorder. He showed it to Gilmore, who blanched when he realized what it was.

Relief poured through Raven. They had Gilmore dead to rights. It was over. They were alive and safe. All the weight seemed to lift off her shoulders.

Then Dax clicked the recorder unit off and raised his gun to Gilmore's head. "Now we don't need you either."

Raven's heart stopped. Dax's face was painted in harsh black and white. He was serious.

Gilmore scoffed in disbelief. "You aren't going to kill me. You're a cop."

"Not anymore. Thanks to you."

Gilmore's arrogant smile faded to terror. He backed up to the wall. "You can't. The model said you'd always be a cop."

Dax smiled. "Fuck the model."

"Dax?" Raven said, panic drowning out the fire in her leg. "What are you doing? We have a confession."

"Until some hotshot lawyer gets a hold of it and decides that we coerced the confession. And then Gilmore will walk."

She limped toward him. Tears blurred her vision. "You don't have to do this. Don't throw your life away for him."

Dax slid her a glance, despair in his eyes. "He won't get what he deserves."

Her body trembled from fear and shock. "Maybe not, but we will. I want a future, Dax. And I want it with you."

Dax squinted as if he couldn't believe he'd heard her right.

"She's right. You kill me, and they'll arrest you," Gilmore said, nodding repeatedly in agreement.

Dax glared at him. "I might shoot you just to shut you up."

Gilmore shut up.

Raven said, "Murdering him isn't going to give you what you're looking for. It won't bring Nick back."

"But it'll make me feel a whole lot better," he said.

"And it'll kill me," she said, her voice breaking.

Excruciating moments passed before warmth replaced the darkness in his eyes, and he lowered the weapon.

Sirens wailed in the distance, and Raven gave silent thanks. Dizziness started to cloud her mind. Through the fog, she heard Dax say, "Be grateful you didn't kill her, Gilmore. She just saved your pathetic life."

CHAPTER
24

Dax paced the hallway outside Raven's room at St. Joseph's Hospital in Yonkers. In shades of gray, the sterile walls and ceiling looked a lot like his recent nightmares. Only this time, he was free. No restraints, and he planned to keep it that way.

A couple of detectives stood at the end of the hall but didn't approach. He'd already given his statement, and he wasn't in the mood to talk to anyone except Raven. Unfortunately, he'd have to wait. He was second in line.

He stopped in front of a window overlooking the parking lot. The place was hopping with midmorning traffic and visitors coming to see if their loved ones were well. He never fully realized how important that one thing could be.

She'd come through surgery to remove the bullet all right, and at this moment, that was all he cared about. Everything else was a bonus.

When Dax rounded the stairs and saw Gilmore standing

over her, he'd thought she was already dead. His heart had all but seized up until he heard her voice.

All along, he thought he was prepared to kill the man who murdered Nick. It had been in his mind from the beginning—the only form of justice he had left after he'd pulled his hand out of Nick's chest, having failed as a cop and a friend.

But when it came time, when he had Gilmore in his sights, he realized that wasn't why he was there. And now, he only felt pity because the kid would never understand love. Never embrace something so remarkable or protect something so fragile. Gilmore wouldn't appreciate the tears of a woman who was afraid he'd do something stupid to screw up their future.

Sunrays filtered through the gray clouds and warmed his face. He breathed deep, feeling lighter than he had in months. He'd done right by Nick, or as right as he could. No more second guesses on what he should or shouldn't have done.

No matter what he did, murder would continue. Death would come. All he could do was his part.

Then he smiled a little. However, he wasn't above scaring the shit out of Gilmore. Dax had wanted to give him a small taste of the terror Nick felt in that slow-motion, split-second moment just before certain death. And since the little bastard pissed his pants, Dax was pretty sure he'd succeeded. Even if that was the only justice he could get, it was worth it.

"Mr. Maddox?"

Dax turned to find a willowy, light-haired woman standing next to him. The body type was longer and leaner, the oval face a little softer, but the eyes had the same intelligence and watchfulness.

"David," he said, and shook her hand. "You must be Jillian."

She smiled Raven's smile. "I wanted to thank you for getting us out of the vault. And saving my father. Everything."

"No problem. Sorry you got dragged into this mess."

"Actually, it was kind of exciting. Except the shooting part." She looked around him down the hall toward Raven's room. "Is she awake?"

"Your father is with her now."

Jillian's eyes widened marginally. "They have some things to work out. Family issues."

Dax nodded. "I know. I think she's ready now." And he was going to have to face his family, too. He wasn't hiding anymore.

"You know her pretty well." Jillian studied him as if trying to picture him in Raven's world. Her eyes narrowed. "Did she tell you about her gift?"

Dax eyed her. "You mean the psychometry?"

Jillian slowly beamed, every emotion clearly visible on her face.

Don't ever play poker, sweetheart.

"She told me about that," he said. "It's okay."

"I'll be," Jillian said in wonder. "So I guess I'll be seeing you around."

"I think that's up to Raven."

Jillian's expression turned serious. "Don't give up on her."

It was more of a plea than a request. "I don't plan to."

Jillian lifted an eyebrow. "She won't make it easy."

Dax grinned. "She never does."

Raven woke up in a hospital bed with sun streaming through the windows. She must have dozed off again after giving her statement to the police following surgery.

Memories returned slowly and in no particular order— some good, some bad. But the only thing that mattered was that everyone was safe. She smiled. It was a new day.

"How are you feeling, girl?"

Her father's voice brought her head around to where he was standing next to the bed, looking old and worn. His bright blue eyes had faded to pale over the years, and he stood a little less tall than she remembered.

"I'll be fine."

He nodded. "I know. I never had to worry about you, but I did anyway."

Raven noted the sadness in his voice. "Is that why you asked Bigley to hire me?"

He gave a guilty grin. "Figured that one out, did you?"

"I found the e-mails on your computer."

"Don't blame Bigley," her father said. "It was all my fault. I guess I didn't want you to end up like me."

"This was why you left, wasn't it?" she asked.

"I was afraid if I stayed, someday someone would come after your mother and you girls."

She shook her head. "So you left us alone? What if someone *had* come after us? What would we have done?"

"I knew Clayton was crazy. We all were back then. I just didn't know how much. I thought by the time he got out of jail, things would be different." Her father pursed his lips as if trying to hold in the emotions he was feeling. "I'd be better."

"Better than what?"

"I had a problem. An addiction. I couldn't stop stealing even after what happened with Clayton. Your mother, God rest her soul, believed me when I told her I'd stop." He bowed his head. "But even her love wasn't enough."

"She knew you were still stealing," Raven said.

He nodded, looking older by the minute. "She had the gift. I couldn't face her. I couldn't disappoint her. So I left, because I knew she wouldn't."

Raven shook her head slowly, unable to believe her father walked out because of that. Why didn't he stay and let them help him? Why didn't he trust them?

"She loved you. You destroyed her when you left," Raven said, her voice a whisper.

He rubbed his upper lip with his hand, and his eyes began to water. "I didn't think I'd be gone that long. I sent her money every month, hoping it would be enough. I thought she was stronger. And then when Clayton forgave me, I wanted to come back, but I didn't know how. But once she died—" He wiped his tears on his sleeve and looked away.

Raven clenched her fists, willing herself not to cry, but it was impossible. Her father loved her. He'd done what he thought was best, and he'd made a mistake he had to live with for the rest of life. He'd left when he should have stayed. How many times had she done that? How many times had she walked away, never knowing the grief she was leaving behind?

Tears burned in her eyes and anguish in her chest. She

opened her hand and placed it over her father's, feeling the strength and the warmth. She squeezed it gently.

He looked at her hand and nodded in silent understanding. "Don't do what I did, Rebecca. Don't throw love away. Give up everything else, but don't give up on that."

"I won't."

He focused on her. "It's a terrible curse, this obsession. And whether or not you want to admit it, you have my blood."

The words settled between them. He thought she stole because of a compulsion she couldn't control. Despite everything, she couldn't bring herself to tell him her only obsession had been trying to fix the past.

"I'm done."

"Good." He gave her a weak smile. "I don't know what's going to happen to me with the authorities, but I was hoping that after everything settles . . ." He cleared his throat. "We could have dinner."

He said it so quietly, so desperately. She could almost hear Jillian in her head. *Because someday you might say yes, and I don't want to miss it.*

Raven could say no and push the past aside. Or she could start a new future. Right now. Right here.

"I'd like that," she said.

His face turned red, clearly overwhelmed. He patted her hand and left quietly. Raven wiped the tears from her eyes, took a deep breath, and accepted the string that wrapped around her heart. It felt good, not strangled. There was no panic. No fear.

Jillian was going to be so proud of her.

The hospital door opened, and Dax walked through. He smiled, and her heart soared. He looked like he'd slept in the collared navy shirt and jeans from last night. He hadn't shaved since yesterday, and his thick hair was ruffled, and he was the most beautiful man alive.

He leaned over and kissed her softly with just enough edge to make her wish she was feeling a whole lot better.

"I saw your father leave," he said. "Are you okay?"

"Fine. How are we doing?"

Dax pulled a chair up to the bed and sat down. He ran his fingertips along her wrist. "Fauss is in critical condition but expected to survive. Gilmore only had a flesh wound and is under arrest. So far they are up to four counts of kidnapping, possession of stolen art, and attempted murder."

Dax was doing amazing things to her arm, and her concentration was split. "That should keep Gilmore and Fauss out of trouble for a while."

"It gets better," he said. "When Gilmore realized he hadn't actually *killed* his father when he shot him, he started talking. Hasn't stopped since. Probably doesn't want to be on the receiving end of one of Fauss's models."

She loved it. "You want me to talk to Fauss? Maybe I can get him to flip on Gilmore?"

Dax gave her a warning look, his blue eyes sharp. "No. And by the way, don't ever do anything like that again. You took ten years off my life. I wasn't real pleased when you lured Gilmore away either."

"I was trying to save you," she said, slightly indignant.

"You don't get it," he replied. "We're a team. Your problems are mine."

"And yours are mine, partner," she countered. His eyes softened, and her heart jumped.

Then she asked the really hard question. "So how much jail time are we looking at?"

Dax laced his fingers in hers. "Hopefully none. It's going to take the authorities forever to piece this together, and they'll still never figure it all out."

She shook her head. "What about the model on Fauss's laptop? The incriminating video of us stealing a painting in Richmond? Someone is going to find that."

"Paulie checked. The hard drive was shattered." Dax gave her a little smile. "There might be a few pieces of it missing, too."

Paulie. She was going to give that boy a big hug when she saw him. "What if that wasn't the only copy of the video?"

Dax shrugged. "Fauss was the buyer. Since he sent us to get it, technically it's not stealing. It would be up to Yarrow if he wants to press charges on the breaking and entering. I'm more worried about the part of the model that showed us going to Cuba."

"Cuba? I've never been," she said, batting her eyelashes innocently.

He smiled. "Me neither."

She looked at her hand wrapped in his, marveling at how wonderful it felt. "You can't fix the hair they found on Walter though."

"Wasn't yours."

She blinked at him. "Then whose was it?"

"Fauss's," Dax said. "I figure Walter was attempting to ID his killer. Miami-Dade is working the case now, trying to place Fauss in the vicinity. Gilmore already pegged Fauss for the kidnap and murder. I think you're off the hook."

She'd forgotten Fauss had long hair, too, and felt a pang of gratitude for Walter. "And what about Nick's murder?"

"We got Gilmore's confession on tape. It should be admissible in court. The investigation is being moved up to the state level. Maybe they can pull a conviction together."

She noted the surrender in his statement. "That's all Nick would have wanted you to do."

"I know. It's out of my hands now," Dax said, and brought her fingers to his lips to kiss. "I didn't mean to scare you."

"You never would have shot Gilmore."

Dax's eyebrows rose. "You sure about that?"

"Positive. Good acting though. Scared the shit out of him. It was the highlight of my day."

He grinned wide. "I aim to please."

He looked so good. So relaxed and at peace. Some-time in the past few hours he'd found a way to forgive himself. She didn't know how, but she was grateful. It was going to be okay. They could have a future. If Dax wanted one. He hadn't answered her when she said it. She knew what he was waiting for—her.

The people she loved were all safe today, and that's the way it was going to remain. She took a deep breath, and said, "I'm terminating Raven Callahan."

Dax stilled. "Come again?"

"After all this is over, I want to create a new identity. A clean slate. A fresh start." She smiled, hiding the fear in her heart. God, what if he said *no*? "In fact, I was thinking of moving to Florida."

He grinned a little and gently caressed her fingers with warm, strong hands. "You know, I hear there's a lot of uncharted shipwrecks off the Keys. Good business in that."

She noted the gleam in his eye. "Need a boat."

"I happen to have one of those," he said, and pressed his lips to her palm. "And an opening for a first mate."

"Are you sure you're staying in business?"

Dax kissed her wrist, sending shivers all over her body. "I'm sure. Sounds a little boring for you though." He looked up. "You'd be happy with that?"

I'd be happy with you. She didn't realize how much until this moment. There was room around her heart for more strings.

"Yes," she said. "What about you? Is this what you want?"

He turned serious and thoughtful. Silence stretched between them as he let go of her hand and sat back to study her.

She held her breath at his uncertainty. Then he pulled something out of his pocket and looked down at it. After a few seconds, he leaned over the bed rail and placed a set of warm car keys in her hands.

He folded his hands around hers. "What do you feel?"

He wanted her to use her ability? Now? She hesitated for a moment, fearful of what she might find. But his face was full of expectation, and she realized that she trusted him—mind, body, and soul.

"Have faith, Raven," he said.

I do. She opened up and inhaled sharply at the powerful surge of love and desire, all the emotions he'd imprinted on the keys for her to find. For a moment, she sank into the wonder of his thoughts. She'd found love.

Then he kissed her with equal parts patience and passion. She laid her palm against his cheek and kissed him back.

"I don't care what you've done in the past," he murmured against her lips. "I don't care what you are going to do. I love you, and, God help me, I'm willing to endure whatever hell that brings."

Raven peered into his clear blue eyes. "I love you. I promise I will never do anything that could get you killed."

He laughed, and she reveled in the rich timbre of it. She held the keys in her hands tightly, feeling the certainty and depth of his conviction. "But there is one condition."

He raised an eyebrow.

She gave him a slow smile as she leaned forward to kiss him. "The next fifteen minutes are *mine*."

The Top Five Things I Learned While Writing This Book

Every book requires many hours of research to make the story as accurate as possible. Here are the top five things I learned while writing this book:

1. How to hot-wire my car. And pick a lock. And defeat a motion detector. And where to shop for totally cool spy gadgets.
2. Be very careful when using an Internet language translator. There's a big difference between pressing the French button and the Spanish button.
3. Actuaries are frighteningly smart folk. Do not mess with them.
4. Everyone should have a safe house, even if you have no mortal enemies to hide from.
5. Don't ask your local hardware guy what would happen if you threw a screwdriver at his fluorescent ceiling lights. He'll never trust you in his store again.

There you have it. My new life skills. I hope you found a few, too. Thanks for reading.

Sam

About the Author

Samantha Graves turned a lifelong love of daydreaming into writing fiction. After penning an award-winning Futuristic Romance series as C. J. Barry, she now brings her unique blend of high adventure, sizzling romance, mystery, and humor to her first contemporary romantic suspense.

Samantha is a former IT manager and was a computer geek long before it was cool or lucrative. While searching for a fulfilling creative outlet, she discovered writing eight years ago and has never looked back.

She is a member of the Romance Writers of America and several chapters, including Fantasy, Futuristic & Paranormal, Kiss of Death, and Central New York Romance Writers. Samantha resides in beautiful upstate New York with her family and cat.

Visit her Web site at www.samanthagraves.com.

The suspense and
romance never stop
with Samantha Graves!

• • •

Please turn this page
for a preview of

Out of Time

Coming in 2008 in mass market.

CHAPTER
1

Simon had been asleep exactly twelve minutes when the doorbell started to buzz.

Go away, he thought through the fog of exhaustion and slipped back into the peace of safe, sound sleep.

Bzzzzz.

He surfaced long enough to register the rain pelting his bedroom windows and the fact that he hadn't eaten today but was too tired to do anything about it. Should have taken that sexy flight attendant up on her offer for more nuts. Now *there* was a good point to go back to sleep.

Bzzzzzzzzzzzzzzzzzzzzzzzzzzzzz.

"Son of a bitch." He tossed the covers aside and looked at the clock. 7:15 P.M. Who in the tristate area would be standing on his doorstep at this time of day in the middle of a thunderstorm?

Whoever it was laid on the buzzer with a vengeance. Simon sat on the edge of his bed and rubbed a two-day-old stubble. He didn't need this. Three months he hadn't been home. All he wanted was one solid night of sleep without worrying about someone shooting at him. Was that too much to ask?

Simon grabbed a pair of jeans off the floor and pulled them on. He stuffed his gun in the middle of his back and walked to the security panel. If it was the old bat next door nosing around in his business again, he'd seriously consider killing her. Okay, maybe a warning shot. But someone was going to pay for waking him.

The front door camera showed a lone figure huddled and leaning against the outside wall, his hand pressed on the doorbell. The man's face was hidden in shadow.

The good news was, assassins rarely came through the front door. The bad news was, it sure wasn't the Avon lady.

Thunder and rain echoed down the hall as Simon made his way through his Bayridge Tudor, adrenaline pushing fatigue aside. Thunder rattled the windows, and a funky green color tinted everything. He pressed against the steel door and peered out the one-way transom window. He still couldn't recognize the visitor.

He hit the intercom. "Who is it?"

The incessant buzzing stopped, and a muffled male voice answered, "It's Jackson. Let me in."

The name made Simon frown. The only Jackson he knew worked out of South America, and it had been years since he'd seen him. In fact, the last time they'd met, the bastard had stolen Simon's hard-earned loot out from under him. And then he'd stolen his fiancée. Simon's chest tightened. Okay, so maybe she was already gone, but still, Jackson had a lot of balls showing up at his home.

Simon yanked open the door and aimed his gun at Jackson's head. "What the hell do *you* want?"

The man stared back, eyes red and heavy and full of pain. Rainwater had plastered short black hair to his head. His face was pale, and the long overcoat hung shapelessly over a well-honed tomb raider's body. He'd aged twenty years since the last time Simon saw him, and he smelled like wet dog.

The hair on the back of Simon's neck prickled. Trouble was a-brewing.

Jackson raised one hand wearily. The other hand he kept inside his coat. "I'm not armed."

"You'd be surprised how often I hear that and wind up in ICU," Simon said. "What do you want?"

Jackson turned his head and surveyed the quiet neighborhood. "I'll tell you inside," he said, his voice rough. Then he stumbled past Simon without waiting for an invite.

Simon kicked the door shut, keeping his gun leveled at Jackson, who gave a painful groan before settling on the stairs in the dark entry. His breathing was labored, and he looked like death warmed over.

"Bad job?" Simon asked him.

Jackson rested his head against the wall and peered up at Simon. "You're the only one I can trust."

"You jumped my find and my girl. We're a long way from trust, you and me."

"Hey, you poached on my turf. Can't have other raiders thinking I'm soft. As for Celina—" Jackson gave a guttural groan and clutched his stomach. The hairs on the back of Simon's neck prickled. He reached over and hit the vestibule lights. The trail of rainwater that stretched from the door to the stairs was turning bright red.

"Christ, Jackson," Simon said, stowing the gun in his jeans. He knelt and ripped open the trench coat. Blood soaked Jackson's shirt and pants from the gaping hole in his belly. "What happened?"

Jackson gave a weak laugh. "I forgot to duck."

"No shit." And recently, too, Simon noted. This didn't happen in Peru. The fact that Jackson was still walking meant it had been only a few hours at most. "You need to get to an ER."

He stood up, but Jackson grabbed his forearm with surprising strength for a man bleeding all over his floor. "No. Listen to me."

He reached into an inside pocket, pulled out a small cloth bag, and gave it to Simon. "You can't let them have this."

"Who?" Simon asked, feeling the weight of the single smooth object inside as he untied the leather strings.

"Don't know," Jackson said, rolling his head from side to side. "Some group. Secret society."

A glass lens dropped out of the bag into Simon's palm. It was perfectly concave and clear. Simon held it up to the light and peered through it, but all he could see was a distorted view of his hallway. "You got shot for this?"

"More than it appears, my friend. It's old. Real old," Jackson replied and gave a sickly, hacking cough. "It's a key—" He started gagging.

Simon slid the lens into the bag. "I have to get you to a hospital."

"No!"

He froze at the raw fear in Jackson's voice. The rain had stopped outside, and it had become very quiet in his house. The hairs on his neck were standing straight up.

"What's going on, Jackson?"

His breathing was slowing down. "This is big. Bigger than anything you or I ever did. You gotta get there before they do. There's a woman. Name is Jillian Talbot. Works at the MET. I was going to see her, but—" He winced. "Find her. You'll need her."

"For what?"

Jackson's eyes began to close. Simon grabbed his shoulders and shook him. "For what?"

His eyes popped open. "I don't know. All we got was the piece and a name. But a lot of people died for that alone."

Including you, thought Simon. Didn't he realize that? Why wasn't he trying to save himself? Why the hell would he use his last bit of strength to find Simon and give him a stupid piece of glass?

"Where did the lens come from?"

"Mexico." Jackson's pasty face crinkled into a smile. "Celina found it."

Celina. It figured. That woman had a nose for trouble. "Where is she?"

Jackson sobered, sadness washing over him. "They ambushed us. She didn't make it out."

"Hell," Simon muttered and rubbed his eyes. She'd burned him good, but he would never wish her dead. Celina's only crime was being as crazy as she was beautiful.

"She still loved you, you know," Jackson said.

Right. She'd sold him out for Incan gold. *That's love for ya*.

Jackson added, "But I didn't care. The last two years with her were the best of my life. You gotta find out who killed her. You gotta find out why." He looked at Simon with sudden clarity. "*Promise* me. This was important to Celina. She died for this."

Simon clenched his teeth. He used to keep his promises. That was before Celina. Besides, this smelled bad. She had been into some weird stuff last he knew. Weirder than usual, even for her.

"I promise," he lied.

"Thank you." Jackson coughed, and then gave a short, bitter laugh. "You want to know something funny?"

Simon couldn't think of anything funny at the moment. Celina was dead, Jackson wasn't far behind, and Simon was getting a bad feeling that he might be next in line. "What?"

Jackson beamed for a brief moment. "I finally did the right thing, and it killed me."

Outside, Simon heard car doors slam. He stood up and looked through the transom. A black Mercedes was parked across the street behind a green Volvo that Simon didn't recognize. Must be Jackson's. Two men in long coats—one tall and thin, the other bulky—checked the inside of the car and the area around the vehicle. Every self-preservation fiber of his being kicked into high gear.

"Friends of yours?"

Jackson replied weakly, " 'Fraid not. They're after the crystal."

What have you gotten me into this time, Celina? It was bad enough she'd almost killed him while she was alive. Now she was messing with him from the grave. Well, guess what? He wasn't playing the fool again. If the Men in Black wanted the lens, they could have it. Hell, he'd even throw Jackson in for free.

"I know what you're thinking," Jackson said. "Won't do you any good to hand it over. You already know too much. You're a marked man."

Simon gave him a hard look. "You son of a bitch. You knew that when you came here."

He had the nerve to grin. "So shoot me."

"I got a better idea." Simon went back to the stairs to collect Jackson. "You're coming with me."

He pushed Simon aside with a wince. "Don't bother. I'm a dead man either way. I'll just slow you down." Blood dribbled out the corner of his mouth as he talked. "Your only hope is to find the answers first. Do the right thing, Bonner."

Screw that. Doing the right thing had brought him nothing but pain, misfortune, and medical bills. Survival, however, was an excellent motivator. "We really don't have time to argue. There's an escape route through my basement—"

"Good. Use it," Jackson said. He took a rattling breath and gave Simon a final peaceful look of a man with nothing left to lose. "Get out, Bonner. Get out now."

Jillian loved the MET at night, after all the crowds had left and most of the staff had shuffled out. By 8:00 P.M. on a Tuesday night, the place was empty. This was when she could be alone with the finest that history had to offer.

Her footsteps echoed across the marble tiles as she made her way through the European Sculpture and Decorative Arts gallery. Long shadows prostrated themselves across the floors of every room as if paying homage to the treasures within. It was one of the benefits of being an assistant curator. She had all the good stuff to herself.

She entered her favorite room, the Sculpture Court, and stopped in front of the *Nymph and Angel* by the French sculptor Emil Crozalles. Unabashedly naked and intimately tangled in spontaneous celebration, their unbridled joy shone through an amorous embrace. Every piece the master sculptor created was playful and full of motion, but this was her favorite for a whole other reason.

She glanced around to make sure no one was nearby. Silence descended over her as she concentrated on the marble lines. Slowly, a vision appeared as if through rippled glass—hands chipping, rubbing, and caressing the marble with a lover's touch. Then the face of the young maker, his hair white from dust, his expression feverish with excitement. The vision grew, blocking out the present as it stole into the past.

After a few minutes, Crozalles turned away from the statue, and Jillian held her breath. This was the moment she waited for every time. As if sunshine warmed his face for the first time, the sculptor smiled at the woman entering the picture. Seconds later, she joined him as they fell upon the marble and kissed like the Nymph and the Angel.

And the artist becomes the art.

Jillian gave a sigh. That Crozalles. He was crazy as a loon, but the man could still steal a woman's breath away two hundred years later.

So many times, Jillian had wondered who the woman was. His wife? His lover? Must be a lover. Married people didn't have that kind of carefree passion. There was just too much baggage and pain between them. Too much weight. Too many tears.

Heavy footsteps wrenched her back to the present. She put her hand to her heart when she saw who it was. "Hello, Charlie."

The veteran security guard smiled, his ruddy Irish complexion reddening and making his white hair whiter and blue eyes bluer. "Evening, Miss Talbot. Working late again?"

"A whole shipment of terra-cotta vases came in from Colombia today. I couldn't seem to pull myself away."

He chuckled. "You know, that happens a lot, missy. This *is* a museum." He winked at her. "You should be out enjoying yourself and breaking hearts."

Any time the conversation turned to her personal life—or the lack thereof—was a signal that the game had begun. It was a battle of wits Charlie and she had played many times. The man was a happily married hopeless romantic.

She said, "Hearts come along every day. Ancient vases don't."

"Yes, but vases are the past. Used and discarded that no one wants. Hearts are the future."

She countered, "At least you can fix a broken vase. You can't mend a broken heart."

"Then that makes hearts far more valuable."

She laughed. He had her there.

Charlie grinned in victory. "Would you like an escort out?"

"No, but thanks anyway."

He tapped his hand to his hat. "Have a nice evening."

"You, too, Charlie." She hiked her bag over her shoulder and headed for the employee side entrance.

October rain pelted the concrete as she exited the building and stood under the overhang for a moment. She looked at the dark, angry skies, hoping the shower would ease up. Instead, it turned into a torrential downpour. *Rats.* Usually she took the subway home. Not tonight.

She cinched the belt of her lightweight trench coat, popped open her umbrella, and ran down the stairs to catch a cab on Fifth Avenue. The sounds and perpetual motion of the city engulfed her. Traffic was heavy in front of the museum so she walked farther up the block where it was less congested.

Cold rain pelted her high-heeled boots and chilled her to the bone. Tonight would be a good night for some homemade apple and brie soup while she studied for her Conversational Spanish class tomorrow night—

She felt someone move behind her. A strong hand clamped onto her arm before she could turn around. A hard object pressed through her coat and into her ribs. She inhaled at the sharp stab of pain.

Gun.

A man whispered in her ear, "Jillian Talbot, do not scream."

THE DISH

Where authors give you the inside scoop!

♥ ♥ ♥ ♥ ♥ ♥ ♥ ♥ ♥ ♥ ♥ ♥ ♥ ♥

From the desk of Samantha Graves

There are some characters who will haunt a writer
until their story is told. Raven Callahan from SIGHT
UNSEEN (on sale now) was one such character.

She was born from a One-Page Workshop exercise
at my local writing chapter, where she fended off an
attacker in an underwater cave. Call it intuition or
inspiration, I decided that psychic touch was the edge
Raven needed to be a world-class art thief and give
her a humanity she didn't always welcome. Fearless,
capable, and fiercely independent, I knew I had a
character I would never forget. But when the workshop was over, I filed her scene into the "Someday"
folder on my desk as other obligations called.

For three years, Raven waited impatiently for me to
create a story worthy of her courage and skill, full of
high-stakes adventure, danger, and a hero who would
challenge her at every turn, yet accept her just the way
she was—the one man she couldn't walk away from.
Enter David Maddox, an ex-cop surviving on guilt
and vengeance. With nothing left to lose, he needed
redemption as much as Raven did, even if she would
never admit it. They would learn the hard way that the
only thing they could depend on was each other.

But I have to admit that half the fun of writing

this book was the opportunity to research some remarkable locales I have always wanted to visit myself. From the excitement of Miami to the tropical paradise of Key West to the sultry heat of Havana, I made their adventure mine.

So now their story is told in SIGHT UNSEEN, and although my "Someday" file doesn't look much smaller, Raven Callahan can finally rest.

Happy reading!

Samantha Graves

www.samanthagraves.com

♥ ♥ ♥ ♥ ♥ ♥ ♥ ♥ ♥ ♥ ♥ ♥ ♥

From the desk of Sarah McKerrigan

In KNIGHT'S PRIZE (on sale now), the final chapter in my Warrior Maids of Rivenloch trilogy, Rand la Nuit, infamous mercenary and expert swordsman, hunts the elusive outlaw known as The Shadow. But who is the mysterious, quick-as-lightning thief? And what is sweet Miriel of Rivenloch hiding from him? The quest draws Rand closer and closer to a shocking truth—that the seemingly innocent woman he's falling hopelessly in love with knows more than she's letting on about The Shadow.

Writing KNIGHT'S PRIZE presented a fascinating challenge for me—intertwining the cultures of East and West in a medieval setting. The Silk Road trade route was established at this time, so I imagined that some martial arts might have been imported along with the silk. Thus was born a very different type of damsel in shining armor—a medieval heroine who kicks butt Chinese-style!

Why martial arts? As a kid, I always thought Kato was way cooler than The Green Hornet. My guilty pleasure is Jackie Chan movies, which I watch with my teenage son. And I could watch that beautifully choreographed foyer fight scene from *The Matrix Reloaded* a hundred times.

The best thing about martial arts is that size doesn't matter. I learned that as a pint-sized girl, studying judo. It's all about momentum, strategy, grace, speed, agility, and surprise, using an attacker's own strength against him. And as you can imagine, martial arts are also the great equalizer of the sexes!

As a reader, I love surprises, so I've packed plenty of them into KNIGHT'S PRIZE. No one is who they seem to be, twists and turns abound, and the story has an explosive ending! The romance and adventure should keep you up all night. Let me know if it did at www.sarahmckerrigan.com.

Sarah McKerrigan

♥ ♥ ♥ ♥ ♥ ♥ ♥ ♥ ♥ ♥ ♥ ♥ ♥ ♥

From the desk of Elizabeth Hoyt

Gentle Reader,

Whilst going through some old papers I found the pamphlet below. Although the author chose to remain anonymous, I have reason to believe that Lady Georgina Maitland, my heroine from THE LEOPARD PRINCE (on sale now), in fact wrote it.

Advice for the Landowning Lady of Means on the Hiring of Land Stewards

by an Anonymous Lady Who Knows

1. When hiring a steward the genteel lady should keep in mind that there are many Aesthetically Pleasing gentlemen who are just as much in need of work as those that are older, surlier, and not nearly as pleasant to look upon. It is your duty to hire them.
2. The Feminine Employer should remember that it is she who is in charge. Do not be afraid to issue orders to your Male Employee, although there are times when it may be to your advantage to permit your steward to issue orders to *you*.
3. Do not under any circumstances enter into an Intimate Relationship with your land steward.

4. However, should you succumb to broad shoulders, a dry tone, and a knowing gaze, do try to be discreet.

5. Whatever you do, do not let your brothers become aware of the liaison.

6. Or your sister.

7. Or your aunt, your family, your friends, your lady's maid, or indeed any of the other servants, passing strangers, and the public in general. *Discretion* should be the watchword for the Genteel Lady desiring Further Acquaintance with her land steward.

8. It is This Author's opinion that it is of Paramount Importance that the land steward be skilled in kissing and other Intimate Arts. She cannot stress this particular point enough.

9. The Lady of Means should try to refrain from mooning about and thinking obsessively of her land steward. This behavior is apt to attract the notice of Other People (see points 5, 6, and 7 above).

10. Finally, the Genteel Lady Landowner must never, *ever*, fall in love with her land steward. That way lies disaster—or at least a very good book.

Yours Most Sincerely,

Elizabeth Hoyt

www.elizabethhoyt.com

Want to know more about romances at
Warner Books and Warner Forever?
Get the scoop online!

WARNER'S ROMANCE HOME PAGE

Visit us at www.warnerforever.com for all the
latest news, reviews, and chapter excerpts!

NEW AND UPCOMING TITLES

Each month we feature our new titles
and reader favorites.

CONTESTS AND GIVEAWAYS

We give away galleys, autographed copies,
and all kinds of fun stuff.

AUTHOR INFO

You'll find bios, articles, and links to personal
Web sites for all your favorite authors—and
so much more!

THE BUZZ

Sign up for our monthly romance newsletter,
and be the first to read all about it!

VISIT US ONLINE
@ WWW.HACHETTEBOOKGROUPUSA.COM.

AT THE HACHETTE BOOK GROUP USA WEB SITE YOU'LL FIND:

CHAPTER EXCERPTS FROM SELECTED NEW RELEASES

•

ORIGINAL AUTHOR AND EDITOR ARTICLES

•

AUDIO EXCERPTS

•

BESTSELLER NEWS

•

ELECTRONIC NEWSLETTERS

•

AUTHOR TOUR INFORMATION

•

CONTESTS, QUIZZES, AND POLLS

•

FUN, QUIRKY RECOMMENDATION CENTER

•

PLUS MUCH MORE!

BOOKMARK HACHETTE BOOK GROUP USA
@ WWW.HACHETTEBOOKGROUPUSA.COM.